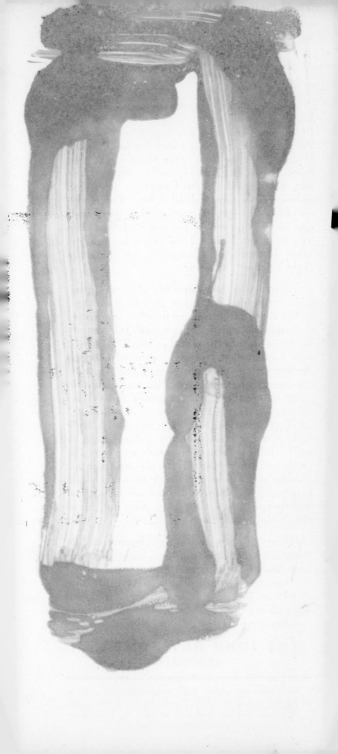

# THE HIDDEN FLOWER

## by PEARL S. BUCK

Josui was a lovely Japanese girl of good family. She had been born in America and lived here until she was fifteen, when, after Pearl Harbor, her father took his family back to Japan rather than have them go behind barbed-wire. In Kyoto, spared by the war, she met Lieutenant Allen Kennedy, who had aristocratic Virginia blood in him. Theirs was no cheap or casual romance. They were married in all dignity by solemn Buddhist rites in a temple in Kyoto. Then Allen brought his bride Josui back to America, and here the child Lennie was born.

"When was the mortal life of the child begun? They did not know at which moment in the day's brightness or in what shadow of the night his spirit stepped from the eternity before birth into the world of life. Whether it was in that first screened room now across the sea, or in the high room looking toward the west, whether it was in the mountain cabin where they spent a handful of days, reluctant to leave the snow-crowned peaks. whether it was in the upper room in a little hotel in a small town on the endless plain, or in the rolling hills of the midwest, they did not know. Somewhere in the glorious months, at some place of love in the chain of days and nights of love, the world child was living, but still they did not know. They were not thinking of him but of themselves."

Beauty infuses the story — beauty of the Japanese landscape, gardens, home life, and later beauty of the American scene, beauty of the human spirit in Josui, in Cynthia, the American girl, in the Jewish woman doctor who brings the child to birth, and throughout, beauty of style and vision.

## THE JOHN DAY COMPANY
### NEW YORK

The illustration on this jacket is adapted from a design on the binding of *Art of the Landscape Garden in Japan*, by Tsuyoshi Tamura, published in 1935 by The Society for International Cultural Relations, Tokyo.

# GOD'S MEN

## A NOVEL

### by Pearl S. Buck

This is a massive novel, in length, breadth, and depth. It sweeps from China to America to England, and in a half-century of colorful action it ranges from the Boxer Rebellion of 1900 to the critical struggles of 1950. The author brings warmth of feeling and the light of understanding to many and varied characters, including Franklin D. Roosevelt, Sun Yat-sen, and Chiang Kai-shek.

Two American boys are born into missionary families in the ancient city of Peking. Both driven by inherited consciences, both shaped by childhood in China, they work out opposite destinies. Each has his romance and the wife he deserves, with whom to enjoy life after his own fashion. The one becomes powerful, for power is what he craves, being a man who doubts himself. The other pursues a simple idea which makes him rich in spite of himself, and which he dreams of spreading to the whole world. Each goes back to China at the time that seems to him crucial. They are never able to understand one another and inevitably they come to clash. At the end of the story, we ask which is the victor, and answer according to our own views of man's purpose. For with her insight into hearts and minds and springs of action, the novelist tells about two strong characters such as those we see opposed everywhere in these tense days. They stand strangely alike, yet in conflict as wide as the world and as close as church and home town.

## By Pearl S. Buck

# THE HIDDEN FLOWER

# The Hidden Flower

## by Pearl S. Buck

THE JOHN DAY COMPANY

NEW YORK

# Part I

Part I

THE garden was quiet. Beyond its walls no echo of footsteps could be heard above the soft incessant splash of the waterfall. The silence was planned, as everything in the garden was planned, though all seemed nature itself. Thus, on the street side of the garden the water had been lifted by the most modern plumbing, concealed behind rocks, to make a brook running apparently from a height. A truncated hillock, half hidden by bamboos, built against the high stone wall, was so designed that it took on the dignity of a spur of the mountains behind the city. Over its rocky side the water splashed in a storied waterfall into a deep clear pool. Three large pines, curved with age, leaned over the pool to make reflection. Though so few, they conveyed the atmosphere of a forest in the distance.

The house, north of the garden, was entirely Japanese. It was large, but the roofs were low. Bamboos softened their sloping corners and like drawn curtains revealed the paper-latticed walls. The house was of wood, unpainted and aging a silvery gray. The season was spring and against the softness of the gray wood masses of azaleas bloomed. The sun shining down upon them lit them into brilliance of scarlet and orange and honey yellow.

The hour was noon. In his study Dr. Sotan Sakai lifted

3

his head from the manuscript upon which he worked and gazed through the open doors. The garden was irresistibly beautiful. He put down his fountain pen and rose from the floor mat, noticing, with some inward pride, that his long legs were not stiff. It had taken him several years to return to the ways of his people, after his youth in the United States. At first it had been unbearable to fold his legs before the low table and write for hours at a time. But he had made up his mind that he would do it, even as he had decided, when he chose to leave that country to return to the land of his birth. He had made the choice because he was a proud man and he could not brook the notion of a concentration camp in Arizona. They had given him the choice, either the camp or repatriation to Japan. He chose Japan.

The iron pride had made him return completely to his ancestry. He had bought the ancient family seat of Baron Kazuko, outside the city of Kyoto. The Kazuko family, impoverished by the war, had gone into final retreat when the sons were killed in China. The Baron himself had entered a Buddhist monastery in the mountaintop near Unzen, on the island of Kyushu, and his wife returned to her own family. The family of Kazuko was no more. In its place now lived Sotan Sakai and his wife and their daughter, Josui. He had once a son, Kensan, older by five years than Josui when they left America. Kensan had not been willing to return to Japan. He had gone to the concentration camp, and there had volunteered for service in the war. He had been killed in Italy.

His son's death had confirmed Dr. Sakai in his determination to be Japanese. Kyoto had been spared by the war. The ancient capital stood as it had been for a thousand years and more, except for a few modern buildings. These could not prevail, however, against such old and honored buildings as the Higashi-Hongan-ji Temple, or the palaces whose thick thatched roofs had been the pride of generations of imperial thatchers. The gardens of the palaces had given to Dr. Sakai the present source of discovery of his ancestral country, and from them he had brought back ideas in rocks, water, dwarf trees, and moss. The garden of the Shokintei House, in the Katsura Imperial Detached Palace, had seemed especially beautiful to him, the calmly flowing water, the footbridge, the rocks, the spare use of trees and shrubbery combining intimacy and distance.

When the end of the war came, he remained aloof from the Occupation troops and their commanders. Since he had established himself as the leading doctor of western medicine in the city, his position was secure. People could not do without him. He treated all who came to him with equal care, or very nearly, but prudent in the realities as he found them, he made it his duty to revive the ancient courtesy toward the aristocrats, the great families who were now in retirement. He did not feel their trust incongruous.

After his work each day in a large modern hospital, he returned to his home, changed his garments, and wrote on his book, entitled *Diseases of Deficiency*. He had accumulated much knowledge upon the subject during the years of his return. Now he wiped his fountain pen carefully before he went into the garden. The pen was his only concession, at home, to American ways. The traditional brush was too slow. But perhaps this was not a concession since most Japanese used pen and pencil instead of the brush. Indeed, these were made in Japan and the pen he considered superior to the American ones. The lead in the pencils, however, was too hard.

At the wide door, which was only the latticed wall slid back like a screen, he enjoyed again his garden. That is, he almost enjoyed it. Knowing its every detail, he could not refrain from searching for the fallen leaf, the possible overnight anthill, which could mar its perfection. He did not wish to disturb himself to find the gardener and to demand of him why he had not removed such accidents. He closed his eyes and meditated for a moment, murmuring the fragment of a sutra. When he opened his eyes again he saw his garden with fresh perception, glowing in the sunlight, exactly as he wished to see it.

Meditation was not easy for him. His youth had been spent in the busy streets of Los Angeles, peddling the vegetables and flowers that he helped his parents to raise on five acres of land outside the city. He had worked his way through college and had won scholarships in medical school. In America there had been no time for meditation. He had been compelled to learn it when he came to Japan, as one learns to play a musical instrument, the five-holed flute, for example, which he enjoyed in the evenings.

He had only one anxiety left, now that the war was over. This was his daughter Josui. At fifteen she had been a child, following her parents when they chose Japan. She had not been docile in other ways and only bewilderment and fear had made her willing to leave America. She had been terrified by her American schoolmates, always so pleasant, so

6

friendly, until suddenly one day they had changed into enemies. Their charming faces became ugly and scowls took the place of smiles. This she could not understand, and she had complained to her best friend, Polly Andrews, the daughter of the grocer who bought vegetables from her grandfather. "But, Polly, I am the same person I have always been."

"No, you are not," Polly had retorted. "You are a Japanese and I hate you."

Josui had said no more. She did not go again to school and a few days later when her parents took ship she followed them in heartbroken silence. The country she had taken for granted as her own, where she had been born, whose language alone she spoke, had rejected her and despised her. Yet she was not ready to accept Japan, because her grandmother had told her too much of the lot of women there. She remained in a state of doubt, safe while she lived in her father's house but uncertain of her future.

Dr. Sakai himself divined the state of his daughter's mind and this was his anxiety. Now that Josui was twenty, what would they do with her? Marriage could not be far off, especially for a girl so pretty, but what marriage? He had received offers for her and he had been too prudent to present them to her, expecting her instant rejection. He had never even discussed her marriage with her, and he had forbidden his wife, Hariko, to do so. The matter was delicate and he wished to undertake it alone. Were the wrong word spoken Josui might refuse marriage at all.

He lingered at the door, and then changing his straw slippers to wooden clogs, he walked down the path to the pool

7

and stood watching the splash of the water. The air of spring was rich with renewed life. He was a man of imagination strictly controlled, and he did not allow himself to feel the season. He was simply the more anxious about Josui. What would the spring do to her this year? Last year she had broken into restlessness which he had understood very well, for he had studied psychology as a necessity for medicine. Mind and body were well or ill together. He had given her sedatives of a harmless sort and had set her to typing the first hundred pages of his manuscript each day as soon as she came home from school. The hot weather began early and her restlessness sank into listlessness. He became convinced, however, that beneath her gentle manners she concealed a passionate nature. Marriage was therefore imperative and soon.

He glanced at his gold wrist watch, hidden under the falling sleeve of his robe. In the hospital he wore western dress but he had learned now to prefer the robe of dark silk, belted at the waist, his feet in heelless slippers in the house, or outdoors, in wooden clogs. He felt free, thus clothed. It was nearly one o'clock. Josui was late. Where had she loitered? The meal must be ready although the servants, directed by their mistress, had not summoned him. They were waiting for Josui.

He frowned, forgetting the garden. If she did not come within fifteen minutes, he would wait no longer. He loved his plain and silent wife, but he enjoyed his meals more if Josui was with them. Nevertheless, he would not indulge his child. He would go in without her, in fifteen minutes, and he would order the food put away if when he was finished she had not come. The order of his house must not be disturbed. At two o'clock he would return to the hospital to see his patients.

He was spared the decision because Josui came in exactly ten minutes. He heard the brass bell fastened on the other side of the gate tremble into sound, then the gate opened and closed. Her western shoes clicked briskly upon the stone path and the maidservant exclaimed in welcome.

He waited, still gazing into the pool, his back to the house. It was the duty of the daughter to search for her father. In a moment he heard her soft voice.

"Father, I am home."

He allowed himself to turn, without smiling. "You are very late."

"Father, it is not my fault," she replied. In the garden, the sunlight streaming down upon her, he was frightened by her beauty. She had walked along the street from the college, looking like this! Her hair was shining black, her great eyes were bright and dark, her cheeks were pink with heat, her lips red. She had changed her school clothes, even in the few minutes she had been home, and she wore a soft green kimono. At least she had not worn this garment upon the street. Her school clothes were ugly.

"How is it not your fault?" he demanded in a stern voice.

"American soldiers were walking down the street," she explained. "There were many of them. Everybody had to wait."

"Where did you wait?" he demanded.

"I stepped into the doorway of the hospital so that I would not be in the way."

9

He decided to say no more. "Let us go in and eat. I have little time left. I do not like to be late at the hospital—it makes a bad example for the younger doctors."

She knew her father's strict sense of duty and made quick apology. "I am very sorry, Father." She spoke in Japanese, because she knew he wished it, but she would never speak it as willingly as she did English.

"You have explained that it is not your fault," he replied. He walked in front of her, his hands behind his back, looking to one side and another as he went. "Observe the azalea," he said. "It has never been finer."

"It is beautiful," she agreed.

He weighed the sound of her voice, as later he would watch the look upon her face, the pace of her every movement, to gauge, if he could, the temperature of her heart. He would have no peace until she was married, and he could not endure another spring in this anxiety. A daughter was a burden, precious beyond any other, and so the heavier.

Josui was aware of her father's secret observation during the noon meal. She was always aware of him and she knew very well his anxiety concerning her, and acknowledged to herself the reason for it. She hid herself from him. He did not know what she was thinking or what indeed she was. Though her conduct was perfect in his presence, he suspected, without accusation, that this perfection was not at all what she was. In this he was right. She lived a double life in this house, not from discontent, but from overflow of energy. This energy, she often thought, must be because she had lived in California until she was fifteen years old, drinking the milk of cows fed on clover and grain and eating fruits and vegetables and meats. Her body was bursting with feeling and strength. Her mind was intense and curious. Thus she was entirely different from the Japanese girls, pale and quiet, who watched her with admiration and dislike. She was called The American, and she did not deny the charge.

"You walk like American women," Haru Mishima said.

There were some American women to be seen in the city, although not so many as in Tokyo and Osaka. Josui observed them and felt that she did walk like them. She did not turn her toes in and her legs were straight. But she loved little pigeon-toed Haru, although she did not know why, except that she loved people easily, it might be, from the very excess of her energy. Though her food was no longer milk and bread and butter, eggs and meat as it had been in America, she ate heartily of rice and fish and vegetables. Her mother laughed at her today.

"Who would think you are the daughter of an educated man?" she now said. "You eat like the child of a peasant."

They sat on their legs around the low table upon which the food was placed. The maidservant had put before each of them a lacquered bowl of clear soup, in which floated a scalloped slice of radish and a bit of green sea lettuce. Three bowls of fish and vegetables were set in the center of the table and into fresh wooden bowls, lacquered black and gold, Yumi the maid dipped white dry rice from a wooden container. She bowed only slightly as she set each bowl in place. The deep bow was no longer proper since the Occupation and democracy. A slight bow, however, Dr. Sakai required. The maid was pleased that he did so, for it meant that the house had a master, even though it was not usual for the master to eat with the mistress and the daughter. Americans did so, she had heard from other housemaids at the market. Her master was therefore something less than real Japanese, but something more than American. She classified him thus and felt content.

Dr. Sakai, secretly observing his daughter, thought her color too high. Her cheeks, always pink, were red.

"Did you stand in the sun while the Americans passed?" he asked.

"Yes, I did," she admitted. "I left my parasol at home this morning. I did not think the sun would be so bright. There were clouds over the mountains when we breakfasted."

"Such clouds always mean clearness by noon," he declared. "It is from the sea that we must expect rain."

Mrs. Sakai looked at Josui. "You are certainly quite red. After the meal you had better put some white powder on your face. It makes a girl look coarse to have such cheeks."

"I wish I were not an only child," Josui said, pouting and smiling. "You have nothing to do, you two parents, but to examine me."

Both parents looked away from her.

"The tokonoma must be freshly arranged tomorrow," Mrs. Sakai said.

The tokonoma alcove faced the garden. From the end of the room where they sat at the table budding willow and plum blossoms leaned above the small incense urn. Yesterday Josui had placed a bronze frog under the drooping plum. Three objects could be placed in the tokonoma but never more. Her father had employed one of the best teachers in the city to instruct her in such matters. The teacher was a widow, slight and small, who lived with her son and his family in a small gray house by the Katsura River.

"Tomorrow I will cut peach blossoms," Josui said.

"With peach blossoms the bowl of rose quartz would be suitable," her father replied.

The atmosphere, which had been growing difficult, was thus restored to calm. Josui said no more, she made herself assiduous in offering the dishes to her parents and averted their displeasure by silence. Had her brother lived, she might have shared with him the burden of their intense love. With him, too, she could have shared her memories of America. He might even have invited her to visit him, for by now he would have been married to his fiancée, and there might have been children. The fiancée, after proper mourning, had married another man and they no longer heard from her. Nevertheless, Josui could remember her quite well. She was a small, lively girl, who wore her black hair heavily curled about a round pale face. She wore bright American clothes and little high-heeled shoes, and once she had been chosen May Queen at the Los Angeles High School. When Josui thought of her it was as May Queen, wearing a spangled silver dress and a crown of polished tin upon her freshly curled hair. Her father was the minister at the Christian church. The Sakai family had always been Buddhist and this had troubled the Christian family. Was Buddhism not heathen? It had been a matter for dissension between her brother and her parents. Dr. Sakai did not wish to see his son married in a church. None of it now mattered, since the marriage had never come to pass. When the wedding day came, her brother was dead, the Christian family was in Arizona behind barbed wire, and the Sakai family was here in Kyoto. Nobody in this house had mentioned the wedding day but she knew that her parents remembered, and she herself had gone alone into the garden and behind a tall rock she had wept for her brother.

"Takashi Matsui invited me to take tea with him," her father remarked at this moment. "Since the invitation came five days ago this afternoon is the time." He had finished eating and was sipping the pale green tea he enjoyed.

Takashi Matsui was his richest patient, who had a rebellious gall bladder which he would not have cut out. He was a man still not old, and he had three sons, one a prisoner in Russia, one who had been killed in the attack upon Nanking, and a third who was now a young man. This third son made the father cheerful, for he believed that never again would Japan go to war, and so he could keep at least the one son. Was it not written in the new Constitution that Japan was never to rearm? This had been demanded by the American conquerors. So upon the third son Takashi Matsui lavished love and money. It had seemed useless to him to educate his other two sons, since they would inevitably be compelled to be soldiers who would probably die in the vast wars then being prepared by the men who were in power, but Kobori was now at the university in Tokyo.

The Matsui family was very old, and the Kyoto branch was not the most important. It was, however, the most conservative and Takashi Matsui was certainly the first and still almost the only man to begin again the tea ceremony after the war ended. Under his instruction Dr. Sakai planned, after the Occupation was over and independence restored, to build a teahouse of his own in the far corner of the garden where was the most quiet spot. Many of the new Japanese ridiculed the ancient tea ceremony but Dr. Sakai did not tolerate this attitude in his presence. He believed it important to revive the old rites and customs as soon as possible in order that the Japanese spirit could revive also. In the tea ceremony meditation upon art and nature mingled with pleasant social intercourse and delicious food. He ate sparingly of his noon meal now because he knew that in the late afternoon he would enjoy a menu which began with a soup of bean paste, was carried through fish and game and vegetable dishes, to end again with a light soup and sweets. There was also the thick green tea, made from powdered tea leaves, gathered from the most tender leaves of shaded ancient trees and mild of flavor.

After the four-hour ceremony he might or might not have time for private talk with his host. If the opportunity came he would allow the old gentleman to begin to talk about his sons. When such talk began inevitably it would lead to talk about the precious third son, and this might in turn lead, as it almost had before on two occasions, to the subject of Josui, the precious only daughter.

Neither father nor daughter spoke of what was in their minds as they finished the meal in silence. Mr. Matsui's third son Kobori was now of an age to marry. He was in fact two years older than Josui. In the old days the two fathers would have arranged the matter but in these days they knew they could not do so. The atomic bombs that fell on

Hiroshima and Nagasaki had destroyed more than bricks and mortar or even human flesh. Dr. Sakai had not yet spoken to his daughter of the young man, but he had told his wife that Kobori wished such a marriage, and that Josui should consider it. This the mother had repeated to the daughter. Josui had considered, but she could not make up her mind. She felt restless and unwilling even to think of Kobori. Certainly she did not hate him. No woman could hate a young man who was handsome and well educated, earnest and proud. She met him often, never by engagement, but by chance. He went to the university in Tokyo, but he came home for holidays. She had met him at the cherry blossom festival only a few weeks ago, a large young man, whose eyes were brown. She had felt quite at ease with him, the more so because he blushed when he saw her. He had unusually white skin and a high forehead and anyone could see him blush. She had admired the clearness of his red blood and white skin, and she had complimented him in her frank American fashion on his pale-gray American suit. In spite of her admiration she had not fallen in love with him, which made her wonder at herself, for she yearned to fall in love. Her heart was trembling and ready. She wanted to love a man and be his wife. She knew desire and the longing to be subdued by love and so to yield herself. Nevertheless, when she looked at Kobori her stubborn heart withdrew from him, and desire grew cold.

She suppressed a strange inclination to be brusque in answer to his mild voice and to look away from his large long eyes, moist with love. What right had he to love her so much

16

and so openly when she had given him no sign of encouragement?

Such rebellious thoughts fought in her bosom while in continuing silence she finished her meal and rose from the table to bow to her parents. She must return at once to the college, for she was already a little late. They accepted her bows and lingered over the tea bowls. She left them thus, and went to her room and changed her kimono for her school dress. She did not, however, wear a hat and this time, mindful of the comment upon her red cheeks, she took her green silk parasol to shade her face. The dress itself was striped green and white and made with a skirt and blouse in the American manner and yet she felt sure that it was not what girls of twenty were wearing today in America. The sleeves were long and buttoned at the cuffs and the edge of the full skirt hung just below her calves. The neck was high but today as soon as she left the gate she unbuttoned it so that the air could reach her throat.

The street was quiet as she came out of the garden gate. The Americans, she supposed, were scattered through the city, sight-seeing. Often enough they came clattering in from Tokyo or Osaka, to spend a holiday in Kyoto where, she supposed, their guidebooks told them the ancient Japanese culture still remained. She had heard that the American bombers had been ordered during the war not to destroy Kyoto, just as the Japanese had not destroyed Peking. Her father had not believed that Kyoto would be spared because he did not believe that Americans understood culture. "We are compelled to choose," he sometimes complained, "between the savagery of Communism and the vulgarism of America."

Her father was an extremist, she often repeated to herself and always with satisfaction, knowing that above all other accusations this was the one, did she dare to make it openly, which he would have most violently denied. He strove for tranquillity, he struggled for calm, he was punishing America, she thought, for sending him away and the punishment was to love Japan only and all the old Japanese ways and beliefs. What nonsense the tea ceremony was, and how foolish it looked for grown-up men to sit solemnly in a little house in a garden gazing into space and waiting to drink a green soup made of powdered tea! Her father said that the tea was rich in vitamins, and aside from the beauty and the spiritual meaning of the ceremony, the tea itself nourished the body. She did not like it. Last autumn she had gone with her parents to Mr. Matsui's tea ceremony, which her father insisted on calling Cha-no-Yu, although it was nothing but a tea ceremony whatever it was called. The conversation, so carefully spiritual and mental and solemn, was only boring. Mr. Matsui spoke little four-lined poems as though he were composing them at that moment, whereas she knew that he had spent hours on them beforehand. If ever she knew Kobori better she would say so. But why wait? She would say it the very next time she saw him.

She walked down the street thinking such thoughts and enjoying them, emphasizing them to herself because she knew she would never dare to speak them aloud. Even her mother would not listen to them, and if she insisted on speaking, her mother would shake her head and cover her ears with her hands and sit patiently thus until Josui stopped. Sometimes she wanted to scream at her mother and pull her hands away from her ears, but she could not do it. All over the soft hot American inside of her there was a crust of hard Japanese. She was like a volcano, sealed by its own cooling hardening lava, and yet boiling and surging within.

She glanced about the streets as she walked in the sun, her parasol making a moving circle of shade as she went. Yesterday there had been rain and now the green of old trees and gnarled shrubs, the brilliance of the azaleas everywhere blooming in the parks and gardens sharpened the spring. She walked quietly, her head high while she breathed in the sweet air of the day. Energy strengthened itself in her blood, and urged her. She wanted to run, to fling out her arms. She used to run like that in America, a crowd of the girls around her running. They ran, their arms outspread like wings, down the tree-shaded street of the suburb where they lived, running as though they were flying like birds, laughing about nothing. She had never run like that in Japan and she never saw girls running, not even little girls. They plodded in clogs or in heavy leather shoes, or they slipped along in rubber-soled cloth shoes, which would have been nice to run in.

She reached the gate of the hospital beyond which was the college. Here she had stood in the morning when the young American men passed by. She had not looked at them, beyond a quick glance of curiosity. They looked alike, all laughing, talking, pushing each other. People said they were like schoolboys, always pushing and laughing and shoving, pretending to fight. People asked each other, "Are the Americans only children?"

Over the hospital gate the wisteria was in full bloom. The purple clusters, heavy as grapes, hung thick among the pale-green leaves. It was the season of wisteria and iris and peonies, and she loved them. Her father did not care for flowers. In their garden the beauty was austere, rock and pine and water, with only the bamboo for softness. Her mother grew the flowers they used for the house in the kitchen garden, except for a clump of blue iris on the north side of the house.

As usual when she thought of her father, Josui felt a strange mixed love, admiring and resentful. She wished continually that they had never left America. Her father did not understand and would not try to understand how much more difficult it was to be a woman in Japan than it was in America. When she thought of the girls in California as she remembered them, it seemed to her that they were young queens. But here the women were never queens. They were subjects, waiting, doing their duty. It was doubtful that they would ever be queens, for when the Americans went away, her father often said, the old Japan would come back, or much of it. Then the young people could not behave as they did now, he said. The Americans were like guests in the house. One was compelled to allow the children apparent freedom when strangers were present, but when the guests were gone the children would be punished.

She sighed and then she smelled the penetrating yet soft sweetness of the wisteria. She had reached the hospital gate and she drew down her parasol. Someone stood beside the gate, a tall, thin young man, an American, wearing a uniform. He leaned against the wall, one foot crossed over the other, and his hands in his pockets. She looked at him, startled, and he smiled at her.

He said, "I've been waiting for you."

She was too surprised to speak. She stared at him, her mouth frankly open. He was blond, young, and quite beautiful. Yes, he was that. His eyes were blue, as blue as the iris. His skin was smooth and fair. He had big white teeth, and his mouth was pleasant. He looked strong and healthy, his shoulders wide and his waist thin, though the leather belt was tight enough.

His eyes were laughing. He said, "Will I do?"

She blushed. She had been staring at him as though he were some sort of strange sight. But it was because he was not strange that she had looked at him so long. He made her think of all that she had forgotten, the boys at the school in California, those boys whom she had just begun to notice when her father decided so abruptly to leave America forever. His voice was like her brother's, his words spoken as she remembered.

"Or don't you speak English?" the young man went on.

"I do speak English," she said easily.

The young man took off his cap reverently. "I've never had a prayer answered before," he said. "It is too much."

"What is too much?" she asked.

"To find that the one girl in Japan I've wanted to meet can speak my language."

She smiled. "How have you wanted to meet me? I never saw you before."

"You looked at me this morning but you didn't see me," he said. "I saw you, though, standing under this bower. It is a bower, isn't it? We have one in our yard at home, a wisteria bower, and I looked at it this morning because it made me think of my mother and there you were, standing under it, looking—well, beautiful."

"I was waiting for the Americans to pass."

"We passed. But I came back. They are on their way to Nara. A pleasure expedition, you know. We had leave. I can go to Nara any time. But I figured that if I came back here and waited long enough you'd come this way again."

"I am on my way to school."

"You still a schoolgirl?"

"College, please. I must go on. I shall be late."

He was still standing with his cap in his hand and the sun shone down upon curly yellow hair, a light yellow, because his eyes were blue. His face was thin, the jaw square, and the cheekbones somewhat high. He looked very clean.

"I want to make your acquaintance," he said. His voice was deep and big, but he kept it soft.

"I cannot," she said simply. "I must pass, please."

"Why not?" he persisted. He moved along at her side. Much agitated, she put up her parasol again. What should she now do? If someone she knew saw her with this American at her side and told her father, she would certainly suffer his most terrible anger. "Please go away," she said. She hurried along without looking again at his tall figure beside her.

"There must be some way to meet a nice girl in Japan,"

22

he insisted. "Suppose I call at your home, send in my card, meet your parents."

"Oh, no," she cried. "How angry would you make my father!"

"Why?"

"Oh, because so," she answered, distracted.

"Doesn't he like America?" he demanded with some sternness.

"He knows America very well," she replied.

"He does?"

"Once we lived there. Then when war came we left there to live here."

She had reached the college gates and here really she must shake him off. It was only her luck that no one had seen them at this early hour in the afternoon, when most people were sleeping for an hour or so.

"You must not come with me, please," she said desperately. "It will truly make trouble for me if you come."

"Then I will not come," he said at once. "But I shall be here again tomorrow. And here is my name."

He took a small leather case from his pocket and drew a narrow card from it and held it up to her until she could only take it—Second Lieutenant Allen Kennedy.

"Will you tell me your name?" he asked.

She wanted to refuse, but she lifted her eyes to his. He was so nice, so courteous, she thought, his mouth, half smiling, was so gentle. And she had been secretly longing to meet some Americans. She was lonely. It was hard to find friends among Japanese when none of them knew anything about the life she had lived in California most of her years.

They even disliked her for that, envied her while they pretended to like her.

"My name is Josui Sakai."

"Josui Sakai," he repeated. "You wouldn't tell me where you live?"

She shook her head in a panic and then could not resist the handsome pleading eyes. She felt warm, she wanted to laugh, and not knowing what to do, she put down her parasol and ran into the gate and slipped behind a mass of bamboos just inside. He came to the gate and stood, gazing this way and that. Then, hesitating a moment longer, he went away. But under the wisteria bower he paused. The sweetness of the flowers was suddenly penetrating. He had not noticed the fragrance before. Yet how had it escaped him? He breathed it deeply into his lungs, an intoxicating sweetness, always, forever, to be associated with the lovely hidden girl. He lingered, hesitating, overcome with a portent he could not comprehend. What was he getting into here, entangled in what fragrance of desire?

From her hiding place she saw him look upward in some amazement and then suddenly she saw him go away.

She came out from behind the bamboos then, half expecting him to be hiding near the gate. But he was not there. She felt sorry, though relieved, and believing she would never see him again, she sat through her afternoon classes, remembering his young and beautiful face, which though every feature was different from her own, still seemed so natural to her, a part of her childhood and never yet forgotten.

Dr. Sakai, refreshed as always by the tea ceremony, sat in a meditative silence with the other guests. There were few homes now where the ceremony was performed with its full spiritual meaning. He considered himself an amateur, since in his childhood home in California there had been no such place as a teahouse. His parents were too busy and too wearied in coping with the new country to teach their children even what they remembered. Therefore it was with humility that Dr. Sakai had become the friend as well as the physician of the Matsui family. He confessed to the aging Japanese gentleman that though he had returned to his own country it was as a stranger and that he must learn again how to be a Japanese.

"It is not that I have forgotten," Dr. Sakai explained. "I have read and I have studied about Japan all my life, so that when the choice was given me, I knew that I must come home. Alas, now that I am here, there is much I must learn how to do."

"You have the spirit and all else can be mastered," Mr. Matsui had replied.

He himself had never left the shores of Japan, and it was with curiosity that he welcomed the tall somewhat severe-looking doctor who with all his effort to be wholly Japanese would remain American, without knowing it. In the teahouse on this very afternoon he observed, for example, the too zealous spirit of Dr. Sakai. The meditative spirit does not come upon demand. Instead of saying this, Mr. Matsui endeavored to guide the conversation into peaceful ways. Thus he took out of its silk-lined box his tea bowl, a treasure which he prized above all else he had.

"This bowl," he said, "belonged to a friend of mine who is now dead. He was a master of Cha-no-Yu and it was from this bowl that he always drank. When he died he gave it to me, because his son, though an only son, would not learn the rites."

Dr. Sakai received the bowl with exaggerated care, leaning his elbows properly on the floor mats. One does not hold a valuable bowl simply with the unsupported hand. When Mr. Matsui drank from the bowl he placed it in the palm of his left hand and held it with his right. Dr. Sakai contemplated the bowl, a pale-green shape upon which was no carving or design. It was as restful as still water, pure circle and curve. When he handed it back to Mr. Matsui he sighed and looked about the room. The hanging scroll, the tea caddy, the vase, the kettle brazier and tray, and all the implements of the ceremony were beautiful in their simplicity. The five guests, all men, sat erect upon their folded legs and yet at ease, their spirits calmed by the perfection of their surroundings. These were men who understood beauty. They were connoisseurs, comprehending that form without spirit is void, and this comprehension led them from one step to another in pursuit of beauty for spirit's sake, man and nature in complete unity. Thus they believed that the principles of beauty must permeate every detail and article of life, architecture, ceramics, decoration. The iris today in Mr. Matsui's teahouse were arranged in two stalks, one in bud, one in flower, combined with a long leaf and a short one. Seeming artless, leaf and flower were placed with reverent care, but all knew that while this simplicity appeared natural, it was beyond nature. To achieve simplicity was the ultimate of sophistication. The fully matured mind reaches simplicity as its final development.

During the long ceremony and the feast there had been no conversation which was troubling. When it was over, however, and the sun was about to set, the friends rose and making the proper bows of thanks to their host, they left the teahouse and went out into the waiting room. There they could talk as they wished, and there Mr. Matsui joined them after a few minutes.

This talk, among men who had never left their country and were intent now upon preserving the culture of their people throughout the years of foreign occupation, was deeply satisfying to Dr. Sakai. He had emptied himself of America. Heart and soul were empty, and the long quiet conversations about the old Japan, the ancient ways, the evil and the good, created a new man within him.

Thus he understood how it was that the people of Japan had allowed themselves to be tricked into ways of life which were not their own. "Every people has its evil spirits," Mr. Tanaka explained today as they sat in the waiting hall. "Into every country there are born some rude souls who cannot be taught. They are wild from birth, doomed doubtless by some crime in a former existence. They cannot be controlled. They distress parents and family, they are a menace to their communities, and they draw to them the weak and the restless. These among us, more than a century ago, seized upon the evil mood of the times, they declared to our people that the western powers who were dividing up Asia for themselves would also take Japan. It may be that they were right—who knows? At least our people grew afraid and out of this fear the wild ones were allowed their way. Thus they built up army and navy, they seized Manchuria, they hoped to make an empire for their own protection. This was the beginning of the great change. Had we dared to reject fear, perhaps we would have remained invulnerable. Fear is the beginning of all weakness."

Mr. Tanaka was old, a small withered man who had lived through seventy years of the great change. He had never worn western dress and in his house there was not a chair or a western bed. He had inherited a moderate wealth and he had lived upon it, though with increasing difficulty. He had lost all his sons in the recent war, and his own father had been killed in the first war with China, many decades ago. He himself abhorred all war and in his revulsion he had become a Buddhist, refusing to follow Shinto, because it insisted upon a patriotism which he denied. He declared himself a humanist, a lover of all men, and he was scrupulous even toward the Americans.

"There has been so much cruelty in the years in which I have lived," Mr. Tanaka said thoughtfully. No one interrupted him. He sat, a small folded figure, facing the open door into the garden, now filled with the yellow light from the setting sun. "When the atomic bomb fell upon Nagasaki, I went there to see what it had done. You know that Nagasaki is the home of my family. The old house is gone, and it was the tomb of my oldest relatives, six of them, who had lived there all their lives. Since my visit, I have not been able to tolerate the smallest cruelty. I cannot, for example, push my way into the tram car, however crowded. Such a small cruelty, even to push someone for a moment, and being so old, it may be said that I cannot hurt anyone by a slight push. Nevertheless, I cannot perform it. It would add, for me, the final last cruelty which would make the world too much for me. I cannot crush an ant or kill a fly, or allow a child to weep. Any cruelty, more than has been done, not only here but everywhere in the world, you understand, would be too much for me. No more, O Buddha God!" He lifted his thin old face and closed his eyes, and Dr. Sakai bowed his head. He felt deep in his breast a wrenching sadness that was somehow strengthening.

When at last they rose to make their final farewells, he had seen no opportunity to talk with Mr. Matsui about son and daughter and he had no wish to make the opportunity now. The afternoon had been pure. He had bathed his soul in the past and he had learned still more of what it was to be a Japanese. He did not want to think of the young or of tomorrow. There was time enough.

He walked home slowly and at peace.

In the main room of the house Mrs. Sakai awaited her husband. How would she tell him what had happened this afternoon in his absence? She was afraid of him because she admired him above all human beings and had she dared, she would have loved him wholly. But it was impossible to love anyone whom she admired so much. So intelligent a mind as his saw every flaw and she was humble. Moreover, she carried within the silences of her heart a secret sin which she could never confess. She did not like Japan. She had not wanted to leave America. She would have preferred even the concentration camp, where all her friends had lived. It was uncomfortable, of course. She knew all the hardships because he told her of them. Nevertheless, she would have been with her friends, and they could have done their cooking and washing together, and there would have been plenty of time to talk. She would have had more time than ever before, because there was no need to earn their food. Food, however poor, was provided. Also the weather in the desert was dry and warm. Here in Kyoto the climate was damp and the house cold, even now. The water in the garden, the fogs from the sea and the mountains made the house damp.

She sat properly on her folded legs, wearing her second-best purple kimono, the neck band of white silk very clean, waiting for her husband. Upon her feet were snow-white socks of cotton cloth, the soles double and stitched. She made the socks herself. She knew how to do everything properly because she had been reared in Japan, her family poor, and living upon a tiny mountainous farm in the high hills above Nagasaki and near Unzen, near enough to the hot springs there so that sometimes in the spring or the autumn when they took a holiday to see the flowers or the coloring trees, they had stopped to cook their fish in the steam rising between the rocks.

So poor had her father been, with so many daughters, that one day when he read in a newspaper that brides were wanted for young Japanese men in America, he had sent her picture and registered her name. That was how she had gone to America. Dr. Sakai's mother had chosen her and he had approved her gentle face. She had as a young girl a very pleasant face, though not pretty. It had not occurred to her that she would be sent to a man who was a doctor and who therefore disliked her bowed legs and short thick feet and hands. He had inquired into her diet, which had always been rice and fish and a few vegetables. Sotan Sakai was very easily in a temper when the children were born and she was not careful to feed them exactly as he said, although in the boy's case, none of it had mattered, since he was killed. How she had forced him to drink the abomination of cow's milk and how he had cried! She wished that she had not made him do anything he did not like, for it was no use now. She could never see even his grave. As usual when she thought of Kensan, her son, the tears came. She wiped her eyes cautiously on the inside lining of her wide sleeves, and blew her nose on one of the bits of paper tissue she kept in the bottom of her left sleeve. Then she wadded the tissue and dropped it into a waste jar near by. She had taken up many American ways but not the dirty one of cloth handkerchiefs.

At this moment she heard her husband's footsteps and the maid hurrying to meet him and take off his shoes. She rose and went toward the entrance and bowed. He nodded at her and made the sound of greeting which was not quite her name, in the presence of the maid. She followed him then into the room where she had been waiting and when he sat down, she knelt and put her hand on the teapot in its padded cover. The pot was hot and she was about to pour him a bowl of the tea. But he put up his hand.

"No tea now. I have drunk of the best."

For one thing she was grateful to Japan. The kimono hid her crooked legs. In America she had worn cotton house

31

dresses as the other women did and she was always conscious of those legs, exposed to his disfavor, though he never spoke of them any more. He had merely looked away, and this was more cruel than speech.

How would she tell him what had happened this afternoon? She coughed behind her hand.

He looked up sharply. "What is the matter, Hariko?" he asked.

"I scarcely know how to tell you," she replied. She looked at him and he saw her eyes were troubled. She was still a pleasant-looking woman; that is, she had a gentle face, and her eyes were round and childlike. Round eyes were not considered the most beautiful in a Japanese woman's face, but he liked them.

"Is the Sung vase broken?" he asked in alarm.

"Oh, not so dreadful," she said quickly.

"The big carp is not dead?"

"Oh, no," she said again. "Nothing is dead."

"Come, come," he said. "I will not kill you or even beat you."

This was good humor and she was encouraged. "A young man came here this afternoon asking for you," she said with much caution.

"A patient?"

"Not a patient," she hesitated, and then said it all at once. "An American soldier."

Dr. Sakai's thin, handsome face lost all expression.

"I do not know any American."

"He did not say he knew you," she replied. "He only wishes to know you."

"How did he know my name?"

"It was given to him, he said, by a friend."

"What did you tell him?"

"I said you were out. Then he wished to wait, but I would not allow it. I feared that Josui would come in at any moment. It would not have been well."

"Certainly not."

"I told him that I would tell you and he said he would come again. He asked at what hour are you at home? I said it is best to go to your office at the hospital at ten o'clock in the morning. I said you do not receive unknown persons here at home."

"Very right," he paused and pursed his lips. "An American! Probably someone over there gave him my name."

"Yes," she agreed. She felt her heart lighten. She had done well, she had told him, he did not feel angry with her. It was wicked to think of anger, for he never spoke to her one angry word, and yet she was so sensitive to his disapproval that she felt the slightest shadow of its darkness over his spirit. His self-control was absolute but it concealed nothing from her. She rose gracefully in spite of her short legs.

"I will now excuse myself. There are things to be done."

He nodded without reply. He did not wish to lose the mood of the afternoon spent with his friends. He sat facing the garden after she had left the room, motionless, and deliberately he put out of his mind the thought of the intruding American. The gardener had sprinkled the stones with water and had wet the rocks and the shrubs.

Mrs. Sakai, watching him, slid the latticed screens softly behind her. He had not asked her what sort of a man the

33

American was and she had not told him, and this, it now occurred to her, might be a sort of deception. She had liked the young man. She used to see rich young men in California, although when she asked him he said he did not come from there. She had asked him almost at once, "Do you come from California?"

"You speak English?" he had exclaimed.

"A little," she said, trying not to smile because of her bad teeth. Americans liked nice white teeth but the same lack that bowed her legs, it seemed, had also spoiled her teeth. It had not seemed important to anybody when she was young because countrywomen blackened their teeth anyway when they were married. Her own mother had black teeth, as black as lacquer.

"You come from California, too?" she had asked again.

"Why, too?" he had asked. "Are you from California?"

"We came from there," she said.

"I am from Virginia," he said. "It's a nice place."

"I do not know," she replied.

Then she had checked this informal conversation. She was always too friendly with Americans. She became cold. Still she liked him. He was so young, so fresh looking. His name, written down upon a card, which he had handed to her, was Allen Kennedy. He spoke it for her and she repeated it. She had never learned to read English.

Now she pattered noiselessly down a narrow corridor to the room in which they slept. It could be thrown into the house by drawing back the screens which were its walls, but she usually kept them closed, so that she had a place for retirement. She had nothing really to do, since Sotan had told her not to prepare a night meal. Josui ate bread at night and some foreign jam and tinned milk in her tea. She herself drank a bowl of rice gruel before she went to sleep. She drew out a chest of drawers so small that it could be set upon a low table, and kneeling she slowly rearranged the contents, bits of jewelry and ribbon, some photographs of Kensan, a picture of their house in Los Angeles which was no longer theirs. Negroes lived in it now.

The screen slid back a few inches and she saw Josui smiling at her.

"Mamma-san, here you are."

"Have you seen your father?"

"No."

Josui came into the room. Her mother saw at once that something had happened to her, something pleasant. The long widely opened eyes, too large for Japanese eyes, were bright with secret joy. Josui had not yet learned to hide herself behind a calm face.

"You look happy," Mrs. Sakai said. "Something nice has come."

Josui shook her head. "Only the spring, Mother."

But could the spring alone curve into tenderness every line of that soft and pretty face? Mrs. Sakai doubted. She continued to gaze at her daughter pensively, trying to remember how she had felt the spring when she was twenty. At that age she had worked as hard as a man upon her father's farm and spring meant plowing and dragging the heavy harrow and scattering the seed. When early summer came the fields were flooded for rice and standing deep in the muddy water she had helped to plant the seedlings. No, she could remember nothing about the spring.

She did not press her daughter. Josui belonged to her father, and it was Kensan who had belonged to her. Had her son lived she would now have had grandchildren, dear little ones looking American, which she would not have minded at all. In America the women had washing machines and electric stoves.

Josui was standing beside her and she picked up the pictures of Kensan. There were several of them, some taken when he was a little boy. There was one of him with Setsu, his fiancée, her hair freshly cut and curled.

"I wish my father would let me cut my hair," Josui said in sudden discontent. She wore her hair straight and long, brushed back from her face and rolled into a round heavy knot on her neck. She could never curl this long hair.

"He will not," her mother said. She, too, was looking at Setsu. "I suppose she has children by now."

"Born in the concentration camp," Josui reminded her.

"Yes," her mother said. But still had Kensan lived and had they all stayed together it might have been pleasant to have the children though in camp. The Americans did not kill anybody. It was not like Germany. There was enough to eat. "I think the camp was not too bad."

"Oh, I don't know." Josui sighed restlessly. She frowned and the light went out of her face, in spite of the spring.

Her mother pondered the sigh. Should she tell Josui about the American caller? It was better not to do so, even as interesting news. She began putting back the trinkets and the pictures, each carefully wrapped in tissue paper.

"I am going to change my clothes," Josui said.

She went away and pulled the screen shut again. Mrs. Sakai was glad that she had said nothing at all. It was indeed better never to speak.

In the particular corner which was her own in the wide-spreading house Josui was looking at herself in the mirror. She knelt facing the garden, the late sunlight falling full upon her. The mirror stood on a low Chinese chest of drawers, not more than a foot high and made of polished blackwood. She had changed her school clothes for a pale-pink kimono, across the skirt of which was embroidered a branch of peach blossom in a deeper pink.

What did Americans call pretty? At least she was fair, her skin as white as almond kernels. Her lower lip was perhaps too full. She was perhaps too healthy looking. Her cheeks were as pink as the peach blossoms, pinker than the silk of her kimono. Her eyes were Japanese, and perhaps he would think them ugly, although they were double lidded, as many Japanese eyes were not. Certainly her nose was too low, that an American would say. If she were in America now, would she have made friends again? Everyone was out of the camps at last. They said the Americans were kind to them once more. There was no trouble, or very little. A great many newspapers had printed stories of Kensan's battalion in Italy, telling how brave they were. Some had told about Kensan himself. He had been among the first to attack the hill they had been ordered to take. He had led the others, and so he was killed. "It is better not to be too brave," her mother had said, weeping, as she

37

looked at his picture in the American papers that they had received.

If tomorrow the American met her again, what should she do? She should not have told him her name. Yet not to do so would have seemed too rude. She drew from her bosom the little narrow card he had given her and she spoke his name softly—Allenn Ken-neddy. At home he would be called Allenn. What did the name mean? She did not know. The family name, Ken-neddy, must also have some meaning. And Virginia? She knew it was far from California. It was a distant state, in the eastern part of America. She could not remember anything else from her schoolbooks. Tomorrow she would find it in the college atlas. She put the card into her bosom and looked into the mirror again. She saw the curve of her lips, and the droop of her eyelids. She put her palms to her cheeks. They felt hot. Her hands were small and cool. She had always cold hands. If he should want to touch her hand, shaking her hand in greeting as the Americans did, she would not let him. The palm of a girl's hand is a private place. It is not to be touched carelessly or by a stranger. Only her husband is allowed to stroke the palm of her hand.

While she mused upon this the screen slid back and the maid Yumi stood there, stolid in her blue cotton kimono. She stared at Josui before the mirror.

She said loudly, "Your father asks you to come. He is in the pines."

Josui closed the mirror set in the lid that covered the top of the small chest. "Tell him I am coming."

Dr. Sakai was walking in the garden under the pines

when Yumi came to report. The green moss lay deep and soft under his feet and the air was tinged with the clean smell of the fresh resin, heated by the day's sun.

"The honorable daughter is coming," Yumi said with her slight bow.

"What was she doing?" Dr. Sakai asked.

"She was looking at her face in the mirror," Yumi replied.

She went away and Dr. Sakai stopped still. Josui, looking at her face in the mirror! Was this not significant? Could it have been that she saw the American, too? There might have been an acquaintance this morning, some slight word spoken. The American soldiers thought nothing of speaking to any girl they saw, and Josui was very pretty—too pretty. He must find out. There must be no secrets. Americans could not be trusted where women were concerned. Josui, his daughter, must not be taken for a geisha or a street girl.

Thus Josui, walking very slowly indeed toward her father, met his dark piercing eyes. His eyebrows were tilted sharply upward. He was frowning, a knot between the brows, from which the two black lines sprang upward like wings of a bird, or of a butterfly, but who could imagine a butterfly poised above the black eyes of her father?

He began impetuously, unable to restrain himself, "I feel you are hiding something from me!"

She was so unused to this sudden attack that she was startled. In America he had been a man of high temper, often angry, quickly repentant, and yet unable to control his anger when he was annoyed. Only in these years since

39

the return had he grown into the silent and restrained man, striving through meditation for self-control.

She lifted her head. "What do I hide from you?"

"I am not stupid," he declared violently. "I am more than a physician, I am also a psychologist. Your mood has changed. You are not the girl you were even yesterday. Something has happened to you."

He was proceeding on instinct but she was amazed at his insight. Did she so easily show herself to him?

"Nothing has really happened," she said. "Yet perhaps you are right. The sight of the Americans today has made me remember much that I thought I had forgotten. Father, I spent fifteen years of my life there, and only five here."

He jerked his head to signify that she must walk beside him. He felt irritable, overspent, too restless to sit down. She understood and they paced together under the pines. It was late twilight, and the afterglow of sunset caught the green of the moss and made it almost phosphorescent.

"You can trust me," her father said. "Indeed, you must trust me. In a sense you are all I have, and even all I ever have had. Your mother has been a good wife, an excellent mother. What more does a man ask? But your mind is like mine. You are also a companion. Your brother was like his mother, but you are like me."

"I am very different," she said with instant rebellion.

"You are more different now than you will be later," he agreed. "The difference in the generations is now most acute in you. Later, when your life is arranged and you do not need to rebel against me in order to show your independence, then you will discover how like you are to me."

40

She felt the strong gossamer of his love wrap her too closely. She pulled away with all her strength and yet in his superior way he enfolded her the more closely. There lay in her bosom the small weapon, the little knife which could cut the net, though it seemed no harsher than a cloud as he drew it about her. She put her hand into her bosom and took out the narrow card. She held it out to him, not saying a word. He bent to peer at the name, and then knowing instantly what it was, he put his hand into his own bosom and took out another exactly like it.

"Where did you get that?" she cried, undone by surprise.

"I may also ask the same question of you," he replied gravely.

"Someone—gave it to me," she said.

"He came here while I was away, and he gave this to your mother," he said, still more gravely.

They looked at each other, he bending the ferocious eyebrows down upon her and she gazing up at him, determined not to be afraid.

"Ah, Josui," he said in his deepest voice.

She drooped, and without a word she put the narrow card into his hand. He took it and put both of the cards into his bosom. "You see, I was right." He spoke tenderly and sadly. "Now tell me, my child, what has happened to you?"

But she could not tell him. The tears spilled out of her eyes and ran down her cheeks. They began to walk again and she lifted the sleeves of her kimono and wiped her eyes.

"I beg of you not to hide yourself from your parents," he said after a long silence. "I will not forbid you anything which is for your good. I think now it will break my heart

41

if you leave us, but doubtless it will not. My heart has been broken before."

She lifted her head. "Because Kensan is dead?"

"No. Long before you or Kensan were born. When I was a young man I—never mind. It does not matter any more."

It did not indeed matter. He was nearly fifty years old, and what had happened when he was young, Josui thought, could not matter now. She shrank from knowing what it was. Her father, she felt, could only have been the man she had always known, imperious, fiercely tender, obstinate, controlling everybody around him. She would think of herself.

"Tell me why you kept the card?" her father was saying, almost coaxingly.

His kindness moved her and she began to sob and talk at the same time, trying to stifle her sobs with her sleeves at her mouth.

"How do I know? There is nothing to tell. He stopped me under the wisteria and asked me my name. I—I—told him. That is all."

"How many times have you seen him?"

"Only the once—today—I promise you. He saw me this morning and he came back. There were so many—I did not see him—the first time they passed."

Her father was kind now that he had the truth. "I do not blame you for what he did. Perhaps you might have refused your name. Nevertheless, as you say, you were too many years in America."

"I did not say so!"

"Many years, then," he conceded. "But we will never return. We shall stay here always. Your life is here, my child.

You will marry here. I shall not force you to marry, I promise you. You may take your time, except, speaking psychologically again," he was trying to lighten his mood for her, "it is best to marry young, when the first desire comes. It is not well to wait too long, especially for a woman. The natural desire wanes, other interests take its place. I saw many women in America who had lost all natural desire. They were absorbed in careers, good enough in some ways but destructive in their effect upon their womanhood. So, let us see what we can do. If it is not to be Kobori Matsui, let us find some other. You shall choose—I am not to be considered an ogre."

She pitied so much his wish to pacify her, discerning behind it his unutterable love, that she had not the heart to refuse his mood. "It is only one more year until I finish at college. I should like to finish."

"Certainly, I agree," he said. "Now shall we say no more? We understand each other?"

"Yes," she murmured, but unwillingly.

"Then—" he paused, and while she looked, he took the cards from his bosom and tore them into fine small pieces. When this was done he stooped and lifted a piece of the deep moss, and under it, as into a little grave, he put the pieces. He covered them with the moss and stood up again. "Come," he said. "Let us go into the house. The night has fallen."

It had, indeed. Under the pines the first fireflies were beginning to gleam.

Allen Kennedy turned restlessly upon the thick quilts.

Japanese beds were deceptive. They seemed soft when one lay down upon them, the quilts filled with down and covered with silk, the mats beneath so deep and yielding. But when he had lain awhile the hardness of the polished wooden floor underneath mats and quilts crept through and defied a man's bones. He was not tired enough, that was the matter. Enemy and ecstasy, desire burned in his blood. The beautiful girl had upset all his careful controls, his schemes, his habits. He loathed the coarse and casual ways of common men in wartime, and yet he felt the same lusts in himself. He would not believe that he was capable of taking a woman's body, however refined, impatiently for his own sake, and yet of course he was. His ever-present need, which he would not again try to slake in a brothel, however urgent it became, had risen against him tonight. He wanted to think of the girl as a pretty picture, but he thought of her only as a female, a creature made for taking.

He sat up abruptly and wrapped his long arms about his legs and bent his head on his knees. He wished that he were not so confused, that he did not at least so confuse love and desire. Some delicacy instilled in him, he supposed, by his mother, that small and dainty creature of immense will nevertheless, had made love and desire inseparable for him. Confronted with a harlot, as he had several times chosen to be, he was impotent. It was so. He was compelled to love before desire could be fulfilled. Here was cause for shame. He envied heartily the coarse louts who went in thirsting and came out boasting. He envied them most of all because they did not know they were louts. The army was full of them and they lived a fine life. But he was made as he was. Ariel could not become Caliban.

He got up, too restless to pretend that he needed sleep. He wrapped about himself the bedroom robe which every Japanese hotel provided for its guests. Good taste was invincible in Japan and it perhaps was why he loved this country. The cheap cotton garment was beautifully designed in blue and white. It was only when they tried to be Western that the good taste faltered. His mother, if she let herself, would enjoy the exquisite pottery, the fine prints, the delicate silks, above all the houses. Mrs. Sakai had not let him come in this afternoon but he had seen behind her bowed head vista upon vista of rooms, lit by the pearly sunlight falling through paper lattices. The vistas ended in a garden. He had seen the silver streak of a waterfall. He had had no opportunity to know educated Japanese. The rules were strict against bringing any Japanese into the quarters Americans occupied. Even on trains they were not allowed to mix. He did not care to mix on the lowest levels. A low-down Japanese, especially female, was for him a degree lower than the low-down American.

But the lovely girl under the wisterias belonged in just such a house. And her name, Josui—he would not have known how to pronounce unless she had spoken it for him. Her face he could not forget, so pure, so pretty, the great eyes, the full lower lip. He had learned to like Oriental eyes. And she spoke English like an American, though not easily. Her accent was good and her voice was soft. She was well bred, and that, too, was unusual. The well-bred girls hid themselves and gave the Americans no opportunity for meeting them. But Josui had been in America and she knew better than that. All the same, she was shy. He would not have liked it had she not been shy.

He stood at the door, open to a tiny corner garden, no more than a curve in the outer wall of the hotel. Still, there was a pool, basin size, and a dwarf tree or two. He had better ask himself what he wanted of this girl Josui. Suppose he allowed his desire to grow—put it, rather, that he did not suppress it utterly and immediately—what would be the end? It would be an embarrassing and even heartbreaking affair. It could be nothing else. She was no Madame Butterfly, he thought, to be loved and left.

The night was dark and still. The faint outlines of the mountains, darker even than the sky, rose beyond the low wall. He had come to Kyoto to see historic beauty and he had seen nothing. Why not let it be as he had planned? There was no need to decide anything now in the small hours of the night, a bad time, as he well knew, to decide anything, a depressing melancholy time of the night, the worst in the twenty-four hours, when the worst in him, too, rose up to make him doubt his own soul. He shrugged his shoulders. Tomorrow he would get up and study his guidebook and make a plan. He would stay as long as necessary to see Kyoto and then he would go back to Tokyo. If he were busy he might forget the girl. Or she might hide herself as the others did.

He felt better as soon as he had made up his mind. He lay down again upon the quilts and closed his eyes. His muscles relaxed, his bones no longer resisted the bottom hardness, and the down quilts were light and warm. He had got quite cold, standing in the open door.

Had the next day been rainy it would have been easy to stay at home. Josui had only one class, mathematics, which she disliked. She had even a little cold, or she could imagine that she had, for she had been restless in her sleep and when she woke before dawn the quilts had slipped away. She slept with a soft pillow. Had she used a hard Japanese pillow, her neck would have been firmly placed, so that she could not turn. Other girls learned to sleep thus held, but she had not. This was her trouble, that she did not make up her mind to accept life whole as it was here. Her father and mother were both more brave than she. That is, her father insisted and her mother obeyed. For this reason she had kept her small rebellions, of which the pillow was one. She rebelled also for her mother's sake.

But the day was fine. The sun rose from a cloudless sky and only upon the mountains was there a wreath of gossamer, soon to melt before the sun. She was compelled to get up, and because the day was so fair she felt compelled also to put on a fresh dress of pale yellow. She would for some wayward reason have liked to wear a kimono today, but her fellow students would have been surprised. Life was clearly divided.

The yellow dress was soft, however, and there were no hard white buttons. A narrow collar of white embroidery made it pleasant with her black hair. She put no oil on her hair, and this too made her different from the others. Small

47

soft hairs were at her temples, not curled but not quite straight.

Her father looked at her when she came to breakfast and sharply.

"I will not go to college at the usual time today," she said. "I am going very early so that I may study my geometry for an hour."

He understood that this meant she would avoid any possible meeting with the American. If the foreigner sought her it would be at the hour when he had seen her yesterday.

"It will be cooler if you start early," he replied. "Today will be warmer than yesterday."

The meal was eaten in silence, her mother saying not one word. In silence they rose and immediately afterward Josui went into the back garden to find flowers, branches, leaves, whatever the season might bring, for the tokonoma. This was a pleasure as well as a task. Her father criticized what she did, sparing in praise so that when he gave it, it was a treasure to remember. Today, wandering in the large garden, she searched for suitable plants. The season was spring, therefore she must not use many flowers. Flowers were abundant only in summer, and the arrangement must always suggest the season. She decided for the informal arrangement of moribana, she decided against water plants. These must never be combined with flowers that grow in dry earth. Searching she found what she wanted, blue myrtle, blooming upon its glossy vine, half hidden by a drooping scarlet maple. She cut a branch of the maple, careful that it would not be missed, and then she cut the vine in two lengths. With these she had enough, and for half an hour she stood at a table on the porch by the kitchen, making her arrangement. As she had been taught, she stood exactly in front of the low oblong bowl of green pottery she had chosen for the day, this that she might arrange the branches, the vine, the flowers as though they were facing the sun, toward which all growing plants turn by nature. The arrangement was in three, the maple branch taller and spreading behind the vine, the blue flowers lower on one side than the other. She was absorbed in what she did, unaware that she was watched by her father from the room of meditation, where he sat for a space before he went to his office in the hospital, and by her mother, lingering in the kitchen. Satisfied suddenly by the turn the smaller vine took as though of its own will, Josui carried the bowl carefully into the alcove and set it a little to one side. She would not change the scroll. It was of willows in a mist. But she changed the ornament. She chose a piece of uneven jade, set into a rosewood stand. Then she stepped back to survey what she had done.

"Very good," her father's voice said.

She turned to smile. He stood there in his western clothes, ready to leave the house. He looked well in the harsh garments, his felt hat in his hand, his stick, his gloves, his carefully pressed suit all correct. But he was not quite Japanese. No Japanese could wear the garments so easily. It was he who had kept alive in her the memory of America, but these were words not to be spoken and she did not speak them.

"Very pleasant," her father said. "I am not quite sure that the blue of the myrtle and the red of the maple—but it will do. It is original. And the jade unites them with the willows in the mist."

He nodded, smiled slightly and left the room.

So the day began and so it went on. She would not allow to herself that she searched the streets as she entered one after the other, but at least she did not change her usual way. She came early to the school and she went to the girls' day room and to her desk and began diligently to study. Geometry was useful to occupy the mind. She drew the circles carefully, she studied the triangles within, she computed the angles. It was formal, it was cold, in its own way beautiful, but lifeless. Crystals thus composed were lifeless, the fossils of what once had been, symmetrical shapes from which the spirit had departed, cooling nevertheless to the quickened imagination, the excited heart. She worked steadily, not looking up except to answer a greeting, and the day went on. She went to classes, she came away, she felt distant, detached, uncaring. At the end of the day, a little earlier than usual, she went home again. The streets were quite empty. Doubtless today, she told herself, he had gone to Nara to join his comrades. There was no reason why he should not. Doubtless she would never see him again.

The next day she did not feel well. It was a morning even lovelier than before but she woke feeling chilled and spiritless. She stayed in her room and when she did not come out, her mother sent Yumi to discover why this was.

"I feel sad," Josui said. "I think I am ill."

Yumi took this alarming news to the parents and they looked at each other.

"You have been harsh with her," Mrs. Sakai declared to her husband. So mild was she that even such a reproach was spoken in a gentle voice.

"I was not harsh," Dr. Sakai retorted. "I scarcely spoke to her yesterday except to praise the flower arrangement. You know I returned very late last night."

"It was the day before," Mrs. Sakai persisted.

"We were in agreement," Dr. Sakai said firmly. "Remember how she looked yesterday morning and how well she arranged the tokonoma. She was entirely calm."

"This morning the flowers are dead," Mrs. Sakai said. "Observe for yourself. This means her hands were feverish even yesterday."

She rose as she spoke and pattered away, her footsteps almost silent upon the mats. So she came into Josui's room and stood looking down upon her daughter. Josui's hands were lying outside the silk quilt, the fingers curled and motionless. Mrs. Sakai knelt and put three fingers into her right palm.

"You are feverish, your skin is dry. I shall tell your father."

"He will only give me bitter medicine," Josui complained.

"It is for your own good," her mother said.

She stood up and continued to look anxiously at the pretty face on the white pillow. "Tell me what troubles you," she coaxed.

"Nothing," Josui sighed. "That is the trouble—I feel nothing, nothing. I am empty of all feelings."

"This is bad," Mrs. Sakai said. "You should feel something at your age, even if it is only discontent."

Josui did not reply and Mrs. Sakai went away, agitated, to her husband. "You must go and see for yourself. The child feels nothing. She lies there. Her palms are hot. She does not know what is wrong."

"Then it is nothing," Dr. Sakai said briskly. He got up and went out of the room, stopping on the way for his physician's bag. It was in order, ready to use, the thermometer in alcohol, everything sterile. He went to his daughter's room, knocked lightly on the wooden lattice, and then went in.

"So you feel nothing?" he said kindly.

"Nothing," Josui said without looking at him.

"You are not hiding something from me again?" he asked sharply.

"Nothing," she repeated.

He put the thermometer in her mouth and knelt beside her, his face severe with anxiety. "You did not see the American yesterday?" he inquired bluntly.

Unable to speak she shook her head.

He waited, then removed the thermometer. "I saw no one," she told him. "I went to school, I worked, I came back."

"When did you feel this strange nothingness?" he inquired. "You have no fever."

"I woke this morning and did not want to get up."

He did not, in prudence, reveal to her what he was thinking. Was this nothingness because she had not seen the American yesterday?

"It is wise to stay quietly here in your bed, if you feel so," he said. "Eat very lightly, sleep if you can, and do not trouble your mind. I will come home at once if you send for me."

"Thank you, Father."

He rose and continued to look down upon her listless face. She did not look at him. She let her eyelids drift slowly downward until they closed. Her face was pale, so much he acknowledged. Therefore a day's rest would be good for her. He took his bag and went away, and finding her mother waiting outside the lattice, he said casually, "She is not ill. It is an exhaustion due perhaps to the intensity of spring. You know how late the winter was and how suddenly the air changed. This is always exhausting to a young girl like Josui, who is too sensitive. I have told her to stay in bed."

"Thank you," Mrs. Sakai said gratefully. "Now I know what should be done."

The house was very still after he left. Mrs. Sakai changed the blue myrtle, then decided against the whole arrangement. She emptied the oblong bowl and washed it and put it away. In its place she chose a tall narrow vase into which she put a spare branch of bamboo, the new leaves very green, and two white starlike flowers that grew in the shade of the bamboo grove. She had never learned flower arrangement, and so very seldom did she try to make the arrangement. But this one pleased her, especially since her husband was not there to point out its flaws.

When it was done she stood admiring it for a moment, and Yumi came in.

"We have no fish," she said flatly.

"What do you say?" Mrs. Sakai asked in sudden agitation. "There was a fish yesterday. I put it into the small pond. It should be enough."

"It is dead," Yumi said.

"Impossible!" Mrs. Sakai exclaimed.

53

But so it was. For some unknown reason the fish had died. Yumi had taken it from the little pond, which was only a jar sunk into the earth by the kitchen and used to keep fish from the market fresh and alive. The fish lay in her hand, motionless, the eyes like marbles, the scales dull, the body swollen.

"Bury it," Mrs. Sakai said sadly. "I will go to the market myself and complain to the fishman. He must have fed it to make it weigh more."

The market was not far away, and Yumi was here in the house. Nevertheless she went to tell Josui that she was going. When she drew the screen, the girl was asleep. She lay on her back, her eyes closed, breathing peacefully, and Mrs. Sakai would not waken her. She slipped away softly, grateful that whatever Josui's trouble was, it did not keep her awake.

"She is asleep," she told Yumi. "I shall be back very soon."

"Good-by, Mistress," Yumi said. She prepared to wash some clothes in the back yard. Then she would be ready to clean the fish and the vegetables when her mistress came back.

The day was very fine. The sunshine in the back yard was warm and Yumi had risen early as usual. She felt overcome with sleep when the wash was done, which took only a few minutes. The house was quiet. She could sleep for a few minutes behind the kitchen stove and no one would find her. If her mistress came upon her she could say simply that she was waiting there to make the fire. So she laid herself down upon the floor, her head upon a stick of wood and was instantly asleep. She was a country girl, healthy, ready at any

54

moment to eat or to sleep, and when she slept, it was so deeply that she could not be wakened. Thus she did not hear the sound of someone knocking at the front entrance. The garden gate was never locked, and Mrs. Sakai had left it slightly ajar.

It was Josui who waked. She slept lightly and her room was around one side of the house only from the front door. She heard a hard thumping, first of a fist, then of the flat hand upon the wooden doors, then the clanging of the bell. She woke, listened, and called first her mother and then the maid. No one answered. The knocking went on more loudly than ever. She was compelled to get up herself, and putting on her pink kimono she smoothed her hair and went out and around the house on the narrow porch, to see who was there without being seen herself. She went noiselessly, and when she reached the corner of the house she peeped around the corner without indeed being seen.

It was he! He was here, knocking at the door, and there was no one to answer him. She drew back, close to the wooden wall of the house, where he could not see her. If she kept still, he would not know she was here. He would go away again. She stood thus until the knocking stopped. Then she felt she must see if he were gone. She put out her head again, very carefully, only enough to see. He had not gone away. He was sitting down on the step, looking this way and that. She drew back quickly, but not quickly enough. She heard him laugh. She heard him say in his deep laughing voice, the words so slow, so teasing.

"I see you—Josui Sakai!"

She did not move. She could not breathe. If she ran back

to her room would he follow? But that would be very bad. He must not come to her room. Where was her mother? Where was Yumi? They would not both go out together, leaving her asleep.

The deep voice spoke again lazily, still laughing.

"Will you come to me or shall I come to you?"

She gathered herself together at that. She fastened her kimono tightly at the belt and the throat. He would not see her bare feet thrust into pink slippers under the long skirt. She came out with dignity.

"My mother is gone out for a moment. She will be back soon. I will send the maid to you."

With these words she went instantly away and into the house, looking for Yumi. "Yumi!" she called softly, but there was no answer. The kitchen seemed empty. Yumi was not to be found. So what could she do except go to the front door herself?

"My mother will be back very soon," she faltered again, her face all hot with blushes.

"I don't want to see your mother," he said. He got up, took off his cap, and stood holding it in his hands, turning it round and round.

She stood helplessly. What should she do with him? She could not ask him to come in. Her mother would not understand. No one would.

"You didn't go to school, Josui Sakai?" he asked.

"No, I—I felt somewhat tired," she faltered.

"You look like a blooming rose," he replied.

She clasped her hands, wringing them without knowing it.

"You don't want me here, I reckon," he said, seeing the hands.

"It is not that," she protested. "It is that I am alone for the moment and so—"

"You don't know what to do with me, being a nice girl."

It was entirely wrong to tell him that she was alone. She had told him without thinking. "Please go away," she whispered.

She did not know, of course, that her eyes were shining, that her lips were soft and red, that her whole little face was a flower opening to the sun as she looked up at him. He took one step toward her, and all the agony of his desire, so long suppressed, came rushing up into his body. It could not be denied. He was suddenly blind with it. He could not see her face, he could not stop his feet. He leaned over her and above her, trying not to yield to the insatiable demand and knowing he must yield. To kiss her lips would be enough, a girl's lips, delicate and pure, in this lovely garden, where the very air was fragrant, and the only sound was that of splashing water. She was alone. She had told him she was alone. He groaned and put his arms about her swiftly with a terrible tenderness, crushing her slowly against him. Then he saw her face beneath his, her lips there. He bent his head and put his lips upon hers, drinking in her gasping breath, freeing one hand to hold her head still, while she tried to turn it this way and that, until suddenly she ceased her struggle and let him hold her.

This was the long moment of which he had dreamed all night, the long moment which she had not known enough even to imagine. She all but fainted in his arms at last, and

57

gently he withdrew, though holding her in the circle of his arms.

She would not look at him. She did not try to escape from him, but she turned her head away, her cheek against his shoulder, so that he could not see her face. He leaned his head down upon the crown of her head, upon her hair, so black, so soft.

"It had to be," he muttered.

She could not speak, and when she did not, he turned her face up to his again, seizing her by the chin, a round soft chin. "You know it had to be?" he demanded.

"I don't know," she whispered. "I never did so before."

To hear her thus confess her innocence filled him with delight again.

"Oh, you darling," he muttered, and bent his head.

"Not again," she begged. "It is enough—for the first time. What shall I do? I must think what it means."

"It means I love you."

"You don't know me!"

"A man doesn't need to know a woman to love her. He learns to know her by loving her."

"Ah, this is Japan!"

"You and I—man and woman."

She was watching the gate. Her mother would be coming back. Doubtless she had gone to the market as she usually did, and Yumi perhaps had gone with her.

"I cannot wait here. My mother will come back."

"Let me meet her," he said at once.

"No, no," she said as quickly. "It is not easy like this. My father hates Americans. He loves me too much."

58

At the mention of her father she drew away and he let her go, feeling the change in her.

"Do you always obey your father, Josui?"

"I wish to do so."

"Will you give me a chance?"

"A chance?"

"To let you know me."

She sighed. "How can we?"

"I will find the way, darling."

She had forgotten that word "darling," but now she remembered it. Once Kensan had used it to the girl he was engaged to marry. It was a word of love. To hear it made her tremble, spoken in this deep voice, filled with yearning. Where could she find love like this? It was only in America that it could be found. They were not afraid there of love.

She looked at him suddenly and fully. "I will trust you, Allenn. Do I say your name right?"

"As I like to hear you say it."

She saw him bending to her again, "Ah, you must go—"

"Where shall we meet? Shall I come here?"

"No, no—I must think now."

"Under the wisteria again tomorrow."

"Yes!"

He bent his head now and she felt his lips once more, gentle but how powerfully demanding. They were lost together. This time she knew. She loved him! Suddenly there was the sound of rustling leaves. They heard it and were startled. Their lips parted, they looked into the bamboos that hung their branches above the door. The new green leaves were twinkling and dancing, caught by a small circular breeze, a minute whirlwind. "How strange," Josui cried softly.

"Is something there?" he asked in wonder.

For a moment they forgot each other, and watched the dancing leaves. Then remembering that she still stood within his arms, she pulled herself away and ran into the house.

Her wickedness was inconceivable. How was it she had agreed to this? Miraculously recovered, she set forth for the college the next morning again in the yellow dress and carrying a small white parasol embroidered in yellow flowers. Her parents had said nothing and she said nothing, since she had an armful of books under her arm and a box of freshly sharpened pencils. It was evident that she was going to work hard. This she intended to do.

He met her, however, before she reached the gate. He was there very early, waiting, his uniform this morning fresh and clean and he more handsome than ever. His eyes were as blue as sea water on a sunny day.

"I am here to tempt you," he said boldly when he saw her.

She was frightened. On such a day could any temptation be resisted? She must remember that she was a good girl. She tried to look grave. She was sorry that she did not wear spectacles, as many of the girls did.

"I am glad you are so beautiful," he said. "It makes temptation easy."

"Please, I must go to school," she entreated.

He grew earnest. "Josui Sakai, I have only five days left of my vacation. I have seen nothing of Kyoto, one of the world's most famous cities. Will you come with me today and show me what I ought to see—as a patriotic duty?"

She was speechless with horror.

"Is it not a noble thing to do?" he urged. "I am an ignorant American. I will not remind you that I am occupying your country. For the moment, let us say I am a visitor. I wish to carry home with me a good impression of Japan. So I have come to this most beautiful of all cities. When I am in America once more, never to see Japan again, I will tell everybody of Kyoto, how my visit here was one of the happiest times of my life, and how I saw all its beauties— that I shall never forget."

She broke down under his laughing bright blue eyes, not at once but with a preliminary of laughter running through her body, responding to his laughter. "You are too tempting, but I cannot. What will I tell my instructor? Suppose also someone should see us together? My father would be too angry."

He shrugged his immaculate shoulders. "Please forgive me. It is the woman, as usual, who takes the risk. We will forget the temptation. You should go to school." The laughter went out of his eyes. They walked side by side toward the gate. He reached for her books and she remembered that in America boys had sometimes carried her books. It was the custom there. She walked along, ashamed that she wished he had not given up so easily. She was doing right but she wished that she were not so able to divide right from wrong. If one did not make such divisions, it would be pleasant to do wrong.

She looked at him from the corners of her long eyes, and

he was looking at her. His eyes were blue again, and his mouth pursed, as though he wanted to laugh.

"I could put these books under the wisteria root," he suggested. "It is thick and twisted and big enough almost to hide even you. I looked under it."

"I will do it," she exclaimed. Incredible words!

But she did hide the books. No one saw her. The hour was still early. She put the books under the roots and then she came back to him and they began quickly to walk down a small narrow side street.

"Tell me about Kyoto," he said, quite as though he wanted to know. She answered seriously to quiet her astonished conscience.

"It is a very old city, once our capital for a thousand years. It has fourteen hundred old Buddhist temples. There are more than one million people living here. There are the ancient imperial palaces and the old gardens, the best in the world."

"My little guide," he said, "take me to see the gardens."

In a garden, he thought, there will be hiding places, grottoes, rockeries, quiet pools, hedges, banks of shrubs. He suspected her of mischief when she led him to no such place.

"The Ryoanji Temple," she explained. "This is the Stone Garden. It is one of the most famous." She gazed at an arid rectangle, a desert enclosed by a low wall. Dry rocks stood like islands in a dead sea of white sand. Upon the sand a wide rake had drawn static waves, motionless in long curves.

"A garden?" he inquired. He forgot for a moment the purpose of the day. There was something here he did not understand, a dignity immense and incomprehensible.

"You will see," Josui explained gravely. "Count the stones, if you please."

There were fifteen groups of five and two, of five and three, and three and three.

"They are not all islands," she explained. "Some are made to look like resting water fowl," she pointed with her little finger. "There, if you please, wild ducks."

The stones were natural, uncarved, shaped only by wind and water and brought here to sleep, but it was true they looked like waterfowl.

"Do you understand this garden?" he demanded.

"Not wholly," she confessed. "I know only because my father has brought me here. He understands. At least he knows. This garden explains the pure soul of the man who created it. It is famous and very old. If we stayed here many hours, in silence, we would begin to understand."

He shook his head. "Not me! I like more life."

So in patience she took him to a green garden in an old palace, an enchanting place, where low hills united ancient gardens with the sky. Yet even so, it was no place for love. It was a garden watched, its every leaf secured. He saw no workman, no one except a few like themselves who seemed only sight-seers, but there was no wildness to provide freedom. He walked constrained, impressed, admiring but confined. He did not dare to touch her hand. She too seemed remote. He felt that she belonged here, but not he.

By noon he wanted no more of palaces and temples, not gardens or gods, either. "I'm hungry," he said suddenly. "Also I have walked miles enough on polished stone. We will go somewhere to eat, and then I shall hire a carriage and we will go outside the city. I want to see some wild country."

She was almost dreamlike in her acquiescence. Having yielded so much, having committed the monstrous sin of the stolen day, she seemed willing now for anything. His blood ran a little faster for this thought.

She was gay enough at lunch, answering his sallies, replying to his questions, telling him who the few people in the small restaurant might be. She had never been there before, an obscure place on a hidden street, where only the excellence of the shrimp tempura made it possible to remain, that and the pale green tea and the dry and snowy rice. A clerk, she suggested, when he nodded toward a pallid little man in a gray canvas suit, perhaps a clerk in a small shop; a servant girl, stopping by to buy a few shrimps; an old man, lonely, eating here instead of at his home; a man of middle age, greedy for a taste of good food that he could not afford at home because of many children.

But later, on the mountain side, he found her still remote.

They left the rickety carriage at the foot of the hill, the old white pony half-asleep, the aged driver incurious, mute at least before an American in uniform. They climbed the hill by a path of brick laid through the bamboos. It seemed a lonely place and yet he suspected it. The bricks were swept too clean, the ferns were planted too amiably through the bamboos, there was no underbrush, no thicket. He found a plot of moss and stopped.

"This is good. Soft as a cushion, isn't it? Sit down, Josui."

She obeyed, seating herself on her knees, a little distance from him. The fine hairs about her forehead were wet and

64

clung to her smooth damp skin. Her lips were very red. He looked at her a moment, daring himself to cross the distance she had made. Abruptly he moved himself near her and took her hand.

"Josui!"

She turned large clear eyes. "Tell me about America," she said.

America! It was far from his thoughts at this moment.

"All morning I have been showing you Japan," she said. "Now show me a little of America. I can remember California. But tell me of Virginia, your home, your parents. Are they alive?"

She did not withdraw her hand, nor did she move away from him. But to talk of Virginia, to ask about his home was to send him far from her.

"I am so curious," she begged.

"Well," he said most unwillingly. "I live in a small town. That is, our house is in a small town, not far from Richmond."

"Richmond?"

"Like Tokyo," he explained, "but not so big, the capital only of Virginia."

"Tell me how is your house," she coaxed.

He looked down at her hand and began to play with the fingers gently, her little left hand, wearing no rings. She wore no jewelry of any kind.

"A big house made of wood," he intoned, "painted white. Six big white pillars, an old house, my great-grandfather's house. Around it acres of land, a thousand, I reckon, woods and hills, a river."

"It sounds beautiful," she sighed.

"Inside the door a hall, a wide stair winding to the very roof, all the usual rooms."

"Where is your room?" she asked.

"Upstairs, left, at the front."

"I remember carpets in America, pictures, curtains, and so forth," she said.

"And so forth," he agreed.

"Bed and chairs with legs, also tables?"

"Also and all with legs."

"Your family is what—father and mother?"

"And me—no more."

"You are the only child?"

"The only."

She looked solemn after this. "You are perhaps too precious," she suggested.

He laughed. "Sometimes I have thought so."

She pondered awhile. "And your mother—how is she?"

"Well, I believe."

"I mean, looking?"

"Oh!" He understood. "Rather small, slender, quite pretty. But she is strong, very strong."

"Your father?"

"A big man, quiet—lazy, I reckon. That is what my mother says."

"He has some job?"

"He is a lawyer, but he doesn't practice. He doesn't have to, I reckon—since my grandfather died."

She understood this meant wealth but delicately she refrained from mentioning money. She gazed over the tops of the bamboos below a small cliff some yards from where they sat. The city of Kyoto lay far below, but not so far actually as it looked.

"I must go home soon," she said suddenly. "I must go home when the college classes are over."

This reminded him that the day was passing swiftly. He flung himself back upon the moss and pillowed his head on his folded arms. "Not yet, Josui."

She looked at him with eyes he could not understand. Not fearful surely?

"Lie down beside me, Josui."

She shook her head and a blush flooded up her white neck.

"Why not, darling?"

She did not reply but he saw her lower lip tremble and she seized it between her teeth.

"Are you afraid of me?" he asked tenderly.

"Some afraid," she confessed.

"I won't hurt you, sweet."

She shook her head.

He asked most gently. "Have you forgotten that I love you?"

"No," she said in a small voice. "I remember it always. But why you love me?"

She turned and looked at him now, her eyes enormous and grave. He sat up suddenly. Why indeed did he love her? She had made it impossible to do what he wanted to do. "I don't know," he said. "I ask myself. I'm—call it hungry, I reckon. I haven't seen anyone here that I could love. Only you!"

"You are going away in a few days."

"I am coming back."

She smiled. "Then we can wait," she exclaimed. "It is not necessary to decide now why you love me."

She rose almost abruptly and stood looking down into his upturned longing face. Then as suddenly she began to run down the hill, lightly, swiftly, and there was nothing he could do except follow her, half angry, half amused. She did not stop until they were at the carriage, when she cried out, panting, "Oh, I have not run like that while I have been in Japan! I used so to run in California, but not here— never!"

The old driver stared. The horse woke, and blew hard through its nose.

"Is this the end of the day?" Allen demanded.

"Just the one day," she answered, "one day with you, Allenn Ken-neddy!"

She had not spoken his full name before, and she made the syllables separately with a pretty emphasis on each, a promise, perhaps, of many times to come.

The day, which had seemed so impossible to Josui when it was begun, thus ended in a dreamy joy. She found her books undiscovered behind the wisteria root. It was late and everyone had gone home except the old gateman. He was sitting asleep in his tiny room, as he often slept whenever the pupils were gone, and the college yard was quiet. He saw her neither come nor go, and she paused for only a moment more on the street, to bid Allen Kennedy good-by.

"But I have not seen enough," he protested. "I have not seen Nara. Everyone must go to Nara."

"You should have gone with your friends," she said primly. "It was not my fault."

"It was your fault," he argued. "I saw you. I had to find out who you were."

He treated her with a half-joking, half-childish approach, this to defend himself rather than her. He was growing frightened at the intensity of his purpose, unwilling to penetrate his own motives. He did not wish to do what he saw other men do every day. He would not believe he was as other men are. Nor did he wish to believe that Josui was the common Japanese girl whom he saw in Toyko aping the commonest girls of American streets.

To his surprise she was looking at him with a sad surprise, her face grave.

"You wish me to go with you to Nara tomorrow?" she inquired.

"I humbly wish it," he replied.

She continued to look at him. "I must think," she said at last.

"How will I know what you think, Josui?"

"If I am coming I will be here tomorrow morning but without my books."

"I'll be waiting."

They parted without touching so much as their hands, as though each knew the other's reluctant and fearful longing.

Josui was stunned by her own wickedness. For she went home as though she were coming from the college. Her father was late, he had been called to an emergency, and she and her mother ate their evening meal alone. This was hard, for had her father been there as usual, it would have been easier for her to maintain her usual reserve. Her mother was so yielding, so gentle, so good, always anxious only that she be happy. It was hard indeed to meet her penetrating and kind questions. She hated to lie, and yet how could she avoid it now?

"It must have been hot in the schoolroom today," her mother said.

"The room is on the north side," Josui replied.

She busied herself with the small dishes for her mother's tray.

"Please do not trouble," her mother urged. "I have very little appetite. I do not dare tell you."

"Tell me what, Mother?" Josui asked.

"The emergency is in the Matsui family. It is Kobori. Your father fears appendicitis."

Josui must concern herself. "Kobori? Oh, I hope it is not too serious! He is the last son in that house."

"And such a good son," her mother said.

"I have always heard that he is," Josui replied. She bent her head and began to eat, keeping her eyelids downcast.

"Your father feels such responsibility," her mother went on.

"Mr. Matsui is his best friend," Josui replied.

"It is not only that," her mother said. "Your father is also thinking of Kobori. He feels great liking for this young man. He often wishes—many things."

Josui knew what her father wished, but she could not reply even for her own protection. She sat in a dream of secret love, her whole self removed from this place, from her home and her parents. She had already left them, heart and body cleaving to the young American. It was no use to pretend. She could only hide the truth until she knew what he meant to do. She had seen many American young men, though none, no, not one like him. The ones she had seen were the noisy ones on the streets, the louts, the boys, the drunken soldiers, the grabbing, jeering, pushing roisterers. On parade they looked clean, they were silent, always obedient. They marched in perfect lines, feet rising together and coming down in great unified footsteps. On parade they looked neither to the right or the left, unless they were told to do so, and then all eyes turned as one. When they were not on parade, however, they broke into fragments, and each fragment became a noisy unit, still like all the others. She despised them, avoided them, hiding inside a gateway somewhere until they passed. The girls whom they seized, the Japanese girls, were even more to be despised. Indeed, she was not like them. She was unique. But he also was unique. Their love could not be like any other therefore. Only what should they do?

She answered her mother absently, sometimes lying. When the meal was over she saw her mother looking at her with puzzled eyes.

"Is there something you are feeling that you do not tell me?" her mother asked.

"Only a problem that came up during school hours," Josui said. She was amazed at the ease with which such answers came to her. They were couched in truth while they were lies. Someday she would be sorry to know she was a liar but at this moment, when all her mind and blood were filled with the same sweet daze, she did not care.

She withdrew very early, saying that she was tired, and she did indeed go to bed soon. The night was clear and from her pallet on the floor she looked through the open screens into a sky full of stars. There was dampness in the air, perhaps, or some stillness at least, which made the stars hang large and soft. They did not sparkle. Instead they shone with a yellow gleam, like distant lanterns of silk. Was he wondering, too, what they should do? When two people fall into love, as Americans put it, is it possible to do nothing? Something was always done. She recalled the magazine stories she used to read in California. Love there was always followed by marriage. First was the kiss, then the declaration, then the request for the date of marriage. She had received the kiss, he had made the declaration. It remained therefore for him to ask for the date of the wedding, if these customs were what they had always been. In Japan much was changed by the war. It might be true in America, also, especially in Virginia.

She sighed, thought of his face, smiled, and longed for tomorrow.

The weather connived again with sunshine. Waked by the sun Josui rose early, and though she saw her mother, she did not meet her father. He had come in late, her mother said. He had operated upon Kobori, who was not yet out of danger, for the appendix had burst, and he was still anxious. He had not come home until after dawn but he had given orders that he must be waked by nine o'clock if he did not wake himself.

Josui was gone by half past eight. She left suitable messages for her father, and then forgot everything. There had been a small thunderstorm in the night, the streets were still wet, and the sky was glorious. Allen was there, waiting for her. This time the old gateman stood looking thoughtfully into the street. Josui saw him there and stopped, and Allen, seeing her, walked toward her. They met just inside the narrow alley to the west of the college.

"He didn't see you," Allen said.

"We will go by the back streets to the railway station," she said. "The journey to Nara is less than an hour from here."

They joined hands at once and thus they walked in silence along the wet street. Drops from overhanging trees fell upon them in a little rain. She wore a clean blue cotton skirt and a thin white blouse, and the drops made small clear spots through which her skin showed. She never wore a hat and the drops fell on her face and her hair.

"Dew on a flower," he said.

She smiled up at him, her eyes liquid with love.

The early train was not crowded, and he insisted on going at least second class. She saw, or refused to see, the inquisitive gaze of the passengers, wondering that a Japanese girl of good family should be with an American. Nothing could be done about it but it was not approved. Women looked at her haughtily and men half angrily. She tried not to know, she spoke in her limpid fluid English, quickly explaining one place after another as the train passed.

73

"Nara was Japan's first permanent capital," she said in a clear rather loud voice. "At first we had no fixed capital. Each ruler put the capital wherever he lived. But in the first century Nara was fixed upon, and continued for seven reigns as the capital, which was then changed to Nagaoka, also near Kyoto."

"What shall we see in Nara?" he inquired, aware that she spoke for the benefit of others than himself.

"What you wish," she replied. "There are shops, palaces, temples, shrines, the great Buddha, the Imperial Park."

"The park," he said promptly. "Is it big?"

"More than twelve hundred acres."

"Then the park."

She kept talking, seated carefully away from him, until the train whistled shrilly for Nara. They came out, and still somewhat formally she engaged rickshaws and they rode to the park. It was necessary to take even more time to remove the unpleasant memory of the accusing eyes of the passengers. In the park they wandered for an hour, then coming upon a lonely spot, he could not restrain his desire. He was leading the way along a narrow path when suddenly he whirled upon her and took her in his arms.

There was now no question of surrender to the kiss. It was no longer strange. It was known, it was intolerably sweet. She hungered for renewal. It was still an experience, a fulfillment in itself.

To him, however, a kiss was mere introduction, a query made sometimes even to a stranger, an invitation, leading on to further exploration in the quest. He kissed her again and yet again, each time more closely and more intimately, one arm crushing her waist, the other holding her chin. Then reaching the end of kissing, and uncontrollably compelled to what must follow, he lifted her from the path and laid her down upon the mossy bank beneath the pines that covered them. He sank down beside her, half over her, his hands trembling, audacious.

In one instant she divined the reason for his haste. She reached up her hands and pushed his face away strongly.

"Stop!" she whispered. "This is not the way. Allenn Kenneddy! No!"

The reproach in her voice was overpowering. His conscience, made sensitive by a long and happy childhood in a big white house in Virginia, quickened against his will. The toughening of the war years was not deep. He had tried to cultivate a proper cynicism, the brave callow cynicism of the young today who must face life and death at the same time. But his cynicism was a shallow surface. The years had been too few to harden it. Desire cooled at the sound of her sorrowful voice, he hid his face in her bosom and lay still.

She lay motionless for several minutes, allowing the weight of his head upon her breast. Then she moved gently away, and as she had done yesterday she sat up while he lay on his back, gazing up into the trees. It was she who resolutely began to speak.

"I do not know what I am exactly, whether more Japanese or American. I think I am more than anything my father's daughter only. I am a Sakai. We are not common people. We are something better. It is necessary that you and I examine how we love each other. We must decide. Shall we say good-by? Or—"

She could not go on. She could not bear to imagine what would happen to her if he should say, "Let us say good-by." She must think of her father. Let her remember her father's stern good face and gain strength for herself through Sakai pride. Rather than the disgrace of the concentration camp her father had chosen Japan.

"Must we decide everything today?" he asked.

She nodded vigorously. "We must!"

"Why?"

She hesitated and then said firmly, "Because whenever we are alone together you attack me."

He was horrified by this boldness. "Oh, come, Josui!"

"Is it not attack?" she demanded. She turned the light of her large clear eyes upon his face.

"I suppose, if you want to put it in plain words," he said grudgingly.

"I will not excuse myself also," she said swiftly. "If I allow myself to be alone with you, I must accept responsibility."

"What long words they taught you in California!"

"I don't learn this in California. I learn it here, in Japan, from my father."

"A fierce father?"

"Perhaps."

When he said nothing to this she added, "Perhaps, also, that is good—for a girl." She clasped her arms around her knees and bent her head.

The nape of her neck was creamy pale. A few straight soft hairs escaped from the knot at the back of her head and trembled in the pine scented air. Her head sat prettily on her shoulders. Her arms were white and round, the sleeves of her dress only reaching her elbows, and her hands were pretty, too. Most Japanese girls did not have pretty hands or feet. She wore white socks and sandals and he could not see her feet.

"Take off your shoes," he said suddenly. "Let me see your little feet. Are they as pretty as your hands?"

To his astonishment she flushed a quick red. She sprang up, and drew away from him. "Now I cannot stay with you," she said almost violently. "I will not! You insult me too lightly, Allenn Ken-neddy! I respect myself at least. It is enough for me. I know now how you are feeling. Love! What is it? I do not want such love."

She began to walk away, and he jumped up and ran after her and caught her hand. "Josui, what did I say? Why are you offended, darling? Is there something I cannot understand?" He took her by the shoulders. "Josui, answer me!"

She flamed at him, eyes burning, cheeks scarlet, lips shaped to wrath. "You do not answer me, Allenn Ken-neddy! I said, 'What shall we do?' You say, 'Show me your'—"

She faltered, turned away her head, and tears came from under her lashes.

He was moved to tenderness and compelled to truthfulness. "Darling, if I didn't answer, it is because I don't know how to answer."

"If you don't know, then you shouldn't—touch me at all."

His hands dropped. "You are right."

She went on. "If you don't know, then please go back today to Tokyo, to America, to your home. Forget, please, that you have seen me, and let me forget—"

"Can you, Josui?"

"Yes, now I still can. Later—I don't know."

He stood looking at her slender drooping figure. And she, after his silence, said brokenly. "I want to go home."

So they took the next train back to Kyoto, and at the station they parted because she insisted that it must be so.

"I shan't forget you, though, Josui."

"Yes, you will."

"If I can't—may I write to you?"

"You will not write."

She left him, not saying good-by, giving him instead a long inscrutable look, and then, though he stood watching until he lost her among the people in the street, she did not once look back.

As for him, he returned to the hotel and packed his bags and took the next train for Tokyo. He wanted no more holidays. The sooner he got back to work the better for him.


"Kobori is better," her father said. "He has a clean good body and he has responded well to the new drugs."

"I am glad," Josui said listlessly.

He knew that something was wrong with her, and he had consulted with his wife only this morning as to what it might be.

"She has told me nothing," Mrs. Sakai had replied. "If I ask her why she is sad she gets angry with me. She declares she is not sad."

"She does not know what is wrong with her," Dr. Sakai said, with his usual decision. "She is biologically upset. It is time for her to marry and she does not know it. I shall take matters into my own hands."

At any other time Mrs. Sakai would have urged patience. This morning, however, she had only replied, "Doubtless you are right."

"Kobori," Dr. Sakai said, continuing with Josui later in the day, "may be called a perfect young Japanese man. Yet he is modern. He goes to no extremes. He respects his father but he will go further than his father. Someday Kobori will be a very important man. I wish you could have seen the healthiness of his flesh. When I made the incision his blood was such a clear pure red."

"But his appendix was infected, nevertheless?" Josui reminded him somewhat cruelly.

Dr. Sakai was indignant. "The appendix is a vestige of early man. It is no longer needed. For this Kobori can scarcely be blamed. Now he will have no more trouble."

She wanted to avoid the thought of Kobori and yet some instinct to punish herself, even to hurry toward her fate, compelled her to go on. "Father, why don't you say what you are thinking?" she asked recklessly. "You want me to marry Kobori. Why don't you say it?"

Dr. Sakai lost his temper completely. "You are a stubborn troublesome daughter!" he shouted. "You know very well why I don't dare to speak to you truthfully. You are like American girls. If you know what I hope, you will destroy my hope!"

He was dismayed at his anger and now prepared for her return attack. All was lost, doubtless. She would never yield. To his surprise, she was mild.

"Father, I am beginning to change. I have been thinking a great deal. I feel now I had better marry a Japanese, as you have often advised me to do. I have thought sometimes I would like to go to America again but now I shall never go. I belong here. So it may as well be Kobori as anyone. As you say, he is good. I want above all a good man."

She spoke so thoughtfully, almost meditatively, even sadly, that he could scarcely believe it was she who spoke. He stammered, his anger gone, "Josui, my child—such wisdom —I feel taken aback. Shall I—do you wish me to speak to Kobori's father? Tell me, what do you want me to do for you?"

She looked at him with large sad eyes. "Whatever you wish, Father."

This alarmed him indeed. "You are not ill, child?"

"No, Father. I am really very well, better than I have been for a long time." Then seeing him frightened she tried to smile. "I am growing up, at last. Do you know I am twenty?"

He was pleased but still somewhat uneasy. "Be sure I shall not hurry you," he said solemnly. "I shall not allow even Kobori to hurry you."

"Thank you, Father," she said.

She left him then with a little bow and went into the garden to arrange some stones in the pool. She collected stones, smooth and round, twisted and water carved, keeping at no time more than twenty or so and throwing away the less beautiful ones as she found better ones. Under the clear water the colors glowed clearly. Sometimes a stone which looked dull in the air shone under water. She moved the stones so delicately that her reflection in the water was scarcely disturbed.

Allen had not written to her once. Now a month had gone by since they parted and he had not written to her. She was glad that she did not know his address, so that she could not write to him. For there had been hours in sleepless nights when she would have written to him out of her weakness and her despair, and she might have begged him to come back, or even to let her come to him. Had she so written and had he answered, it would have been the end for them sometime or other, however many years hence, for her pride would have risen again, prostrate though it now was. And so at the core of their love would have been the seed of rot.

Gradually through the waiting weeks, one sleepless night conquered and then another, the future had become plain to her, the simple future, the inevitable way of a woman's life in Japan, marriage, husband, children, home. All the talk of modern women did not and could not change the inevitable. So, as she had said to her father, why not Kobori? Gradually she was accustoming herself to the thought of him. She remembered his face, pale, rather large, the features slightly heavy but their expression kind and easy-going. His voice, too, she could remember quite clearly, a pleasant, slow voice, slurring words, perhaps with a slight lisp. He could scarcely speak English. "I am stupid at language," he had explained to her once, without seeming to care that he was. He was not repulsive, at least. He was not aggressive. He would not press himself upon her. So, in time, she could probably love him well enough. At least she could respect him. What she wanted, above all else, was simple goodness, which he had more than any man she had ever seen.

She polished a round greenish stone with the soft palm of her hand and let it sink into the water. The green grew clear, a mild and pleasant color, without hint of violence, sparkle, or glitter.

The summer was hot in Tokyo. The streets of modern asphalt burned with stored heat, and time and again the electric plant broke down so that the fans stopped, usually at the hottest time of day or night. The only way to tolerate the intolerable was to blind himself with work.

"Lieutenant Kennedy, sir!"

A private stood at the door with mail. "Homeside mail, sir."

"Throw it there on the small table. I have to finish this report first."

"Yes, sir." The soldier saluted, put carefully on the table a bundle of ten or twelve letters and went away.

His family! Father, mother, aunts, uncles, cousins, they wrote to him devotedly, making a martyrdom out of his having to stay in so remote and heathen a country as Japan. "Darling, when will they let you come home?" Thus plaintively his mother's letters always began.

He went on writing, tapping swiftly on the portable typewriter. Lieutenant was a convenient title covering many duties, especially those his superior officers did not care to perform, or were too incompetent to perform. He had known even generals who could not spell—or speak cor-

rectly, for that matter. When they found that he had gradu-
ated from the university they heaped tiresome written work
on him. He took a warped pleasure in making of such a dull
report as this one, for example, upon certain civilian organi-
zations of the Japanese under the Occupation, a minor mas-
terpiece of style. Not, of course, that anyone who read it
would know! Yet he found himself taking an interest in
what he wrote about the Japanese now, and this, he acknowledged to himself, was because of Josui. Through her he had
come into some sort of reality of relationship with these
people, though she still remained for him someone special,
the most beautiful girl he had ever seen. She had courage as
well as beauty. For she had loved him, it was hard for her
to resist him, and yet she had done so.

As usual when she crept into his thoughts, as she did
twenty times a day, and in the night how often, he pondered
the possibility. Suppose the end had been different, suppose
he had asked her to marry him, as certainly he would have
done had she been an American girl whom he had loved
as well—what then? He became lost in a maze of thought,
his fingers idle on the keys. They could live here in Japan.
Would he be willing to spend his life in Japan? Or they
could live in America. There were many places in America
where he could live with her very happily, their children—
well, their children! Must they have children? She would
want them probably but then so did he. He had always
supposed that someday he would marry and have children,
not just one solitary child growing up as he did, pampered
in the big house which should have been full of children.

He had taken it for granted that his children would live in that home. Had it not been for the war, he would by now have been married to some girl or other, quite happily, doubtless, for he would never have seen Josui. He might have married Cynthia Levering, who his mother said again and again was like a daughter to her, "a dear daughter," she clamored, with peculiar emphasis when she said it in his presence.

"Don't throw Cynthia at my head, Mother," he said teasingly. "I might really want to marry her someday, on my own."

"Oh, be quiet," his mother said in her sweet gay voice, "You're real mean since you've grown up, I do declare!"

There was probably a letter from Cynthia now in that pile. She did not write often, just often enough, and usually long pleasant letters full of small home-town news. Cynthia lived at home, not far down the wide quiet street from his own house. He had known her all his life. Indeed, three generations earlier, his ancestors and hers had intermarried.

"How far back?" he had once inquired idly of his mother.

"Far enough back to be safe," she had said with quick mischief.

He reached out a long arm and took the letters and ruffled them. His mother, the minister of the Episcopal church where his family had seated themselves on Sundays for generations, two he did not recognize, and yes, a big envelope from Cynthia. There was nothing small about Cynthia except her graceful waist. She was tall and well proportioned, generous and large in mind and heart. Someday he supposed he would fall in love with her. Just now he wished, incongruously, that he could tell her about Josui.

"I'll bet she could understand," he muttered.

He cut open the envelope, the creamy paper too thick to tear, and took out three double sheets, folded and covered with her blue-black handwriting, the letters large but not sprawling.

"Darling Allen," so her letters always began. They had written to each other desultorily for years, she away at finishing school when he was at the university. "Darling Allen, there has never been such a spring. Maybe I have never really seen the spring before. This year I seem to have time."

He read on slowly, seeing the home town, the familiar streets, the well-known faces of neighbors and relatives. Yet they were all as far from him, sitting alone here in Tokyo, as though they lived in another world. That was it. They lived in another world, and they could not possibly understand this one, whose capital was Tokyo, Japan. No matter how much he explained, no matter what he did or even what he did not do, they would not understand. There was no way of making them understand. His only choice was which world he wanted to live in—and with whom.

He folded the letters carefully and put each back in its envelope and then sat looking at the bleakness of his type-writer.

Only his father had not written. His father seldom wrote, as he seldom spoke. As long as he could remember he could not recall that his father ever said anything much, nothing certainly to remember, the least that had to be said about anything, sometimes during a whole meal nothing more than, "Please pass the butter, son," or more expansively, "These biscuits are better than usual, Sugar." Sugar was his mother, whose real name was Josephine, a name which his father declared impossible to any man except a Napoleon in France.

"I declare, Mr. Kennedy," his mother replied with spirit, "as if we didn't always have the best beaten biscuit!"

"So we do, Sugar, and that's why I remark on these being even better."

Twitted often on his lazy silences his father smiled amiably and murmured that Sugar talked enough for two, and was always interesting, much more than he could be.

He did not pretend to understand his father, nor had it ever occurred to him that it was necessary to do so. Now vaguely he wished that he did know his father better so that he could write to him about Josui, and ask him—

What?

There was only one question and that had to be asked by himself and of himself. Did he love her enough to marry her? Was what he felt, this undying longing night and day, was this true love? He had never been in love, that he now knew. But was he in love now?

He put the letters into his desk drawer and then bathed and dressed himself carefully. He had an invitation to dinner with the Colonel and his wife, a decent couple who clearly did not know what to do with the joyous reckless desperadoes who were the privates under the Colonel's command. "They aren't serious about anything," the Colonel's wife complained when last he had dined at their house. "They act as though they were living in the days of Madame Butterfly."

He knew what she meant. He had felt a little like that himself, there in the Imperial Park in Nara. It was impossible sometimes to believe that the Japanese were the same people whose men had mercilessly slaughtered Americans so short a time ago. He found himself forgetting it altogether, although he had taken his share and given it in that warfare. But the ruthless little men who crept up on them out of the jungles of the islands had no connection, or so it seemed now, with the terraced green hillsides, the blue-coated farmers, the pretty girls in kimono and geta, and certainly not with Josui, who was really more American than Japanese in all except looks, and, perhaps, in the rather precious perfection of her English enunciation.

When he let her name rise to the surface of his mind, his heart pounded once or twice and he wanted to stretch out his arms, as though she were there. He wondered, somewhat wistfully, if he dared to bring his question to the Colonel when they were alone after dinner. The Colonel's lady was well brought up and she always left the men for half an hour or so with their coffee, even though she might be the only woman. If there were another woman guest, as often there was, when he was the only other man, then the half hour might stretch another fifteen minutes.

But he did not dare disclose himself, for all that. As far as he could get, after the excellent dinner, cooked by a Japanese chef and served by a white-clad Japanese "boy," was to ask the Colonel somewhat abruptly how many Americans had married Japanese wives during the Occupation. The Colonel looked unhappy. "I suppose we have the figures somewhere. I don't care to face them. Do you mean married or just—"

"I mean married."

"Not many, probably," the Colonel said hopefully. "If it is the other thing, who knows? I suppose even the thousands of half-and-half babies would not be the gauge of what really happens. I don't understand exactly why our men seem so —oversexed, let us say. It has surprised even me, though I am an old officer."

"What will happen to the children?" he asked too intently.

The Colonel looked distressed. "I don't know. Barclay— he's my aide—says that his wife found a child hidden the other day in the house of a neighbor—very respectable people, too, man a merchant or something like that. Barclay and his wife had been disturbed from next door by a baby's wailing all night and she went over to inquire. It was hidden in a closet by the grandmother who was ashamed of it."

"What did Barclay do?"

"I believe he reported the case to the Catholic orphanage and they took the child away. The family was grateful, even the mother, a pretty girl. The child was queer looking, Barclay said, abominable mixture, really. I don't believe in it at all, but what can one do?"

Josui, therefore, could not be mentioned. He left rather early, sitting with the couple only a little while and then getting up on the plea of the unfinished report.

But he did not want to go to Karuizawa for a vacation or even go very often to the motion pictures in the evening. He danced a few times during the summer, seeing no girl who attracted him, and remembering none at home that he cared to see again. Even Cynthia, though it would be pleasant to talk with her, could not now arouse his love, he believed. There was no magic any more in life.

And no sooner did he say this to himself than he knew where magic was. He had felt it electric in his being when he was with Josui, and so one hot and lonely night he let himself remember every time he had seen her, Josui standing under the wisteria that first day when unwittingly, simply staring about him and at a famous old city, letting his eyes rest where they would, he had found her. He allowed himself to remember every glimpse of her, especially the moment when she had peeped at him from the corner of her house. How beautiful she was in her kimono that day, the only time he had seen her in her own dress, in the vast spaces of the house so sparely furnished and exquisite in its elaborate simplicity, her home! Perhaps her world was best, a world of dignity and custom. She had chosen to remain in it, rather than to deny its lofty demands. She was more than merely a "good" girl. Even when he kissed her, because he could not help it, he felt that she allowed it with reluctance in spite of her obvious longing, too, for him. Poor little thing, he thought, bewildered by her own love, and not knowing how to cope with its confusion within herself. He had betrayed her, and his only answer was that he had gone away before it was too late.

Thinking of her thus, picturing her again and again, he

knew it was folly to do so, for as the days passed the habit grew on him in the continuing loneliness of the summer, when one by one the few men he knew best went away to the mountains or the seashore and the Colonel closed his house and flew to America for a fortnight. By the middle of August he felt that he must see her once more, to test himself, to be sure that he could really forget her enough to marry sometime another woman. Surely she was not so beautiful as he remembered her.

The summer had been hot in Kyoto, too, but Dr. Sakai had no time to think of it. Without seeming to hurry, he had proceeded at once with Josui's betrothal. How deeply he regretted his years in America! For now instead of knowing by instinct the marriage customs of Japan he was obliged to study an old book, to inquire of others, to find in any way he could without attracting notice to his ignorance how his daughter should be married to the son of an ancient and wealthy family. Busy as he was every day and always busier because of his fame as a physician, he felt he must himself decide upon the patterns of her new kimono, the silks, and the embroidered satins. He demanded that Josui be present, for he did not wish to be arbitrary. She must have what she liked, if it conformed to the suitable, and her mother must be present also, for propriety's sake. Yet in spite of their presence he made the final decisions always with an eye to the Matsui family and what he knew of their tastes and habits.

Nor would he demand of his daughter, he said, an obedience as blind as that of their ancestors. He was quite willing, if she wished, for her to meet Kobori informally, here in her own home. He would not allow her to be seen in public with him until they were married, but Kobori could call upon her, at such an hour when her parents were both at home. Thus several times before the wedding day, which was set for mid-September, Kobori came, after announcing beforehand the day and the hour and inquiring as to its convenience for the Sakai family.

Dr. and Mrs. Sakai always received him. The first time they stayed throughout his visit. Then they observed that Josui spoke very little. She bowed slightly to all that Kobori said, murmuring yes or no to his questions, but making no remark herself.

"Had we better leave the two alone?" Dr. Sakai asked his wife that night in their own room.

"After all, we were in America so many years," Mrs. Sakai suggested.

"Now we are in Japan," he retorted with some irritation. He did not wish anything to be as it had been in California. He reminded friends and family many times of the concentration camps for Japanese in America and he continued to do this, although long ago the camps had been dispersed and the Japanese had spread all over the United States without much difficulty.

"Josui remembers America," Mrs. Sakai said. "It may seem strange to her that she cannot even speak alone with the man she is to marry."

The next time, therefore, after a few minutes of talk about the weather, the prospect of fine chrysanthemums this year, always completely ignoring matters relating to the Occupation, Dr. Sakai motioned to his wife and they withdrew. When they were gone Kobori Matsui laughed silently and turned to Josui with a gentle gaiety. "Your father is so remarkable," he said in his mild bass voice, a large voice which had he raised it could have been very loud. But he never raised it.

"How is he remarkable to you?" Josui asked.

"He is more Japanese than any of us, and yet he does not know that there is something about him which can never be Japanese, however hard he tries. America has stamped him."

"I suppose it has also stamped me," Josui said.

"Yes, also you," Kobori agreed, "but then I like Americans."

"Even these who are here in the Occupation?" Josui asked doubtfully.

"Even they," Kobori said. "I do not like always what they do and very often I pity them. Their task is so great."

"What is their task?"

Kobori laughed again. "It is to make Americans out of us. How impossible!"

"Still, they are changing us," Josui suggested.

"Some of us," Kobori agreed.

"You mean after they are gone, everything will be as it was before?" Josui asked.

"At first it will even be more so," Kobori replied. "We shall become intensely Japanese, seeking first of all to find our old, our own souls. Then, after a generation or two, perhaps we shall change again. What we rejected we will begin to examine and partly to accept. It will be fifty years until we know what we are to be. By that time who knows what the world itself will be?"

Josui listened. Kobori talked well, meditatively, and without her father's arrogance.

"You are not afraid?" she inquired.

"Why should I be?" he replied. "I belong to an old family, conservative as you know. We shall do very well in the conservative period ahead. The ones I feel sorry for are these thousands of little children now sheltered in the orphanages, whose fathers are American, whose mothers are Japanese, and who are therefore orphans."

Strange she had never thought of them! Had she allowed Allen Kennedy, had he even wished to marry her, theirs would have been these children also. Would he—and she—have deserted their children? No, impossible for them to do so!

"Poor little children," Kobori was saying in his big merciful voice. "Better for them never to have been born."

She longed suddenly to be able to tell Kobori everything. He was so kind, it was part of his goodness. She could imagine him listening with pity, and even perhaps understanding how it had come about. Should she not tell him, since she was to be his wife? She looked at him, not knowing that question shone in her eyes.

He smiled, "And now what is it? You are asking something?"

"How do you know?" She was startled.

"Your face is open. I can almost read what you are thinking."

"Am I thinking?" She delayed, not knowing whether

now was the moment, but indeed she should tell him so that there could be no secrets between them.

"You are asking yourself what sort of man is this I am pledged to?" he suggested.

"Doesn't every woman ask that?" Thus she evaded him.

"Yes, I am sure she does."

They were kneeling in the Japanese fashion. He had placed himself at some distance from her, and this made her feel at ease. Kobori would never allow himself to touch her before they were married. Yet he had said to her father that he believed that they should know each other through talk.

Kobori was considering. Then he said, "I believe I am not very complex. The years during which I was compelled to be a soldier have made me now the very opposite of all that I was taught to be. Now I cannot kill anything. You must not expect me even to kill mice. I let them run about. I have heard for so many years the loud coarse shouting of military officers that there are times when I feel I should like not to speak above a whisper for the rest of my life. I have seen men beaten and kicked for small faults, and so please do not expect that I can ever strike a child. I have seen so much cruelty that the only way I can endure to live is to insist upon my own kindness. This is merely for my own sake. It may be called weakness. Yet while I know that I myself can resist the poison of cruelty, which, like an evil disease, can be so easily communicated from one to another, I can hope that there are others also and that someday human cruelty will end."

She had never heard him speak so long or so seriously,

and she was grateful to him. She knew that he did so in in order that he might reveal himself to her, as his duty. But he had unknowingly answered her question. In kindness, did she tell him of her love for another man, he might insist that she indulge it, or at least that he would withdraw until she had forgotten, or had changed. Surely she would forget and surely she could change. She did not want to wait. She wanted to marry, for marriage would occupy her mind, or at least her time.

"Thank you for speaking to me as you have done," she said. "I respect you, Kobori Matsui. I think that kindness is the greatest quality in man or woman. I hope I, too, am kind."

She allowed herself then to look at him with what she felt was at least the dawn of affection. For centuries marriages in Japan had been made without love. Respect and affection were enough. At least, her ancestors had so considered.

He responded to her with a slight informal bow. It was the end of the second visit.

This month of August continued so hot that old people in the city declared it must be some result of the atomic bombs the Americans had dropped on Hiroshima and Nagasaki. On the sixteenth day of August when the bonfires burn on high Daimonjii Mountain at night above Kyoto, even there it was so hot that those who tended the fires could not find coolness in the wind.

Dr. Sakai was overtired. The hospital had suddenly been

crowded with a rush of patients with old unhealing wounds from the two cities upon which the atomic bomb had fallen. His fame had spread from mouth to mouth, and the incurables had found their way to him in last desperate hope. He had been too zealous in his efforts to save their lives, and added to his zeal had been a continuing and mounting anger against all Americans.

In the accumulating heat he fell ill himself and for several days he was compelled to stay at home. He was, as he very well knew, the worst of patients, and although he struggled against irritation, although he could not stay in bed as he knew he should, he tried to achieve peace through meditation and the enjoyment of his garden. Even the garden, however, had suffered from the heat. Instead of contemplating its beauty he saw the waterfall weakened by water rationing, ferns dried and brown, and goldfish dying in the pool, exhausted by water heated by the sun.

One day, in no good frame of mind, he heard a persistent ringing of the small brass bell hung at the front gate. The gateman was evidently asleep, and although Dr. Sakai felt far from well he strode to the gate and threw it open. There stood a tall American officer in uniform.

Dr. Sakai stared. "What do you want?" he demanded.

"Dr. Sakai?" the man asked.

"Yes, I am he."

He made his eyebrows ferocious in order to discourage the American. Were these men to force their way even into the homes of private citizens?

"I am Allen Kennedy," the man said.

The name remained perfectly clear in Dr. Sakai's mind. He had tried to forget it but he could not.

"I do not know you," he said stubbornly.

The man smiled. "No, but I have met your daughter."

"My daughter is not at liberty."

"May I talk with you then, Dr. Sakai?"

Dr. Sakai did not answer at once. His mind was gathering quickly the possibilities of refusal. An officer, certainly, was not to be easily refused.

"I am not well," he said. "Otherwise I should be at the hospital. I prefer not to be disturbed."

The two men looked steadily into each other's eyes, matching themselves.

"I will call again," Allen said.

"It is not necessary," Dr. Sakai replied in a lofty voice.

"I think it is," Allen said. "In fact, I insist that it is."

He was horrified to feel within himself a real anger against this handsome cold Japanese face. What right had the fellow to refuse to allow him to come into his house? It was Josui's home. He did not forget that this was Japan, whose people were now subject.

"You cannot insist," Dr. Sakai told him with immense dignity.

"I insist upon seeing your daughter," Allen Kennedy retorted.

Dr. Sakai's quick temper rose beyond the bounds of control. He realized this and recognized it in himself as the result of having lived so long in America, where he had not received the proper teaching in his childhood or in the public schools for self-discipline. But it was too late. He could not stop the force of wrath not only against the American but against himself because he could not be altogether Japanese.

"I do not allow Americans here," he shouted, and then he tried to close the gate by violence.

In Allen, too, there was a mixture. Although he sincerely disliked being a member of a conqueror race, yet the effects of it had crept into him. He did not allow himself to remind Dr. Sakai of his rights, but he put his shoulder against the gate, and to the shame and disgrace of both, and each felt this, they struggled, the Japanese to close the gate, the American to force it open.

That part of the house which was nearest to the gate was the kitchen. There Yumi slept peacefully after the dishes for the noon meal had been washed and the floor swept. She woke, hearing the shouting voices speaking the foreign language of the conquerors, and she ran to the door. Now, struck with terror, she saw her master struggling to hold the gate shut against a young strong American officer. She screamed and with loud lamentations she ran through the house to find her mistress.

Mrs. Sakai and Josui were sitting together, sewing on some of the inner garments for the wedding. Upon their peaceful quiet Yumi burst like an explosion.

"Oh, Mistress! The master is fighting with an American officer!"

Mrs. Sakai rose from her knees and hurried out of the room, Yumi following.

Josui did not move. She knew instantly that Allen had returned, and how unfortunately! Why had he come to the gate? Why had he not written to her? But she could not stay here. Whatever the battle was she must join it, or make peace.

So Allen Kennedy saw his love, the slender girl, coming toward him wearing a blue and white flowered kimono, and beautiful beyond his remembrance. Her face was pale and imploring, and as he was now inside the gate he went to meet her.

Dr. Sakai stood exhausted, his lips pressed together. In front of him, a sort of guard, stood Mrs. Sakai and Yumi. He was defeated. He saw his daughter waver, and suddenly she was enfolded in the American's arms. She struggled, it is true, but he divined that it was because of his presence and that of her mother and the maid. Had she been alone he believed that there would have been no struggle whatever. He had lost her, that he knew. It now remained to find a strategy.

He turned to his faithful wife. "Bring your daughter to me," he commanded, and with restored dignity he went inside the house.

First he needed a few minutes alone. He was determined that he would still rout this American. It would not be difficult, strategically. He would simply demand the real intentions of the visitor. He did not believe that anything honorable was intended. Americans did not want to marry Japanese. He knew that, he had proof of it. If necessary he would present his own proof. Yet how could he do so in the presence of his wife? He groaned and sat down upon a low cushion, his legs folded under him in the way it had taken him so long to learn.

Here he was when they came in. The young man was

polite enough now. "Dr. Sakai, I am very sorry indeed. I don't know what got into me for a moment. I really had no right to press myself upon you."

Dr. Sakai did not answer this. He motioned to a guest cushion and noticed with some pleasure that the young man had difficulty sitting upon it properly. He allowed Josui to stand and frowned at Yumi so that she left the room. Mrs. Sakai knelt unobtrusively behind him.

The young man rose suddenly again. His legs, probably —but no, it was to offer Josui a seat.

"Where will you sit?" he asked in a low voice.

"Please don't think of me," Josui begged, in distress.

"I do think of you," he replied.

"Sit down!" Dr. Sakai thundered to his daughter.

She knelt beside her mother and Allen sat down, again uncomfortably, upon the cushion.

Dr. Sakai waited. Let him be approached. It was not he who had sought this occasion. He was the aggrieved. At the same time he intended, once the matter was opened, to be judicious, patient, but inexorable.

"Father," Josui began in a timid voice.

Instantly he frowned at her and so hideously that she stopped.

The American rushed to her defense. "It is not you who should speak, Josui, it is I."

So Allen was compelled to speak. When he came to Kyoto today he was all confusion. His only clarity was that he must see Josui once more and judge, if he could, how deeply he loved her, and whether he could bear to part from her. He knew now that he could not. He had been forced to decision partly because of the struggle with her father, but really because of the sight of her pale and vivid face.

"Speak then," Dr. Sakai said coldly. "I would like to know why you are here."

"I came to see your daughter."

Dr. Sakai turned to Josui. "Do you know this man?"

"We do know each other," Allen Kennedy said quickly. And then he told easily and well the brief story of their acquaintance and how after only a few hours they had agreed to part.

"Then why have you returned?" Dr. Sakai demanded.

"Because I know how much I love her," Allen said.

Dr. Sakai was ruthless. "You cannot love her! She is betrothed to the son of my friend, Kobori Matsui. The wedding is to take place in a fortnight."

The young man sat very still for an instant. Then he turned to Josui. "Is this true?"

She nodded, beginning to weep.

"I wish you had told me," he said.

He sat a moment longer in thoughtful silence. Then he spoke to her again. "Josui, I know I can't see you alone. So I must speak to you as if we were alone and I ask you to answer me in the same way. Do you love the man you are engaged to?"

"No," she said in a low voice. "But he is a very good man."

"Josui, answer me truthfully again. Do you love me?"

She lifted her face, wet with tears. "Oh, yes, Allenn Kenneddy!"

"Then will you marry me?"

The American way, Dr. Sakai thought savagely, always

the attack, the eternal offensive! "A betrothal cannot be broken," he declared. "Not in Japan."

"I suppose, sir, that if the two themselves decided that they did not want to marry it could be done—in modern Japan?" Allen asked.

Dr. Sakai was shaken. He cleared his throat and placing a hand on each knee, he looked down at the floor immediately in front of him. "I wish to tell you something."

"Please, Father," Josui begged.

"It is something I have never told anyone," Dr. Sakai said, in a strained voice. "I have never even told my wife." He glanced from under his heavy brows at that kind woman. "Forgive me, Hariko! I have never told you. I have forgotten it for many years. I remember it now only because of our daughter."

"Do not think of me," Mrs. Sakai whispered.

"Josui, my only child," thus he began. "It is not possible for you to marry an American. I say this because I know. Even this young man does not know what I know. It may be true that he loves you, or even that you love him. But love contains no wisdom. It is only an emotion. It passes soon, and life goes on."

He spoke with such sad gravity that they listened. The silence was so deep in the house that small noises not usually noticed were suddenly heard, a lingering cicada hanging in a tree ground its stiff wings together, a mockingbird called, the trickle of the waterfall suddenly seemed loud.

"When I was a young man in America," Dr. Sakai said painfully, "I loved a young American woman. I may say that she also loved me. We confessed it to each other. My parents objected, but I had been brought up as an American and I felt they had no right to deny me what I wanted with all my heart."

Mrs. Sakai was suddenly rigid. She clasped her hands and stared down at them. Dr. Sakai did not look at her.

"Oh, Mother!" Josui cried under her breath.

Her father went on. "I was prepared to give up everything," he said in a cold steady voice. "I was even ready to leave my parents. Then something happened. Her brother threatened me with a pistol. It happened one night when I came home late from the university. How did he know I passed that way? She must have told him. He put the pistol against my ribs. 'Listen, you,' that was what he said. 'You leave my sister alone!' He said, 'We don't want any damn Japs in our family.' That was what he said. I never saw her again."

"Is that all?" Allen asked.

"How do you ask is that all?" Dr. Sakai inquired passionately. "It was everything to me at the time. It is everything again to me now." He thrust out a long shaking forefinger. "For I tell you, it will happen again to my daughter."

"My family does not threaten people with pistols," Allen said haughtily.

"The same thing will happen," Dr. Sakai insisted. "It will not be with a pistol. It will be something else. They will not have a damn Japanese in the family. I tell you that!"

"I understand how you feel," Allen said with sympathy. "But that was long ago, Dr. Sakai, before Josui was born. Things are different now."

"Ha!" Dr. Sakai said loudly. "I read the newspapers. It is not so different. Many states do not allow marriages between white and colored people. Tell me, does your family sit down at table with them?"

Allen looked startled. "It would not occur to me to think of Josui as colored."

Josui's cheeks grew pink. "I will talk alone with Allenn Ken-neddy," she announced suddenly. "Everything is confused now. First we must be clear with ourselves, Father."

She rose with such decision that her father could not stop her, and would not, perhaps, if he could. Let them go away into the garden and talk. The young had always to talk. But he had told the bitter secret of his own life. They could not forget that.

So he was left alone with his wife. She continued to sit motionless. Then looking sidewise at her and seeing first her clasped hands he perceived that they were trembling. He put out his right hand and covered them. "I bless the day I saw your picture," he said. "I knew the moment I looked at you that you would be a good wife, though it was a poor photograph and not nearly so pleasant as you proved to be. You have been only good fortune to me. How miserable would have been my fate had I pursued another path! I can thank that murderous fellow that he put the pistol to my ribs."

She struggled against her sobs. "I am sure you were not afraid of him," she said loyally.

"I was," Dr. Sakai said. "I retreated at once, I assured him that under no circumstances would I marry his sister. So much was true."

"Please forget," his wife begged. She slipped her hands gently from under his palm and wiped her eyes with the edge of her long sleeve. "We are in our own country. It is not necessary to remember other things."

"You are right," he said. "But you see why I had to tell what I had forgotten."

"Please," she said imploringly.

"If I had not forgotten," he said stubbornly, "I would have told you long ago."

The moment became more than she could bear. She rose gracefully in spite of her short legs and bowed to her husband. "Excuse me, please," she said in a faint voice. "I have some duties."

She left the room and pattered in her soft half-stocking shoes to the room where she and Josui had been sewing. She took up the thin white silk stuff and began to sew, being careful to wipe her eyes each time they filled, lest her tears spot the silk. She had never been a pretty girl. She remembered herself very well, a thickset farm girl, her face square and sunburned. He had not chosen her. His parents did the choosing, she had looked strong and obedient, which indeed she was, but he, so wounded by lost love, had not cared what she was. Then suddenly she put down her needle. This garment, it might not be needed, so what was the use of her sewing?

Out in the garden the two young creatures were behind the bamboos, at this season a thicket against the wall. Side by side upon a rustic wooden bench they clung together, their agony healed for the moment. He could not pretend to understand the nature of his love. He only knew that he loved her as he had never known love, and whatever this meant he must go through with it to possess her.

"You know you can't marry anybody but me," he muttered against her lips.

"I know it now," she said brokenly.

"We'll run away," he said recklessly. "You're American, Josui. We'll act like Americans. We don't have to obey as though we were children."

"No, we cannot run away," Josui said firmly. She clasped her arms about his waist and tilted her head, so that she could see him. "You don't know Kobori Matsui. He is really good. I must tell him honorably. He will understand."

He wished unreasonably that the man were not good. It would be easier to take Josui away from a stiff-necked Japanese like her father.

"I don't want to meet the fellow," he said abruptly.

"Please," she implored, "leave such a matter to me. I must talk with my parents. We must obey my father in every small matter, you understand, Allenn Ken-neddy."

"Listen, Josui, you must stop calling me that. Just say Allen."

"Allenn," she repeated, and went on as though he had not interrupted. "In the great matter we cannot obey my father. We cannot part. But when he sees this, and I will make him to see it, then it is our duty to give him his way otherwise."

He was ready to yield anywhere now that he had made up his mind to marriage. "Whatever you say, darling. Only soon!"

She laid her head on his breast. "Soon," she echoed.

Strange that when so momentous a decision had been made they could not go on with the making of love. They sat gravely, pressing close, he playing with her hand as though it were a toy, and yet not thinking of it. He was becoming aware of immense problems, whose shape he could not see, yet which stemmed from the two of them sitting here in a quiet garden in Japan and, bridging the ocean, centered in the big white house at home. What would his family think? He would not tell them, he decided. He would wait and let them see Josui. It was not a matter to be argued. They must see this adorable woman, this soft and tender girl, who in spite of sweetness had a core of strength in her. Such a wise child, too, though she was shamefully, pitifully young, and this was the only thing that troubled him. But she was brave. He could imagine her going to his mother with that air of gentle pride and resolute docility. Well, it would be irresistible.

So he hid from Josui his doubts, not of her or of himself but of life itself, whose patterns they were breaking. But they were young enough and strong enough and all patterns were breaking nowadays. Other Americans had married Japanese girls and taken them home. Some marriages had turned out well and some had not. There was no reason why theirs would not, if they had the courage. But he would not burden her mind with all that. She had enough to do with her own family and with this engagement which had to be ended quickly. He could not endure the thought that she was promised to another man.

"How could you promise to marry someone else?" he demanded suddenly.

"Why not?" she asked. "In Japan I must marry somebody. You did not ask me, Allenn."

It was his fault, of course, and he must never forget that.

"When can we be married?" he asked restlessly.

"How to do it!" she sighed. "First I must talk with Kobori. He will do everything in the best way."

"Well," he got to his feet. "I hate to leave it to you, darling —I'll have to. I don't understand these things as you do."

But he felt suddenly jealous. "Sure you wouldn't rather marry your Japanese? It would be lots less trouble."

She put her hand over his lips. "Hush! You have told me I am an American. If so, then I want to marry American." She looked at him with trembling love. "I want to marry *you!*"

They sprang into each other's arms again. The old terrible longing rushed into his blood, into the beat of his heart. He felt half choked. "Don't let it be long, Josui. I shall begin the arrangements from my end tomorrow. I'll have to tell my Colonel—get his help. Maybe we can cut some of the red tape. Let's make it quick, darling. You here with your father—don't let him hold out."

"Oh, no," she exclaimed. "He will not if Kobori knows."

"Well, then, I have to catch the five o'clock train. I'm away without leave, in a sense, though I shan't be missed for a day."

"Write to me, Allenn!"

"You write to me, sweetheart."

"I don't write well, I'm sorry. But as well as I can, yes."

They pulled themselves apart, she fearful lest her father shout from the house that the time was long enough, and he that he might miss the evening train. A long kiss, and then another.

"You're learning to kiss like a real American girl, Josui."

"Oh? You know?"

"Silly, anybody knows who goes to movies."

"Oh, yes, but here the kiss is taken away before showing to the people."

"Not in America, though. Write to me tonight, do you hear, Josui?"

"I try. But you, too, Allenn."

"You mustn't mind my typewriter."

"Oh, no-o!" Her no was long drawn, soft as a sigh.

They parted and as she stood alone again she saw her reflection in the pool. Why must love contain so much sorrow? She loved him too much. It would have been better if she had loved Kobori, and by it made everyone happy. If she had not stood under the wisteria bower at that moment when the American soldiers passed, she would not have seen Allen, nor he her, and all would have been happy as now it could never be. Her parents, too, were hurt by the love which filled her with such ecstasy and pain. And on his side, there in Virginia, who could tell? But she would be such a good daughter-in-law that they could not hate her.

She went into the house at last, surprised that her father had not called her. He was nowhere to be seen, and in a few minutes her mother came out from the room where he studied and slept, whose screens were never pushed aside.

"Your father is not well again," her mother said. "The

day has been too much for him. Do not speak to him to-night. If you must speak then let it be to me."

Mother and daughter stood each hesitant before the other. For how, Josui thought, could she inflict still more pain as yet she knew she must? Love was a dreadful driving force, compelling her to the utmost cruelty, although she hated cruelty and had been a most tender child. And now she must wound even her mother who had never spoken any but kind words, and whose whole life was devoted to their family. Tears filled her eyes and she looked at her mother piteously, not able to speak.

It was her mother who spoke for her. "You wish to marry this American, do you not?"

"Yes, Mother. But oh, I wish I did not! I wish I had never seen him. I could then have married Kobori and I could have been happy, because I would never have known anything else. I would have learned to love him, as you did my father. You didn't see Father, did you? Before you married?"

Her mother did not smile. Her patient plain face continued unchanged. "Those were different times. My life was wholly different from yours. I simply obeyed. That was my fate."

"But you have been happy!" Josui cried.

"Yes," her mother replied. "But my happiness has been easy to attain. I did not expect so much good fortune as I have had."

They were still standing and Josui put her hand on her mother's arm. "Mother, do you understand me when I say I love him so much that I do only what I must?"

Her mother looked at her with a strange and unutterable

sadness. "Yesterday I would not have understood. Today, I can understand."

She turned her head away from her daughter, her pale lips trembling.

"Oh, Mother, don't!" Josui cried. "It was long ago. Father had forgotten."

"He had not forgotten," her mother declared in a small tight voice.

"It was only his wounded pride that made him remember," Josui urged. "You know how proud he is."

"Not his pride," her mother replied in the same stifled voice. "It was his love that was wounded. This was why he wanted to leave America. His wounded love—yes, he loved America, and when they turned on him, as—as once the American girl did also—it was all the same wounded love, beginning when he was young and growing until in the end he left his country. America was his country."

"Oh, Mother, Mother," Josui whispered. She did not know how to comfort her mother.

"It is natural for you to love the American," her mother went on. "And so you must marry him. It is not right for you to marry Kobori. You must do what your father never could do, and you must go back to America. It is I who belong here in Japan—only I. And so I will help you."

For the first time in their lives the two women embraced each other and clung together weeping.

In the morning Dr. Sakai rose, exhausted and grim. His wife, who he had supposed always was what she seemed, a simple and obedient woman, had in the night shown him an entirely different creature. She had taken the side of Josui against him and with much injustice she had declared that he was the cause of this desertion. By some twisted sense she said that because he had not been able to marry the American woman whom he had loved as a young and ignorant man, Josui should now marry an American.

In the middle of the night and for hours he had argued with her. "I tell you, Hariko, I am glad indeed that fate kept me from such a marriage. What would have happened to me when they wanted to put me into the concentration camp? I suppose I would have had children. Where would they have gone? Also into the camp? I could scarcely have brought children of mixed blood here to Japan. You know how they feel here about such persons. These would have been children of no country, exiles in the world. No, I am glad that I was shaken from such folly. I will try to save our daughter, also."

His wife had then made a wholly inexplicable declaration. "And I will save Kobori Matsui! I will save a good young Japanese man from marrying someone who is in love with an American! Josui shall not be his wife. I will go and tell him so, if you do not."

He had never dreamed that this quiet creature who had lived at his side for so many years could have concealed such rebellion, such determination. Because he had never so seen her he was afraid of her desperation. He knew the dark strain in their race, the easy transition from despair to suicide. For a Japanese there was a wide and ready bridge between life and death. It took too little hesitation for that brief journey. In her stubborn instinctive unenlightened way, his wife had mistaken completely the purpose of his revelation yesterday. She put into it a meaning wholly different from his own, a personal, female meaning, and he knew he could never dissuade her. It was quite possible that she would go to Mr. Matsui herself, or to Kobori, and if he forbade it or took physical means of preventing her leaving the house she would take her own life in protest.

So in the morning he got groaning out of bed and decided in his heart that his sole hope lay in his daughter, who at least was an educated person.

Then Josui was nowhere to be found. It was late, nearly noon, when he felt well enough to rise, and she had been gone, Yumi said, since ten o'clock. Yumi served his midday breakfast in portentous silence, knowing the disturbance in the house. When he asked where her mistress was, for she had got up early, Yumi replied that she was busy this morning making a fresh supply of cho-yu. Mrs. Sakai refused to buy this essential soy sauce, preferring to do as they had done on the farm, that is, to buy the best of soy beans and set them to the necessary process of aging and fermentation. At this task she did not like to be disturbed. There was no rest to be found in the house as it was, and he decided that he would go to the hospital and to work.

"Did your young mistress say where she was going?" he asked Yumi as she fetched his hat and stick.

"She said she was going to find some books at the college."

This was a lie. Josui had gone out without telling anyone where she was going. Seeing her master's yellow face, however, Yumi felt the lie a kindness. He went away without speaking again.

Josui at that moment was talking with Kobori. She had slept little but lying quietly in bed she had allowed the hours of the night to pass and by morning her determination was crystal. The sooner she saw Kobori the better. Above all, she wished it to be before she met her father again. She wanted to say, "Father, it is finished. Under the circumstances Kobori does not want to marry me. There is no going back."

When she had said this to her father, she would then write a letter to Allen, telling him the same news, though in different words. She would say to him that she was ready. He must tell her where to go to him.

After her mind was clear and her spirit calm she slept. It was still early when she waked and she had risen, washed herself, and put on a dark-blue silk dress in which she felt she did not look attractive. She combed her hair plainly and did not wear rouge or redden her lips. She ate the food that Yumi served and left the house without seeing even her mother.

She knew from Kobori's own description of his day's work that he reached his office late and so she walked into a park and then sat for a while on a bench beside a small lake. A few early chrysanthemums were already blooming in the beds and the goldfish were lively. There was a new coolness in the air. The heat was over at last. Sitting alone in such finality of stillness, she could feel the cessation of growth, the subsidence in the earth, the sinking into sleep. Some part of her own life, too, had ended, indeed, her first youth, her girlhood. She had chosen her fate as a woman. Had she been timid or fearful in disposition, she might have been afraid of her present solitude, but she was neither timid nor fearful. She felt in herself an immense strength, a capacity to cope with whatever came. Her natural fearlessness gave her the capacity, too, for faith, and not only in herself but in anyone whom she chose to trust, and she trusted Allen wholly. The world was changing and together they could deal with whatever came to them.

A little before noon she rose and walked toward the main street of the city to a tall modern building where the Matsui offices were. The elevator carried her to the sixth floor and there opened to admit her to the entrance of Matsui House. A young Japanese in a western business suit came forward.

"May I help you?" he inquired in English.

She replied also in English. "Please tell Mr. Kobori Matsui that Miss Sakai wishes to speak with him for a few minutes."

Had she answered in Japanese it is doubtful whether she would have been admitted so quickly. As it was, he left her at once and then she saw Kobori himself, looking very clean and pleasant in a western suit of gray flannel. He came to her with just the right shade of warmth and welcome. They bowed without touching hands.

"Come in, please," Kobori said.

"I am afraid you are very busy," Josui said in Japanese.

"I am never very busy," Kobori said with a slight smile. "Shall I call my secretary?"

This he said, not knowing whether she might dislike to be seen to enter his office alone with him.

"Please, no," Josui said.

He led the way then into his office and left the door a little open.

"Please sit down," he said and moved for her a comfortable western chair. The room itself was large and all the furniture was heavy. The white walls were bare except for a pair of fine scrolls behind his desk.

He did not sit there. Instead he took a chair like hers and so they sat as though they were in a living room, perhaps in the Matsui house, where there were both Japanese and western living rooms. Thus facing him Josui felt a deep unhappiness that she was here with such cruel purpose. He sat there, a big kind man, his smooth pale oval face smiling, his brown eyes beaming at her. She could see his simple trust in her, his pleasure at their relationship, his complete faith in his own good fortune. It was easy to perceive that he had never known disappointment or pain, the well-loved son of a rich man and heir to all his father had. How pleasant his love could have been had she never met Allen!

Then she reproached herself. How could it have been pleasant? The height of life was love and she could never have known love had she simply married Kobori.

She leaned forward, holding her leather handbag with both hands. "Kobori, I am come to do a strange cruel thing. It is difficult."

He sat quite motionless. "You need not be afraid of me, Josui."

She dealt the blow. "I cannot marry you, Kobori."

He looked at her, still motionless, waiting. Oh, she thought, he is going to feel this too much!

"I take the blame on myself," she said swiftly. "I should

116

never have promised. That was my fault. I knew what I hid in my own heart. But I thought it was dead. Now, without the slightest expectation on my part, and even without my wish, it has come to life."

He spoke carefully, and even dryly. "Will you express yourself concretely?"

She looked at the handbag. "Last spring I met an American. We soon discovered that we loved each other. We decided against our love, and he went away. I thought I could forget this experience, but yesterday he came back. He, too, was compelled. We know now that we cannot forget. It would be an injustice to you to conceal the truth."

He wet his pale lips. "Thank you for telling me," he said.

She waited for him to go on and could not look at him while he delayed. But there seemed nothing more for him to say.

"How do your parents feel?" he asked at last.

"They do not approve," she replied, "but my mother feels as I do—that I must do what I am doing. My father is only angry. He does not suggest anything constructive. He hates America, as you know. It is dreadful to him that I should return there."

"But you love America," he mused. "I have always known that you do. I planned that I would take you there sometime for a holiday. We do business with American firms, and will do more when the Occupation is over. I planned that we might stay several months in California, perhaps." He leaned forward suddenly and hid his face in his hands.

"I am very sorry, so sorry," she muttered.

"Yes," he said behind his hands, "well, it cannot be helped.

It is honorable of you to come and tell me yourself. Of course, for some time I must—collect my thoughts."

"I hope you will find someone else," she said and knew how foolish this was.

"I cannot think of that," he said. He took his hands away and she was relieved to see that he was not weeping, although he gazed at her with sad and loving eyes. "I suppose we shall not meet again alone, Josui?"

"There will not be need, I think," she replied. "It will be easier for us not to meet."

"Then I had better say what I wish to say now, if you allow me."

"Surely I should not forbid it," she replied.

She was aware of a lightening of the heart, and she was eager to be gone. Yet at least she must stay to hear what he wanted to say.

He leaned forward, his elbows on his knees, to look at her the more deeply. "Josui, it is quickly said. Only this— if ever you need me again, for any reason whatsoever, call upon me. Do not let pride prevent you."

"Oh, Kobori," she cried. "I shall be very happy, there will be no need, but how good you are!"

He tried to smile. "Keep the path open, that is all I ask."

She was on her feet now, restless, anxious to escape.

"I promise you that, Kobori." It was an awkward word to use, and she knew it as soon as it was spoken. Promise! She had not kept her promise to him. But now she put out her hand and for the first time felt his clasp, a large warm soft hand covering hers entirely, which was so small and firm within.

He seemed shaken then and his eyes shone suddenly with tears. But he smiled and bowed and she bowed, and so it was over.

After she was gone Kobori sat for some time in the easy chair. He allowed the catastrophe to flow over him like a great wave. Long ago, as a little boy, his father had taught him how to deal with the sea. They had then a house on the shores of Kyushu, and in the summer he spent most of his daytime hours in the water. He had learned early to swim, but it was his father who taught him how to swim without exhaustion.

"You cannot overcome the sea," his father had told him. "It is as endless as eternity, as unchangeable as fate. In comparison to the sea a man is less than a small fish. Do not fight the sea. Do not combat the tides. Yield yourself and as the waves flow, let yourself follow them. Then you will be borne up, the sea itself will uphold you."

He thought of these words now. He was overwhelmed with what he had just heard. He had allowed himself to trust completely the sureness of his love for Josui. He had never loved any other woman. Like most men he had gone to pleasure houses, joined in the feasts that men give each other, laughed with pretty girls and listened to their music. But he had not wanted any woman for his wife except Josui. Now she would never be his wife. The thought was so monstrous that for a moment he felt giddy, as though the sand were being sucked from under his feet, as though the wave were crashing over his head. He closed his eyes and leaned back on the cushion of the chair and remained wholly

passive, allowing the pain to swirl about him. So it must be
—so it must be!

After nearly an hour he opened his eyes and then he got
to his feet and poured himself a small bowl of hot tea from
the padded teapot on a stand near his desk. He sipped it
slowly, feeling himself cold and tired, as if indeed he had
been in the sea itself. He could not recover easily from this
chill.

Nevertheless after another half hour he touched the bell
on his desk. His secretary came in and he began to dictate
his morning letters, thinking as he did so that tonight, as
soon as he reached home, he must tell his father. The arrangements for the wedding must be stopped at once. The
invitations must be recalled. It was too late to return to the
jewelers the gift he had prepared for Josui, a set of pink
pearls, true pearls, gathered off the coast of India.

"I have already told Kobori," Josui said.

Her father had not returned until midnight but she had
waited for him. Her mother knew. They had put away the
wedding garments which now would never be needed. What
her mother had felt, Josui did not know. She folded the garments carefully, not allowing Josui to touch them, and the
rich stuffs were put into camphorwood chests in a storeroom.
The whole evening they had spent at this task, and her
mother had asked not one question of her, not even what
Kobori had said, nothing had she asked.

"It is very late," her father said when she asked him to
hear her.

"I shall not sleep until I tell you what I have done," Josui declared.

So, hiding his despair and his weariness, he had sat down, and she, standing, had told him that she was determined to marry the American.

"I do not know how to tell my friend, Takashi Matsui, nor how he will tell Kobori," he had said.

So she had said that Kobori knew, for she had told him.

"You told him?" her father demanded, unbelieving. "How could you be so bold? See how already you are changed!"

"Kobori is so good that I could tell him," she said drooping her head.

"He is so good—he is so good!" her father mimicked. "But it seems he is not good enough for you to marry."

"He is good enough," Josui said bravely. "It is simply that I love another man and Kobori understands this."

"It does not remove the disgrace," her father declared.

He sat frowning and gloomy but exhausted as Josui could see. His handsome face was as pale as wax and his large eyes were sunken. Then he clapped his hands three times sharply.

"This American will never marry you!"

"He will!" Josui cried.

"How can he marry you?" her father demanded. "In America it is always done in a church. A civil marriage is not enough. They will not consider it enough. And how can there be feasting and guests? Who will even be the witnesses? The witnesses are necessary, from the American point of view."

"I do not want to have a feast or guests," Josui said. "And what is our religion, Father? We have no church."

"I am a Buddhist," he declared. "The Americans have their gods and priests and we have ours. The ceremony would have to be in the Buddhist temple, in the presence of the gods and the priests."

"I am sure my—that he—will be willing for this. He wishes to do whatever you require," Josui said.

"Except to leave you in my house," her father said bitterly. "That he will not do. He has stolen into my house and taken my treasure, and he will not return it. What else do I require?"

Her head drooped still lower. Yet, watching her face, he saw no sign of yielding. That full red lower lip did not quiver. He yielded suddenly and leaping to his feet he swept her aside with his arm, a gesture which was all but a blow. "Have your way," he said harshly. "Go to America. But when they throw you out as they threw us all out, do not come back to me."

She lifted her head, as proud and as angry as he. "I will not come back to you, that I promise—Father!"

In Tokyo Allen was talking with his Colonel. The two men sat alone in the Colonel's office. Piles of paper work lay on the desk and the Colonel eyed it secretly from time to time. In his imagination it grew of its own weight, mounting higher and higher in his distress as Allen Kennedy talked.

"It is your personal affair, of course," the Colonel said reluctantly. "Still, I've had an admiration for you. You have something more than the ordinary military mind. The military mind is all very well, but the best men are the ones who have something more than merely a soldier's mind. You could, if you wanted to, rise as high as five stars—in my opinion. Of course, you won't get the chance if you have a Japanese wife. A man's wife is very important, if he wants to rise in this profession."

"I know you are right," Allen Kennedy said. Cynthia, for example, would have been the perfect wife, beautiful in her large blonde way, tactful, friendly, simple minded without being in the least stupid. Well, he was not in love with Cynthia.

"Can't you make arrangements?" the Colonel persisted. "The Japanese don't look on these matters as we do. The men here have plenty of arrangements. The girls don't expect them to marry. Japanese men marry as high as they can, without thought of love. Love is something else."

The Colonel was an educated man. He knew that sex, while made up always of the same instinctive lust, found its satisfaction in ways as various as man himself. The sensitive and somewhat too delicately handsome face of the young man facing him with such resolute blue eyes revealed a nature complex beyond the soldier on the street. Lust might burn within such a frame but it could be slaked only by the magic of romantic imagination. It was not the need of the bull, yet it was as definite a need, though entangled in the mind and the soul and infinitely more difficult therefore to satisfy.

"I suppose," Allen said reluctantly, "had I been the sort to make 'an arrangement' as you call it, it would have been better. Unfortunately I—can't—"

The Colonel nodded. "Well, men aren't alike. Give me a few days to think it over."

Allen got to his feet at once, aware of dismissal. "Shall I—"

"I'll send for you when I've made up my mind," the Colonel said. He was already sorting the papers.

"There's one more thing, sir," Allen said standing his ground. "We have made up our minds. It is not a question of will I or won't I. It is simply how to do what we have to do. What does an American do, in short, when he wants to marry a Japanese girl of good family? That is all I am asking you, sir."

The Colonel flared at him. "Just leave it to me, will you, Kennedy? I can't see my best officer make such a step without taking some thought. I can't think now—look at this!" He waved handfuls of papers.

"Yes, sir," Allen said, and went away.

Actually what the Colonel wanted was to go home and talk with his wife, but an unmarried man could not know this. As soon as Allen had left the room the Colonel made no further pretense of work. He smoked several cigarettes while he pondered, then he called his wife on the telephone. She was, she said, doing nothing at all.

"I thought you were going to play bridge today?" he inquired.

"That's tomorrow," she reminded him.

"Oh? Well, I think I'll come along early to lunch with you. I've just had some upsetting news."

He left the office, wishing he had brought a topcoat with him this morning. The air was sparkling clear and already early chrysanthemum venders were everywhere on the streets. He had never seen such blooms, bigger even than the big yellow balls he used to buy for Edna to wear to the football games in New Haven. She had been a real success as an officer's wife, always knowing the right thing and doing it, treating the lesser wives without condescension, and the higher ones with exactly the right deference but not too much. She had a sense of humor, although, thank God, not too much of that either. She took military life seriously, as a woman had to, if she was married to a Colonel.

At their house she was pleasantly waiting for him, wearing a nut-brown woolen suit that looked warm without being heavy. She was a brown-eyed brown-haired woman, and though he suspected that she tinted her hair to keep the gray hidden, yet he would not for anything have pried into her little secrets. She was not prudish in any sense. She understood men. Nevertheless she liked to be let alone while she was dressing, and he had learned that he was not welcome when she was fixing herself up, as he called it. He smiled at her now.

"You look nice. Is that new?"

"Heavens, no—ten years old, at least. Don't you remember I bought it in London when we were stationed there?"

"I never know what you buy," he retorted. "Is lunch ready?"

"I made cocktails, just in case."

"Good."

Over their cocktails in the big sunny living room in this house which had been requisitioned from a Japanese millionaire, he told her the unfortunate news.

"Kennedy has got himself mixed up with a high-class Japanese girl," he began abruptly. "He wants to marry her."

"Oh, Robert!" his wife cried reproachfully, as though he could help it.

"I know," he said, "but what can we do? I told him all that you're thinking."

"Can't he just make it—temporary?"

"That's what I suggested."

"Well?"

The Colonel smacked his lips slightly over his cocktail and dried his clipped mustache on the tiny napkin. "It's not that Kennedy is a prude," he said cautiously. "I don't think it is a matter of morals."

"What else?" she demanded.

"He's overbred," the Colonel said. "Know what I mean? He can't just take his women and leave them. The kind that you can do that with don't appeal to him. The only kind that rouse him are the kind that don't expect to be treated that way."

"Oh, he's romantic," she cried, robustly.

"Maybe," the Colonel conceded. "Whatever you want to call it! But I've seen men that couldn't go through the act unless it was romantic. It's a nuisance, to say the least. Unrealistic. You can't count on men like that. I'd rather have a fellow that stands in line for a couple of dollars and gets it over with and back on the job."

She was an amazingly comfortable woman. You could say things like that to her and she didn't mind. She knew what you meant. At the same time, knowing what men were like, she didn't fall in love with them and make talk for him.

"Don't take more than two, Robert," she warned him

when he filled his glass again. "You know what it does for you at noon."

"Yes, dammit," he said gloomily. She mixed a rousing good drink, tangy and on the sour side. He hated sweet stuff. "Well?" he said.

"I'm thinking," she replied. She drank very little, but she never refused to drink with him. She was always willing, though not often enthusiastic. She was too sensible for enthusiasms.

"I'll tell you," she said after a few minutes. "Why don't you wangle him a leave?"

"Now?" he demanded, "When Korea is looming?"

"Get him home. Get him into the home atmosphere. He lives in Virginia, doesn't he? Remember the pictures he showed us of that big white house with the pillars? Get him home quick. Pull your wires, Bob! He'll find a girl at home who will make him forget. My guess is that it is just a case of continence, not conscience!"

Her brown eyes twinkled at him and they laughed. They enjoyed a dirty joke together now and then, each knowing that the other was decent at heart.

"Smart girl," he said feelingly. He was warmed with the alcohol, with the sunshine in the big room, with the general comfort, security, and superiority of his life. He put out his arm, pulled her to him by her neck, and gave her a mighty kiss. "Best girl in the world," he mumbled against her acquiescent lips.

Kobori did not go home earlier, although he was desperately tired. For all his large softness of body he was a healthy and strong man, never tired physically, but easily tired from within. If he had a religion it was that an air of happiness and content must be maintained at all costs. He considered this his filial duty, as the only remaining child his parents had. He admired his father more than any man, knowing that he had sacrificed much for principle's sake. Thus his father, almost alone before the war among the merchant princes of Japan, had declared that the policy of the militarists who controlled the government was wrong.

"We cannot possibly hold an empire by force," Takashi Matsui had declared when summoned before a committee of the Diet.

"England has done so," a general declared.

"But the age has changed," Mr. Matsui had reminded him. "India three hundred years ago is not to be taken as example of China today. The Chinese will not tolerate subjection by Japan. They have never been a subject people."

"If we do not continue with our policy of building an empire," the general insisted, "we ourselves will fall into colonialism. Do not think that the West has given up the idea of empire. The United States is only now rising to power. Americans dream of empire."

"They dream of trade," Mr. Matsui said stubbornly.

"Trade—trade!" the general snorted. "All empire begins in trade. Englishmen went to India to trade but the end was empire for three hundred years. If we do not seize Asia, the Americans will."

"You must remember, sir, that today there is also Russia," Mr. Matsui said gently. "Russia is more to be feared than America."

The general replied in so loud a voice his words rang through the hall. "We will take them one at a time, if you please!"

Takashi Matsui left not quite in disgrace, he was too rich for that, the family too ancient and honorable. But he went into prudent retirement. The Matsui interests were ignored, and only since the Occupation had they begun to be rebuilt. Meanwhile Kobori's elder brother was dead and his second brother was lost in Russia. Seeing the deep sadness of his parents, he tried by all means to comfort them, and the best comfort, he had discovered, was to appear always happy before them. He had never revealed to them, therefore, any discontent in himself, and this stern self-discipline had made him a controlled and seasoned man.

His first thought now as he walked home, according to habit, was of his father and how he would present the blow which had fallen upon him in the best way to assure his father that it was not a crushing one. His mother would feel as his father did. She was an old-fashioned Japanese wife, so long and so exquisitely subdued that now she was only a shadow of his father, a reflection and not a substance.

The evening was clear and cool and the streets were lined with the baskets of chrysanthemum venders. He looked at them as he passed, to see if there were any varieties which his father did not have. He saw at last a very pale and pearl-pink one, the petals quilled around a center as yellow as gold. He stopped to buy the pot and have it wrapped in a bit of old newspaper. Then he carried it carefully the short distance to the gate. Before the Occupation no man would have thought of carrying a flower pot thus, but now it was considered democratic to do so. He enjoyed the freedom of its being convenient.

It would be pleasant, he thought, to present his father with the new chrysanthemum. It would be an introduction, which he could follow later or at once with the evil news. He would let the moment occur when it would. He hoped it might be soon, for it would be easier for him to control himself if his father knew, since he would be obliged to assure his father that he did not mind as much as he thought he would and that certainly he would not have wished for his wife a reluctant woman.

His father was, as usual at this time of evening, walking in the garden. Like most garden lovers, he could never enjoy the perfection of the garden as much as he wished, because his overzealous eye saw always some imperfection, too minute to be noticed by a stranger.

Now Kobori saw his father among the formal beds of chrysanthemums, his lips pursed as he stood above a magnificent bush of red and gold blooms.

"Kobori!" his father cried. "I think these are not as fine as last year!"

Kobori bowed. "I will come and see," he said. "But first, Father, do we have this pink-quilled variety? I have not seen it, I think."

Mr. Matsui put out his hands eagerly. It was those two outstretched hands which startled Kobori. They were so thin that every bone was clear. His father was as thin as this! He gazed at the beloved face and saw the same thinness. As usual Mr. Matsui wore Japanese garments and his neck was bare. Kobori could see the hollows of the collarbone, the sunken temples. He was taller than his father, broader and stronger in body than his father had ever been, and now he yearned over this aging man, transferring himself almost into the position of the parent. He made himself laugh.

"You have not this one? I have actually found a new chrysanthemum for you!"

His father's dry brown face crinkled. "I would not have believed it possible." The Matsui chrysanthemums were famous.

Together they bent over the new flower, absorbed in its fragile beauty.

"Now where shall we put it?" Mr. Matsui asked anxiously. "Certainly not with these red and gold ones. Your mother will like this new one. It looks like her. I shall place it here where she can see it from her window."

He set the plant carefully in another group and then rubbed his hands together to free them from dust. The scene was so pleasant, the air so delightful, that Kobori seized upon the happy moment.

"Father, I am glad I found this chrysanthemum for you. It makes it easy for me to tell you something not so pleasant. My marriage will not take place."

Mr. Matsui whirled on his son. "What is this?"

"Miss Sakai has decided against the marriage," Kobori said calmly.

Mr. Matsui blinked; he could not speak for a moment. Kobori took advantage of his father's instant shock. "You are not to be troubled by this, Father," he said mildly. "I had been feeling somehow that the marriage would never come about. I think Dr. Sakai overpersuaded his daughter, in his devotion to you. You know how he admires you. He will suffer very much. We must think of how to spare him. It is really very good of Miss Sakai to let me know in time."

"Did she, herself—" his father sputtered.

"Yes," Kobori said tranquilly. "She is very American, you know. She came simply to my office and explained her feelings. She prefers to marry an American."

"Is there an American?" Mr. Matsui demanded.

"It seems that there is," Kobori said. "Under the circumstances, therefore, I am sure it is for the best."

Mr. Matsui had now recovered enough to be angry. "It is certainly for the best, certainly so! A young woman such as this would never fit into our ancient family. But what of you, my son?"

Kobori smiled. "You see me. I am quite happy!"

Mr. Matsui put out his hands and clasped his son's arm. It felt reassuring to him, so strong and soft inside the flannel coat sleeve. "How embarrassing, my son, for you, that she came face to face with you."

"Not at all," Kobori said lightly. "I rather liked her frankness. It was something new. She is an intelligent young woman. I think she will be happier in America than here. After all, she spent the first fifteen years of her life in California. She can never be really Japanese, I think, after that. We must think only of her father. A wonderful man, suffering much, I think, because he has lost one country and cannot relive his life in another."

They walked slowly toward the house, arm in arm.

"How to tell your mother," Mr. Matsui murmured.

"Let us not tell her just now," Kobori suggested. "Let us

have the evening meal as usual. Then tonight perhaps you can tell her alone, when you have retired for the night. Tomorrow we will decide how to meet Dr. Sakai. It should not be too soon, perhaps. He must have time to arrange himself and create a proper mood. We should await this mood, in order that we can meet it suitably."

Mr. Matsui leaned upon Kobori's arm. "I think only of you, my son. So long as you are not wounded—"

"I cannot be wounded," Kobori said. He smiled down upon his father's uplifted face.

So clear were his brown eyes, so reassuring was the richness of his mild voice, that Mr. Matsui believed him.

"So, and therefore," the Colonel said. "You may take off for home, my boy, next Thursday. You may have as long as you like, within reason."

Allen grinned at his superior. "Don't think I am fooled, sir."

The Colonel did not look up from the papers he was signing. He was brisk and efficient this morning and very self-confident.

"Who wants to fool whom?" he retorted. "I don't care if you are fooled or not. I want you to go home and think. Get back into your home atmosphere, see your family, look at the girls."

"It won't make any difference, sir."

"It might," the Colonel said. "If it doesn't, then don't come back here."

He added these words in sudden anger at the obstinacy of this handsome young officer. He had put a lot into Kennedy, time and advice and liking. He was angry that it might all be wasted for a Japanese girl. Be refined, he thought, but weren't there refined American girls? He did not believe in mixing the races. Already there were thousands of half-American Japanese babies, thousands of half-American Chinese babies, just as in India there were hundreds of thousands of half-English Indian babies. It was one of the accursed accompaniments of war and even the Pentagon could not lick the problem. While they were trying to keep America safe for the Americans, the men themselves were undermining the whole idea. Even Kennedy! Lust he could understand, when men were in a foreign country, but marriage!

"Thank you, sir," Allen said formally.

"Oh, you'll be back," the Colonel snarled.

Allen went away. Three days! What could he do in three days? He was furiously angry at the trap that the Colonel had laid for him and into which now he was compelled to step. There must have been telephoning back and forth across the Pacific. Whose idea was it? The Colonel's wife, of course! Only a woman could have thought of something so mischievous. Last spring he would have been mad with delight to think of getting home. Now the one thing he longed to do was to stay in Japan—forever, if that was the only way to be with Josui. He was shocked at his own faithlessness, for at this moment he would willingly have sworn never to go home again, never to see his parents, if he could be sure that he could spend his life with Josui. There was something more than love in his anger. He had never been thwarted in so high-handed a fashion. Very little had been forbidden him in life. An only child, he had been too precious for frustration, and he was not inclined to submit to it now. He had always had what he wanted.

Three days!

"Get your things ready," the Colonel had said. "I won't ask anything of you. I advise you just to go off without seeing the girl again."

Well, this he would not do. He would go to Kyoto on the first train he could catch. Of course he had to go home. Not to go would be insubordination to a degree he did not care to face. But somehow he would have to persuade her that he was coming back. He wished that the Japanese fellow were not so near, so powerful, so ready. The doubt was whether Josui could hold out.

The doubt agitated him so horribly that it was intolerable. He would not enjoy anything at home unless he made sure of her and the only way to make sure of her, he knew, was to marry her. They would be married now, as quickly as it could be done. But how? It took forever to get the permission, and probably the Colonel had blocked all that, anyhow. How did the Japanese get married? Or could he persuade her—

He telegraphed to Josui that he was coming on the afternoon train the next day. It was too late to catch the morning train today. He would pack, get ready to leave and spend every moment with her. Oh, he would persuade her, the darling, hold her, entice her, and love her until she could not refuse, marriage or not, make her his own, and when their love was sealed by consummation he could go and come back again quickly.

Or, better still! His mind was working fast while he

walked back to his rooms. He would get transferred. He would stay in America, get a desk job maybe in the Pentagon. He had years of experience behind him in the Pacific Islands, in Japan, in Korea, and now in Japan again. He could make himself useful. Then Josui could come to him. She was an American citizen by birth and there would be no trouble about getting her into the country.

His heart lightened. Perhaps it was all for the best, in spite of the Colonel. He might need some time to persuade his family. Who knew what benighted idea they might have about the Japanese? He was glad that he had taken the trouble to describe to his mother the landscapes, the amusing experiences, the pleasures of his life here. He would like, all things being to his satisfaction, to have stayed here. It was a delightful country, easy to live in, the people charming. Yes, he had grown to find them so. It was strange sometimes to wake up in the night out of a bad dream, a nightmare of the jungles, where the horror, likely to spring upon them at any instant, was a Japanese man, naked, painted with green shadows until he was invisible, a few feet away. He had learned in those days to sleep, half awake, to hear, to feel, the presence of the enemy. Once, still almost asleep, he had sprung up and buried his short-bladed dagger in a thick Japanese body. But he never got used to it. He was not a killer. The nightmare was of the instant when his blade sank into the softness behind the skin. The skin was tough, at the first plunge of the dagger's point, and then—

He turned abruptly into a telegraph office and wrote his message to Josui. ARRIVING TOMORROW AFTERNOON. HAVE BEEN ORDERED HOME. So far he wrote and then paused. This would terrify her and she must not be terrified. He bit the pencil and then added. YOURS UNTIL DEATH, ALLEN.

The telegram arrived that night. Dr. Sakai took it from the messenger and read it before he handed it to Josui. She had heard the bell, had seen the messenger, and suspected that the telegram was for her. It did not occur to her to object to her father reading it first. Sooner or later she would have given it to him.

He handed it to her without comment, but his face brightened.

She read it slowly twice, getting from it exactly what Allen had intended. He had been ordered home because of her. As an officer he was valuable. He would have to go. He wanted her to know that he was determined to marry her.

But how was this to be accomplished? Her quick mind collected the facts and faced them.

"We must be married at once," she told her father.

"I forbid that," he said loudly. "Let him go home. We will wait and see if he comes back."

"If we are not married, I will go away with him anyway," she declared.

"I shall lock you in your room," he bellowed.

She laughed at this, not pleasantly at all. He was shocked to hear the way she laughed. Her pretty face grew scornfully harsh. She looked at him sidelong, her mouth curving downward. "Do you think he will let you lock me up? He will break down the house! Haven't you seen the way Americans can behave? Are they to be crossed? Don't forget that they are our conquerors!"

"I shall have nothing more to do with you!"

"And I will go with him!"

Her mother, hearing the angry voices, came running as fast as she could. Yumi met her in the corridor, and hooked her thumb toward the front door. "The people on the street!" she hissed.

"Josui, Josui!" Mrs. Sakai cried. "Your father! Oh, do not be wicked!" She ran between them, pushing her husband with one hand and her daughter with the other.

Neither paid any heed to her. They continued to glare at each other.

"A god-sent chance to test this foreigner," Dr. Sakai raged. "But she, this shameless girl, insists on marrying him before he goes so that he cannot escape her. I begin to think it is not he but she who has done the evil. She standing at the gate to be stared at, she meeting him secretly—I apologize for my daughter!"

He raised his face to the ceiling and threw out his arms.

Mrs. Sakai turned to Josui. "You cannot marry quickly. It takes time. He must get permission."

"I will go with him," Josui insisted.

She looked at one parent and the other and saw them in sudden league against her. It was a sight she had never seen before, not at least since Kensan was killed in Italy and she became the only child.

"I will do as I wish!" she cried. Then she turned and ran away through the house to her own room.

Left alone, the parents stood sadly together.

"What shall we do?" Dr. Sakai asked in strange humility.

"She is so stubborn," Mrs. Sakai said with sorrow. "Remember that she grew up in America. She cannot be changed now."

"I will go to the temple and see what the Buddhist minister, the *Hosshu,* will do," Dr. Sakai replied, with equal sadness. "She will have to be married."

Allen Kennedy shook the brass bell on the door. He dreaded the hour ahead of him, but he was resolute. If Dr. Sakai forbade him entrance, he would stand his ground. If only Josui were not so young! It was hard to tell a man that his twenty-year-old daughter was old enough to know her own mind. Yet he must himself know the caliber of Josui's will, her firmness, her calm, her strength. There was temper behind the sweet repose of Josui's face. He counted on the temper. Many a time in his own life he himself had been able to sweep aside obstacles which people put in his way if only he were made angry enough, as now he was angry. The Colonel, Dr. Sakai, neither of them or both of them together, could change his determination.

So he stood at the door, waiting. It opened after a moment and Yumi, the stocky maidservant, stood before him. She spoke a few Japanese words which he understood to mean an invitation to enter. He entered and she was not distressed, and so he had understood what she said. She bowed and led the way, beckoning him to follow. He was surprised, but he obeyed. The house was silent. He did not hear the sound of a voice or a footstep. A trap? Fantastic idea, and yet it occurred to him.

There was no trap. He was ushered into a large beautiful room, whose paper-latticed walls were drawn back to reveal the exquisitely ordered garden and the vista of a waterfall falling from level to level down the side of a small hill designed to look like a mountain.

Before the alcove where a flat bowl of early autumn leaves was set a little to one side of a landscape scroll, sat Dr. and Mrs. Sakai, he on the right and she on the left. They rose when he entered. Both were in formal Japanese dress, and soled white stockings. Upon Mrs. Sakai's kimono of heavy purple silk crepe there was a design of wisteria blossoms. Dr. Sakai's robe was dark and he wore a short outer coat. Very formal, indeed! But why?

"Sit down, please," Dr. Sakai said in his perfect English. "Would you perhaps prefer a western chair?"

"I am quite accustomed to Japanese ways," Allen replied.

He returned their bows and then with competence if not with grace he folded his long legs and sank to the floor mats. Where was Josui? He waited. If she had been sent away he would go after her. This formality was doubtless designed to make him understand that he was unacceptable.

To his surprise Dr. Sakai began to speak rather easily and without any anger. "I have been in America for many years, Mr. Kennedy, and I know that Americans appreciate frankness. Let us be frank."

"By all means," Allen murmured.

"After some conversation with my daughter," Dr. Sakai went on, "I have convinced myself that she is certainly in part to blame for this unfortunate situation. It is highly embarrassing to our family, for she is, or was, formally betrothed to the son of my closest and most admired friend. I have been too agitated to rearrange my friendship. At present, compelled by your sudden telegram, I have been able only to consider what to do for my daughter. What are your intentions, Mr. Kennedy?"

Dr. Sakai put this question with hauteur. Allen met it simply and at once. "I wish to marry her before I return to the States, Dr. Sakai. That means today or tomorrow."

"How can this be done?" Dr. Sakai demanded. "You cannot get the necessary permission."

"I know that, sir. But there are many ways of establishing a legal marriage in various countries. I remember that a friend of mine in Formosa, sir, wished to marry a young Japanese girl. He married her according to the Japanese law and only after a whole year was he able to finish the legal marriage in France. Nevertheless, the ceremony was recognized by all as valid. Something like that I had thought of, sir."

His earnestness, his simplicity, above all his courtesy and excellent English confused Dr. Sakai somewhat. He had not seen this sort of American in Japan. Here was a man very different from the gangs of soldiers on the streets, whom he avoided and never recognized by any greeting.

"Nevertheless, it is irregular," he said doubtfully.

"Everything is irregular nowadays," Allen said. "The customs between countries are in great disorder."

He leaned forward to persuade. "Sir, I love your daughter and I want to marry her. I want to take her to my home and present her to my parents. I want them to see her as she is. I am forbidden now to take her with me, and so I shall be compelled to leave her here until I can arrange her coming. I have made up my mind, although I have told no one, not to return to Japan to live. I shall change my assignment and try for something in Washington instead of Tokyo. I want to be free to live my own life with your daughter. I think we shall be able to do that better in my country than here. I hope you and Mrs. Sakai will visit us, I hope we can visit you. But before I leave her, Josui must be my wife, sir. It will be easier for her to rejoin me, if that is an accomplished fact."

What Dr. Sakai would have said cannot be known, for at this moment Josui swept aside a screen. It fell on the floor and she came impetuously into the room and faced her parents.

"Father and Mother, what Allenn has said I will do!"

She stood there, shining in a kimono of silver white, her arms outspread so that she looked like a beautiful bird, a winged creature, her head upflung, her cheeks glowing red, her eyes glowing dark. Allen had never seen such beauty. He rose to his feet, and stood gazing at her in delight.

Now she turned to him, her hands reaching toward him and he went to her and clasped them, held them. This was only for an instant, a bright second of hesitation, and then seeing the utter yielding in her eyes he took her into his arms. Behind them the father and mother sat immobile. Mrs. Sakai looked away but Dr. Sakai continued to stare at them, motionless.

Josui turned in her lover's arms.

"Father, Mother, we are ready."

The parents rose. Dr. Sakai spoke.

"Mr. Kennedy, this was foreseen. We are Buddhists. I have made the necessary arrangements at the Buddhist temple. It is all irregular, you understand. There is no proper precedent. But the Hosshu comprehends the strangeness of these days of foreign occupation. He will conduct our ceremony. For the ceremony in your country we must trust to your honor."

He bent his head and without waiting for Allen's reply he walked to the door. Mrs. Sakai followed him, passing Allen without looking at him.

Josui stood looking after them. Then she turned to Allen and he saw tears in her eyes. "You must not mind them," she said, pleading. "It is so hard for them. You cannot imagine! They have no other child. My husband was to have been their son."

"Can I not be that son?" he asked.

She shook her head. "They are not able to receive you—not yet," she said simply.

She leaned her head against his breast for a moment and felt the beating of his heart against her forehead. Oh, surely she could trust that heart!

"Perhaps they will learn," he said. He clasped her dark head with both hands and pressed it against his breast.

Who can know the beginning of a child's spirit yet unborn? It stirs in the small wind among the wisteria blossoms, distilling fragrance. It glows in the gleam of the first fireflies of spring under the pine trees, in a first kiss in the garden. It gathers form in the drenching pain of separated hearts, it draws near in the final kiss, it waits the sanction of the gods.

In the great temple, under the deep thatch of centuries, the small wedding party stood. Yumi and the gardener were the witnesses. They stood behind their master and mistress, dazed and uncomprehending. The Hosshu faced the lovers, two lower priests on his right and his left. He had not an easy conscience, for he did not approve this marriage. But Dr. Sakai had urged him, reminding him of the strangeness of the times. "It will be necessary for our religion to adapt itself if it is to live," he had insisted. The Hosshu had looked doubtful. He was an old man, a scholar, and a recluse. He had never approved the imitators of Christianity who had invented Buddhist hymns which parodied the Christian ones. Neither did he like the Young Men's Buddhist Association. The gods were not served by such means.

"You cannot imagine how I suffer," Dr. Sakai had said sternly. "My only choice is whether I shall lose my daughter or whether I shall provide some means for making this a marriage."

"You have allowed her too much freedom," the Hosshu had suggested.

"All my past mistakes do not change the present," Dr. Sakai had retorted very sensibly.

A large gift to the temple treasury, his own pledge of loyalty, and his rising impatience combined to make the minister realize that in this one case at least he must change. Therefore he had consented to perform the ceremony which now awaited him. He entered the temple hall with dignity and striking a large gong he waited for the sound to die away in the high roof. Then he turned to the altar and motioned to the couple and to the parents and the witnesses to approach. There he waited, drawn to his height made taller by his priestly robes. The American was not in black garments as he should be, but as Dr. Sakai had said, this was the Occupation and strange things must now be accepted. The woman at least was in a white kimono.

He gave one long look at the young American who stood before him and then he averted his eyes. He did not look at the young woman, he began the ceremony with the exhortation, intoned in his high clear voice, in Japanese.

"Here we are gathered together in the sight of our Compassionate Buddha to bring this couple into a most perfect matrimonial union. The estate of marriage is the most sacred fountain of all life, to which do the successive generations of mankind owe their being, and from which do all the successive codes of morality derive their origin. Nothing happens without cause. Know, therefore, that such a sacred union of two people, which shall last throughout their lives, does not come about through accident. Indeed, it is the preordained consequence of many past lives and the fruit of the benevolent guidance of Buddha."

He dropped his head suddenly and his voice fell to the murmur of prayer. "May this new couple who enter the holy estate of marriage, keeping this blessed circumstance in their hearts, be lastingly true to their vows, love and respect each other, help each other in stress and woe, keep themselves pure both in body and mind, and encourage each other in the promotion of all virtues. These are the essentials to a happy wedded life and the true way of living in accordance with the teaching of the Buddha."

He lifted his head again and looked full upon them, his gaze resting upon Allen.

"Therefore," he said with the voice of command, "before

taking upon yourselves these vows, remember that it is the duty of a husband to support and cherish his wife, to be faithful to her in thought and in deed, to comfort her in sickness and in sorrow, and to assist her in the training of the children."

And to Josui he said, "It is the duty of the wife to love and help her husband, to be patient and gentle in her manner, and to be faithful to him in all things."

"Do you," he continued, speaking to each of them in turn, "do you solemnly declare that neither of you knows any impediment to prevent you being joined lawfully together in marriage?"

Josui looked at him and whispered the words.

"I know of no impediment," Allen repeated in English.

"I do solemnly declare that I know of no impediment," Josui said firmly in Japanese. For had not all impediments been overcome?

The Hosshu turned again to Allen, "Will you, Allen Kennedy, take this woman Josui Sakai as your lawfully wedded wife?"

Josui looked at him again.

"I do," Allen said in English. Now that he spoke the words his voice quivered, though he strove to keep it firm.

"And you," the Hosshu said to Josui, "will you, Josui Sakai, take this man Allen Kennedy as your lawfully wedded husband?"

"I do," Josui said in Japanese.

Allen, prompted before they came to the temple, took from his little finger his signet ring and gave it to the Hosshu, who placed it upon Josui's finger. He joined their hands

146

together and placed upon their united hands his sacred rosary.

"Seeing that you have agreed," he said earnestly, "to marry according to the Buddhist rite, I pronounce you husband and wife. May you always be surrounded with infinite love and compassion."

He stood for an instant, and then turning he led the way to the altar, where Allen, guided by gestures, placed sticks of incense in the ashes of the urn before the gods bending above them, and Josui touched the burning spill to the sweet-smelling incense.

And the Hosshu, standing beneath the great gilt Buddha that towered above the lesser gods, spoke thus: "The blessed Buddha said, 'Support father and mother, cherish wife and child, follow a peaceful calling. This is the greatest blessing.'"

These words he spoke to Allen, and then, the ceremony being completed, he turned and faced the gods, and four priests fell in behind him, making a human screen.

To the Buddha the Hosshu spoke alone now in a voice so low that what he said could not be heard. It was explanation, plea for forgiveness, prayer for blessing if this were possible; if not, then a safe return of the young woman to her own country and her own people.

The Buddha, gilded until the image looked like solid gold, stood immobile as always, the hands in a gesture of eternal and universal blessing, the eyes unmoving and unmoved.

Strange unreality, Allen thought, his head not bowed. He looked at the robed and stooping figures of the Hosshu and the priests, and above them the image. The solid presence made the Buddha no more actual than the unseen deity in a Christian church, and yet no less actual. For the temple air was somehow sacred, not with gods but with the prayers and sorrows of those who came to plead, to beg, to search for what was not to be found. The atmosphere of humanity was here, reaching into the unreachable beyond, asking for the answer never given. Here he stood, too, with Josui, and slowly at last he bent his head. Long ago he had ceased prayer and belief. Yet when he was at home he went to church with his parents, he sang the childhood hymns, and he bowed his head. Today, prayer rose of its own accord out of his personal need. He trembled with its urgency, and in that wordless prayer the son, the world child, came nearer to his life and birth.

In the room where Josui had spent her girlhood Allen lay beside her as her husband. The parents had withdrawn. They had returned after the ceremony at the temple, and in a short speech of welcome Dr. Sakai made it known to Allen that he was now accepted in this house. There would be no further denial. Let him come and go as he would.

Before Allen could thank him he went away. Mrs. Sakai was not seen. Yumi had served dinner to the bride and groom alone in Josui's room, and after the meal, still in utter silence and without a smile, she had spread the silken quilts upon the floor mat to make their bed. Then she bowed deeply to each and drew the screens close and put out the lights in the corridors. So they were alone at last and no one stood between them.

They were not thinking of the child that night. Lovers do not think. They only feel their love, beginning so huge, so vague, pervading every part of the world, and all they see is love and all they feel is love. Then that which is pervading and formless takes form, but it is their own form, the shape of man and woman, the shape of themselves, narrowing and gaining in power and rhythm, in the roar of blood, in the demand of the body alone. The child waiting in the outer air was drawn into being, but they did not know it. The mother was young and a virgin, and it is not every virgin who can conceive so easily as do the mothers of gods. The first visitation is not always enough. Or perhaps the trouble is in the father. Not all fathers are gods. These two did not dream of the child's soul, a nebula moving closer each instant to a fixed point, a shape of permanence.

The parents were unaware of the waiting child, this world child. They were aware only of each other, of trembling hands, and of quivering bodies until they fulfilled the revelation of love.

So far as could be seen, they continued alone in the house. It was a big house and doubtless somewhere in the screened rooms the elders were living apart. But go where they would, Allen saw no one except the silent maid.

"It is rather wonderful of your parents," he told Josui the next day, "but I don't want them to feel they must. You and I could go to an inn."

"Oh, no," she exclaimed. "A strange place? No, since we have no house it is as my parents wish. We must thank them in some way in the future."

Neither of them spoke of children. There must not, of course, be children. He had to go away in a few more hours, she would be left alone.

"Not for long, sweetheart," he told her. "Perhaps only a few weeks."

But weeks are years when there are only a few hours, a day or two, for love. She wept in the night, the second night, the last night, and love waited upon comfort. She was filled with strange foreboding, premonitions that she would never see him again, that he would be lost at sea, or that the plane would crash against a mountain, or that someone at his home would separate them. This, this was their whole life together and there would be no other, she felt it so.

He held her in his arms, she curled against him small and crying upon his bare breast. There was no way to make her believe his promises. She was consumed with fear. The separation of the inevitable tomorrow could continue, she insisted. They were to be cut asunder, never again to be joined. She knew it.

"But how can you, Josui?" he demanded at last in some vexation. "Why should I, of all the other hundreds and thousands crossing the ocean in planes, be chosen to drown, or I be the one to crash against mountains? And how can you suspect my family when you don't know them, or suspect me, for that matter when you do know me?"

He had to be even cruel at last. "Josui, do you think it has been easy for me? If I did not love you, would I be here now?"

There was only one answer to these fears and questions.

They renewed their love again and again, flesh to flesh and heart to heart, while the child waited.

The next day the dreadful parting took place. He would not let her come to the train, nor did she dare trust herself to go. The father and mother appeared for a few minutes, they bowed, the men shook hands, and then the parents went away again, leaving the two alone. He would have sworn that his flesh bled when he tore himself away from her. He felt the pain of raw wounds when he loosed his hands from hers.

"I will write every day," he promised.

"And I, too," she whispered, her face broken and wet with tears.

"We will tell each other everything," he promised. "Think of me, darling, hurrying day and night to get you to America. Now a smile, sweetheart—just for the last minute! Think of last night. Ah, that is my sweet."

He rushed away, turned his head to see her standing half fainting in the doorway, rushed to her again, and gripped her hard once more.

"I mustn't look back," he gasped.

He forced himself to look ahead and caught the train by an inch as it moved out of the station.

*Part II*

M RS. KENNEDY was prepared for her son's home-
coming. The Colonel's wife, whom she had never
met, had written her fully.

"Let me write to his mother," the Colonel's wife had said
to him. "If you write she'll think I've been having an affair
with him and that you want to get rid of him."

So she had written as one old enough herself to be Allen's
mother, she told Mrs. Kennedy, and doing only as she would
like to have been done by, had she been Allen's mother. He
was a brilliant young officer, she declared, her husband's
right-hand man, and one to be saved at any cost. It was difficult to spare him for leave at this moment when so many
new policies were being attempted under the changed high
directives, but her husband was prepared to make sacrifices.

> Your son is so far above the average [she wrote Mrs. Ken-
> nedy] that the usual methods will not do. It is no use just
> talking about week ends or shackups or any of the ordinary
> sort of thing. Your son is a Southern gentleman and he
> thinks even of a Japanese girl with chivalry. Of course he
> believes that she is a superior girl who would not consider
> anything but marriage. But I doubt whether he has proposed
> anything else and of course Japanese are all mad to get to
> the States. They think it is heaven on earth and I suppose
> it is, in comparison.

Mrs. Kennedy was a woman with reserves and she had answered the letter with proper gratitude but with entire confidence in her son's good taste and judgment. It was a noncommittal letter and the Colonel's wife, who had no reserves and was perhaps not even a lady, read it in Tokyo with amazement. She tossed it across the dinner table to the Colonel. "Take a look at that," she commanded. "Does she or does she not want a Japanese daughter-in-law?"

The Colonel read it carefully. "Damned if I know. You'd better drop the whole matter. Kennedy said something about not coming back, anyway. I'm going to replace him."

Mrs. Kennedy showed the letter from the Colonel's wife to her husband and then to Cynthia, secretly, because Mr. Kennedy had told her not to show it to anybody. "This town is as leaky as a sieve," he declared. "For God's sake, Sugar, let's keep our family affairs inside this house. Besides, we haven't heard the boy's side."

Cynthia said very little. She read the letter carefully, and handed it back to Mrs. Kennedy. "Aren't Colonel's wives supposed to be—" she paused.

"What?" Mrs. Kennedy asked.

"Gossipy." Cynthia said at last, trying to find the right word and not quite doing it.

"Perhaps," Mrs. Kennedy agreed. "On the other hand, Allen is a man. He was the sweetest little boy. I used to think he would always be different. But he wasn't. He is just like his father. And he has been cut off from normal society. I wish you would help me, Cynthia."

Cynthia opened her blue eyes very wide. "Why, of course I will, Mrs. Kennedy. I'd do anything for Allen."

Mrs. Kennedy gave her a quick kiss, standing on tiptoe to do so. When the girl was gone she went about the vast and beautiful house, seeing that every touch was perfected. Allen's rooms, a bedroom and sitting room on the second floor, she would have had redecorated, had there been time. But there was not time. She could only see that the linen sheets were aired, that the blankets were fresh, that bowls of small bright chrysanthemums stood on the mantel and the desk. At the last moment she picked a yellow rose and put it in a small silver vase on his chest of drawers. Atmosphere was what she wanted, the family atmosphere, tradition heavy and sweet, love expecting everything of the only son and heir. She knew of old that to cross him, to forbid him, would be to lose. His anger must not be roused. She did not mention the Japanese girl again even to her husband. She would forget. The girl did not exist.

When Allen was there at last she stood in the hall in her silver-gray chiffon tea gown, and held out her arms. He was in them at once, his long young arms were about her, and his face was against her cheek. How he had to stoop, this tall son of hers!

"I do believe you've grown," she said, half laughing, pushing him off ever so little.

"You smell as sweet as ever," he declared. They were never serious with each other, thank God. She made fun of everything, her touch was as light as a hummingbird's wings.

"Oh, your face," she exclaimed rubbing her cheek. "You haven't shaved since you left Japan."

It was true that the delicate skin of her cheek was pink where he had rubbed it. "Give me five minutes," he cried and went bounding up the stairs. His father was just coming down and they met with a mighty embrace. His father had never let him outgrow that expression of love.

"Mother's sending me up to shave," Allen said. "It makes me feel at home."

"I'll not stop you then," his father said mildly.

That was the way it was. When he came home, however long he had been gone, they were just the same. It was as though he had never left. He dashed into his rooms and stood looking at the beloved vista, this, his private sitting room, there his big bedroom with the glorious window toward the west, and beyond the marvelous bathroom. He and Josui could live in their own home within the home. Perhaps his father had been wise just to choose to live here without toil or worry. He had never seen his father unhappy. In a wretched world this place was as near heaven as could be made and there was no reason why he and Josui should not live in it.

"Darling," he wrote to Josui that night. "I am sitting in my own room, the room you will share with me. Let me describe it so that it will be home to you when I lift you over the threshold. Do you know that superstition, I wonder?"

So he described the rooms, the house, how his parents had looked, how the view from the window near his desk rolled over hills and valleys even in the moonlight. There were chrysanthemums on his desk, not the big ones of Japan, but small gay tight little flowers. He had dined alone with his parents except for Cynthia, he told her, Cynthia Levering, his old childhood friend, as nearly a sister as she could be and not bear the family name. She was an only child, too, now, for her brothers had been killed in the war, one in the Pacific and one in Germany. "She will be your good friend," he told Josui. "She is above all else a very kind person. She is only two or three years older than you."

He had been surprised to see how handsome Cynthia had grown. Beauty had come to her late. He remembered her as gawky and pallid, her blonde hair straight, her expression timid and humble with the humility of the young girl too tall for her friends. She was not timid any more and the humility had changed to a sweet modesty. Her hair was shining in short curls, her skin perfected, her mouth soft and not too red. She was slender and graceful, she had learned to live with herself as she was, and she held her head high.

It was pleasant, too, to see that she was glad to see him, really glad and not afraid to show him. He wanted to tell her at once about Josui, but he had not told his parents and it did not seem fair to tell her first. Besides, she made no effort to see him alone and it would have been pointed for him to arrange it.

He finished the long letter to Josui and sat with closed eyes for a while, remembering and imagining her. Oh, it was right to have taken her before he left! She was his now and she would come to him here and no one could separate them. He thought of her stealing about this big house, wearing her little Japanese kimonos if she liked, the darling, for she was such a picture in them. He did not want her to be altogether American. He would keep her what she was, an Oriental treasure, someone who could share that part of his life that he could share with no one else in this house.

He went to the long French doors that opened upon the balcony, and stood looking out into the moonlit night. There were whole years of his life he could not talk about, the war years, when he had been so young and so cruelly separated from life. Scenes were engraved upon his brain, experiences which had shaped him so profoundly that he could never escape from them. He could feel now the miasma of wet jungles, the horrible life of serpents and insects, the constant danger of death not only from the enemy but from disease, and the rottenness of places where the sun never shone. But the memory most fearful was still that of the blade piercing the slight toughness of human skin and then melting into the vital softness beneath. Here where death had never come, still he could not forget.

He wheeled abruptly and went into the bathroom and turned on the hot and cold water together and let the water roar into the huge tub. He would soak himself clean, and he would sleep.

"How do you think he looks?" Mrs. Kennedy inquired of her husband.

"Perfectly well, perfectly happy," he replied.

They were going to bed, she in her own big room, he in his. She stood in the open door between, a lace jacket thrown over her silk nightgown. He was tying the belt of his pajamas around his waist.

"I shan't say one word," Mrs. Kennedy declared. "Let him think I don't know anything."

"Very wise," Mr. Kennedy said. "I have never believed in talk."

He went to the door and kissed her nicely. "Better go to bed," he advised. "You've had an exciting day."

She lingered. "He is very handsome," she mused. "You know, when he was a little boy I didn't think he would be. I'm glad he looks like you."

"Go on," her husband retorted. "He doesn't look like me. I look like my mother and the Lambert side. He looks like my father."

They kissed once more and went to their separate beds, the door open between. Sometime in the night she would wake and steal across the floor and close it. He never knew when she did. But in the morning it was always closed. What that meant he had never inquired. He did not believe in talking if he could help it.

"They know," Cynthia said.

She had met Allen quite by accident the next morning when she was shopping for her mother, who always forgot the essential article necessary for the day's work. Cynthia had from childhood made the extra trip to town to get it. It was not very far. Fifteen minutes of walking down a tree-shaded street brought her to the stores. Even after she had her own car she still walked. It gave her the chance to speak to people. So she had met Allen and they walked together, speaking to everybody as they went. She was still not quite as tall as he was.

Then he had told her about Josui. He had to tell someone. He could not think about her continually, write to her every night, and then tell no one. Sooner or later his parents must be told, but it must be properly done, at the strategic time. His mother, he persuaded himself, would not easily welcome his wife, whoever she might have been. There was no reason to think that Josui would be less welcome than another, once his mother understood that he was already married to her, but there was also no reason to think that she would be more welcome for that.

What he would not acknowledge even to himself was that he wanted Cynthia to know for her own sake. He despised men who imagined that women were in love with them, and yet his sensitive mind told him that had he never seen Josui it might have been easy to think of coming home to Cynthia. Her pleasant and entirely genuine sweetness of manner toward him might mean nothing or anything. He had never cared to discover its depth. It was possible that she was the same to everyone.

He stopped. "They know?" he repeated, unbelieving.

"The Colonel's wife wrote to your mother," Cynthia said in her calm sweet voice with its slight Southern drawl. She had struggled to overcome the drawl but it was born in her.

"The Colonel himself doesn't know," Allen exclaimed.

"Don't stand here, Allen," Cynthia said. "People are beginning to stare."

He moved abruptly forward and she tried to catch his step. She laughed. "Don't let's run, either! What doesn't the Colonel know?"

He slowed his pace. "I married Josui. Nobody knows that except you. I want you to know because I need your help. I went straight off to Kyoto and married her, so that we couldn't be parted. I knew why I was given leave—it was so that I would forget Josui. The Colonel and his wife thought

162

that if I got home to all this—" his long gaze swept the tree-shaded street, the shops, the big white houses set back from the sidewalks. "They thought I'd forget. So that damned woman wrote to my mother!"

He frowned, and Cynthia looked at him sidelong with a rage which made her ashamed. What right had he to go off to a foreign country and find a foreign wife? What of women like her, growing old in little towns and villages all over America? Foreign women ought to marry their own men. Allen belonged to her. If he had not been sent away by force—for what was the draft except force—they would have been married by now, it was inevitable, and she would have lived one day in the Kennedy house where she had almost belonged ever since she had been born. Had he not been so handsome, had his head not towered above hers— she could never marry a man smaller than herself, and nearly all men were smaller—she might not have made the decision she now made as suddenly and as instinctively as though she were not a civilized woman living in a civilized country. She would ally herself with Allen's mother and not with him. She would do her best to keep the Japanese girl from coming here. . . .

He was talking fast in a low monotone. "I am sending for her as soon as I can get her over. Lucky she is an American citizen! She was born here. In fact, Cynthia, she didn't go to Japan until she was fifteen years old. She even went to school here. Her English is perfect—well, almost. She calls me Allenn Ken-neddy, unless she stops and thinks."

"I thought it was rather difficult to marry a Japanese girl," Cynthia said. Under her brimmed hat of cream-colored felt she was smiling steadily, gazing up the street, waving now and again to someone she knew.

They were stopped every few minutes by someone they both knew and before Allen could answer now they were stopped again.

"Allen Kennedy, isn't it?"

A bevy of pretty girls on their way to a Friday morning bridge club surrounded them. "I reckon we won't see you at the club this morning, Cynthia!"

"I reckon we can't blame you!"

Their high sweet voices rang in the cool autumn air, their new autumn garments, the bright little jackets, the flying skirts, the tight gay little hats, the shining hair and bright shallow eyes and fluttering pretty little hands surrounded Allen and Cynthia with a warmth that was innocent and yet shrewdly female. Young female eyes examined Allen and red lips parted. Upon each pretty painted face appeared the searching stare of the young female who stalks alone, ready at any moment to desert her kind when the desirable male appears. It was every woman for herself, but Cynthia was the fortunate one, with whom he walked. The impulse of revenge clung to Cynthia's usually gentle heart. She smiled at them all and said in her lovely voice, "Allen was telling me some wonderful news. He married a beautiful Japanese girl, just before he came home."

It was pitiful to see the changed looks and the striving against the change, the instant effort at control, the bright artificial looks of happiness, the false congratulations. "Oh, Allen, how wonderful!"

"Tell us about her."

"Do you have her picture?"

He cast upon Cynthia a look of outrage. "Well, I hadn't meant to announce it in just this way," he managed to say.

He did have a small picture that Josui had given him before they parted, a snapshot of herself in her school dress. It was not a good picture. Her look was grave, the dress unbecoming, her hair plain. But they snatched it and passed it from one to the other, and seeing that solemn young face they cried out in relief and triumphant pity. "She's real sweet, Allen."

They gave the picture to Cynthia with nods and smiles and went away and she walked along studying Josui's face. The eyes were strange.

"It is a poor likeness," Allen said. "She is really beautiful, and she looks especially so in her own Japanese dress."

"She wouldn't be able to wear Japanese clothes here, would she?" Cynthia suggested. "It would make her very conspicuous, wouldn't it?"

"I suppose so," Allen said. He took the picture from her and put it back into his wallet.

They walked along for a few minutes. "You didn't tell me how you were married," Cynthia said.

"We were married in a Buddhist temple," he said abruptly. "Buddhism is their family religion. "

"How interesting," she said. "Tell me, is it like our Episcopal service?"

"No, well, yes. I suppose the essentials are the same in any religion. There was a minister and his priests, and the gods."

"Gods?"

"Images, like the Catholics have. They don't really worship the images, of course. Images only serve to fix the mind upon some great saint or upon God."

"And did you promise to cherish—and all that?"

"I made all the promises," he said firmly.

Why, he wondered, did she press him so closely, and was she entirely his friend? "What on earth made you tell all those women?" he demanded. "It will go all over town."

"That is why I did it," she said with more than her usual calm. "The sooner everybody knows it the better. Good-by, Allen, this is where I have to stop. It's a hat shop and I don't believe you'll want to come in."

So she was not his friend!

Josui had his first letter. She was at college again, nobody knowing. Her father would not allow an announcement of her marriage, he said, until the legal papers arrived from America. The letter came while she was away. Her mother received it, recognized it, and gave it to her father. Dr. Sakai put it in the top drawer of his desk. He did not give it to Josui for two days. While he came and went to the hospital and busied himself with his patients he thought about the letter and did not touch it. He was visiting Mr. Matsui every day just now, for his old friend had an inflammation of the gall bladder which had flared because of autumn crabs. Mr. Matsui was very abstemious but each autumn he felt he must eat a few crabs with wine. It was one food which he liked exceedingly. Sometimes the crabs made him ill and sometimes they did not, depending upon what they had themselves eaten. This autumn they had been malevolent. He had been extremely ill, and for several days Dr. Sakai had been anxious and Kobori had stayed near him. He was better at last, and although Kobori had not yet left the house, he was working in his study and was no longer constantly beside his father's bed.

Mr. Matsui was grateful indeed that he had not died, and he was ashamed enough of his annual indulgence to declare to Dr. Sakai that this year was a lesson to him and he would never eat crabs again. At last he was so much better that he begged Dr. Sakai today to come in after his hospital hours were over and spend a little time in friendly talk. This Dr. Sakai did. He was tired, but he felt he could never atone for his daughter's behavior to the Matsui family and could never show gratitude enough for their magnanimity. When he had tried to say this, Mr. Matsui had merely smiled and waved his right hand. "Such things are not important," he had declared. He had never allowed the slightest sign of anger or revenge to appear in his manner or behavior. Perhaps the matter was not really important. Nevertheless, Dr. Sakai was too proud to forget.

This day, late in the afternoon, sitting beside his friend's bedside, he felt the impulse to confide. The house was still, the doors closed and because of the rising autumn chill, a brass brazier of charcoal stood on three legs in the middle of the floor, glowing and sending out a shimmer of heat. A slight current of air passed through the room from a narrowly opened window to purify the fumes.

Mr. Matsui lay on his mattress, his head and shoulders covered with a gray silk short coat, crossed on his chest and tied under his arms. He looked almost himself. The yellow-ness of his skin was gone, and his face, which had been agonized with pain, was at peace again.

"I owe my life to you," he said.

"I did only my duty," Dr. Sakai replied.

"Something more," Mr. Matsui insisted. "All debts are now paid."

Dr. Sakai understood and warmth gathered about his heart. He leaned forward to speak in a low tone. "I have to ask your advice. A letter has come for my daughter. It lies in my desk. If I do not give it to her, would it be a fault? It is for her own happiness that I still hope to separate her from the American. For her own sake, you understand. I am sure she will be unhappy in America, as I myself was."

Mr. Matsui considered, merely as a friend. He did not now wish to have this young woman in his family, for he understood that the marriage had been consummated, and only a virgin would be suitable for his son.

"I think you must give her the letter," he said. "After all, she is your daughter. I agree with you, but in a family the correct relationships must be maintained."

Dr. Sakai bowed slightly.

Mr. Matsui changed the subject at once. "I am thinking of enlarging the entrance room to the ceremonial teahouse."

In the evening when Josui came to bid her parents good night Dr. Sakai opened the drawer of his desk.

"This came for you," he said. "It was while you were away."

He did not say what day the letter had come, and she did not stay to ask. She bowed deeply to her father and then to her mother and hastened away to her own room. Oh, the letter! At first she could not open it. She held it to her cheeks, to her breast, and then to her lips. Then she examined it closely. Her name was written so clearly, Mrs. Allen Kennedy, and under it Josui Sakai, just in case, and the street address, Kyoto, Japan, and the bright stamps. It had come by air mail and at what cost! But he wanted her to have it quickly and so she must read it carefully, but not until she was washed and clean. So the letter lay on her little low chest of drawers while she made ready for sleep, and when she was clothed in her soft silk blue and white sleeping garments, and her hair was brushed and braided, but no cream rubbed into her skin for fear of soiling the letter, she took her scissors and cut the envelope carefully without touching the stamps, and then drew out the sheets of paper within.

She read it carefully word by word, each word so indispensable and so precious, trying as she read to see exactly what he saw, and seeing it after her fashion, built up out of her memories of Los Angeles. But in Virginia everything was better than anything she remembered, and she must stretch her imagination to see the rolling hills and the gardens and the palace which was his home, and most tenderly to be dwelt upon were his own rooms, where she would one day be with him. He told her of everything, a great bed hung with a satin coverlet of golden brown, the same golden tints in the curtains and the rugs, and with it were touches of crimson, and pale yellow, but still it was a very plain room, he said, but how could it be plain? A fireplace was in the sitting room. He had two whole rooms for himself—and for her—and they were so big, as big as the garden here, very nearly, and the big window, and books against the walls by the fireplace, and deep chairs, each being wide enough, he said, to hold them both. She read again again and again the pages about the rooms, for there was her house and she must grow familiar with them so that when she entered she would know she was at home. His parents were well. He had not yet told them. But she was not to be frightened for they were kinder than ever to him. They would welcome her first for his sake and then for her own. She must bring many pretty kimonos, not to wear on the street, of course, but here in the house.

She put out the lamp at last, she curled under the quilts and with the letter clasped to her breast she cried quietly for a long time, because she was so far away, so alone, and so happy.

He had to tell his parents—now, immediately. When he thought of his parents he meant his mother. That mild man who was his father could be brought to any reasonableness. He loitered when he left Cynthia. The question was, should he tell his father first and hope for his help or should he go to his mother and tell her abruptly, straightly, taking it for granted that what he had done would be approved? He weighed the relationship between the man and the woman who were his parents. He knew intuitively what this relationship was. All his life in lesser matters he had weighed the very question he asked himself today. When he was a child and something of a coward, or because he had always longed so intensely for what he wanted that he had felt denial was unbearable, he had sometimes gone to his father and together they had approached the mother. In his adolescence he had perceived, again only by intuition and experience, that his father was no help to him. His mother would be hostile if the approach was made through his father. It was better—as for example, when he wanted a convertible car so badly when he was at the university in Charlottesville—to go straight to his mother. It was his father who had been doubtful and the doubt had made his mother firm.

"I think Allen ought to have it," she had declared. "He needs independence."

He drew a deep sighing breath. Well, he had the same need now. He would go straight to her, immediately, because telephones would begin to ring soon and she would be distant with him because he had not told her.

He ran up the white marble steps, into the big pillared porch, and thence into the house, shouting for her. "Mother, where are you?" She liked to hear him calling her.

"Here!" her distant voice answered. "Here in the conservatory."

The house had an old-fashioned octagonal conservatory, built on the back of the left wing by his grandfather, and opening into the present dining room, which in that day had been part of the old ballroom, later built into the library and the lengthening of the downstairs parlors. His father called the ballroom out of style and pretentious.

She was digging at some huge tubs of high ferns, her hands gloved, her brass trowel shining bright. The morning sun shone down upon the ferns and potted chrysanthemums.

"What chrysanthemums!" he exclaimed. "They're almost as big as the ones in Japan."

She showed no interest in Japan.

"I was thinking we ought to give a dance," she said. "Everybody wants to see you. The telephone has been ringing every minute."

He plunged in at that. "I'd better tell you something before the damned telephone does. Cynthia says you already know. But you don't know everything, I reckon. She says the Colonel's wife felt she had to write you."

His mother went on digging carefully among mossy roots. "You mean about that Japanese girl?"

"Yes."

"Oh, I don't take that seriously," she said in her lightest voice. "I know how it was. You were way off there, and I dare say there weren't any nice American girls. But you're home now—"

"Wait, Mother."

She looked up and saw his face white, his mouth drawn and dry.

"Why, what's the matter, Allen?"

"You're all wrong about Josui. That's her name. She's my wife."

"Allen Kennedy!" So she had cried at him from the time he was a baby, whenever he had been naughty, when he had bitten her breast, when he had thrown down his toys, when he had muddied his first little suits, had played hooky at school, had taken a dollar bill from her purse, had smoked his first cigarette, had come home from a dance drunk.

"We are married, Mother," he said. "I want to bring her home right away."

She put down the trowel, she took off the gloves. "Come into the library," she said, "let's talk about this."

"There isn't much to talk about, Mother. It's done." But he followed her and they sat down on either side of the fireplace in which there was no fire.

"Just tell me," she insisted. She sat there, her hands clasped, her voice so carefully light, a slight smile upon her face, but her eyes—he saw her eyes were sick.

So he told her, enraged with himself and with her that he, a man, was haunted by the ghosts of old guilt, the childish sins for which she had scolded him here so often in this very room. He had always to apologize, to tell her that he was sorry and that he would never do it again, and that he loved her. The process had been unchanging, her anger, her hurt, and then her forgiveness and the need to have him tell her he would be good because he loved her.

He would not follow those steps now, he insisted to himself. He would simply tell her. If she did not want him in the house, she could say so. The world was wide, and he had traveled far.

But she did not behave as usual. He had to confess when it was all told, all except the deep sacredly private hours of the two nights he had spent with Josui, that his mother was being very generous. She listened, she was not angry, though he could see that she was dangerously shaken. That she struggled so plainly against herself made him unwillingly gentle. He would have preferred her anger, so that he could have been strengthened by his own.

"You will soon love Josui," he said, and hated the sound of his almost pleading voice. "She isn't really like a Japanese girl, Mother. She speaks beautiful English, she knows our ways."

"Did you say her blood is entirely Japanese?" she asked.

"Yes, but she was born in California. Did I tell you that?"

He had told her, but he wanted to tell her again.

"Then she looks Japanese?" his mother said.

"They aren't dark, Mother. I mean they are nothing like the colored people here."

"They certainly are not white," she said a little sharply. He could not answer this. There was silence between them for a moment. Then she said, still with the touch of sharpness. "It seems so strange that we were fighting the Japanese, they were our enemies. It was no time ago, and now you are asking me to receive a Japanese girl here."

"Mother, I can see how you feel about that. I did, too, I confess. Before I really knew Josui, I used to think about that and wonder why I didn't connect her with—the others. The answer is that I don't connect her with anybody I have ever known. She is simply herself, the woman I love, whom I have made my wife. It happens that her ancestors came from some islands in the East instead of the West. She might have been born in England, for example."

"Our ancestors came from England," his mother said.

"Just a handful of islands," he repeated. Then he thought of something and smiled wryly. "Her father felt just as you do, Mother. He didn't want me for a son-in-law because I am white."

This did not interest her. She could not imagine Dr. Sakai.

174

He continued to look down thoughtfully upon the crimson carpet.

"Mrs. Sakai was very decent," he went on. "She is really a Japanese—one of those picture brides—"

His mother lifted her head suddenly. "A picture bride?"

He wished that he had not spoken the words. "Oh, it was long ago. Our immigration laws forbade the entrance of Asians and the men had to choose their wives from pictures of women in Japan and be married by proxy or something like that."

"She can't have been of a very good family even in Japan," she said coldly. But still she was not interested.

He leaned forward, his elbows on his knees, and tried to smile, searching her face for a gleam of light.

"Well, Mother?"

She met his eyes again. "If, as you say, it's done—"

"It is done," he said firmly.

"The only thing is—"

"What, Mother?"

She would not go on. "No, nothing. A foolish idea of mine."

"But, Mother—"

She cried out passionately at this moment. "No, Allen, let me alone for a while. I shall have to tell your father. It will be a blow to him. We had thought of your marrying somebody here—Cynthia, we hoped—and we had dreamed of seeing our grandchildren running around the house. It's such a big house. I never had as many children as I wanted. I couldn't, you know."

"There may be children, Mother." He spoke for her comfort and then he saw the frightful mistake. For now she really could not control herself.

"Oh, no, Allen!" She cried out the words and sprang to her feet.

"Mother!" He shouted in alarm and sprang to catch her. She fell into his arms weeping, and nothing he could do would stay her terrible sobs. He had never seen her weep, she had not used tears upon him, and he knew that these tears were not for her own defense. He held her hand, muttering over and over again, "Mother—don't! You'll see—"

But she tore herself away from him and hurried from the room.

Mr. Kennedy, coming home from a leisurely walk through the town, was aware of disturbance in the air of his home. The morning walk was a habit established after his father died, leaving him the sole heir to a fortune accumulated as a cotton broker in Nashville, Tennessee, and a horse breeder in Kentucky. Each morning soon after a late breakfast Mr. Kennedy visited certain friends, never the same ones on consecutive days, and by little talk and much listening he was the best-informed man in the county. Several times a year he made trips to different parts of the country to find out what people were saying and thinking. His general wisdom would have fitted him to run for Congress, even for the Senate, but he had no wish to use his information or to impart it. Had he been reared in a different family he would have been a professor in philosophy, or had he possessed a turn for words he might have been a poet. As it was, he was an amiable man with a well of wisdom which was seldom fathomed but which he enjoyed in his profound inner habitude.

So sensitive was his receptive nature that he had only to enter his front door on this pleasant day, near the hour of noon, to know that something was wrong. He walked softly to the coat closet, hung up his gray cloth topcoat and his hat and dropped his walking stick into the large blue porcelain Chinese vase which stood in one corner of the hall. Almost immediately he heard his son's footsteps upstairs and then coming down.

"I'm glad you're home," Allen said, rounding the last curve of the sweeping stairway. "I didn't know where to look for you. I'm afraid I've upset Mother dreadfully. She's locked her door."

The locked door was a signal. They looked at each other. "I don't know how to tell you," Allen said.

"I rather think I can guess," Mr. Kennedy replied.

He led the way into the empty living room and sat down. "I knew it was coming sometime or other," he went on. "We've known for quite some time that you had a private interest in Japan. Colonel—"

Allen broke in, feverish with impatience. "Father, what upset Mother is that I am married to Josui Sakai." He perched on the arm of a big velvet chair, unconsciously disobeying one of the earliest rules of his childhood.

Mr. Kennedy's large pale face with hanging jowls flushed a delicate pink. He had a fine smooth complexion, and a light sandy beard which he kept closely shaved except for a tiny goatee under his hanging lower lip. The lids of his pale-gray eyes were waxen and half closed. He did not lift them unless he was disturbed. He lifted them now.

"Son," he remonstrated, "you might have told us."

"I didn't expect to marry immediately," Allen said. "It suddenly seemed the right thing to do. I still think it was. Her family is a good one. Besides, I am not the sort who could have done anything else. At least I don't think so. Maybe it was just that I saw too much of the other sort of thing and it turned my stomach."

Mr. Kennedy did not reply to this. The relationship between him and his son was close and completely literal. Sentiment had no part in it.

"What sort is the girl?" he inquired. His large pale hands were stretched out on the arms of the chair and they looked peculiarly helpless, as though they had never been used very much, as indeed they had not.

"Mother would like Josui, if she would only let herself think it possible," Allen said, argumentatively. "The truth is, Father, I'm lucky. We fell in love at first sight. She might have been simply a beautiful girl. Instead she is much more."

"How long have you known her?" Mr. Kennedy asked.

"Not long, but enough to know that there is a great deal more to know."

He got up and moved about the room, not looking at his father, talking as he went. "I can't tell you why or how it happened. I worked terribly hard this year, especially after the change in command. Then one day some of the fellows said they were going to take a few days off to see Kyoto and Nara, and I thought to myself that I hadn't had a day off in months and so I went along. I happened to see her going into the gate of a college. I reckon we just—looked at each other at the psychological moment. Heaven knows! I might have passed by without a second thought. But I didn't. I went back again the next day at the same time and so we met. It isn't just that she's beautiful, I tell you. Perhaps it's that she has that touch of the unusual that made me aware. She's not like any other woman I have ever known. Perhaps it's because she is Oriental—how do I know? I've been over there for three years and maybe it has crept into my blood. I've heard men say it does. I've heard them say they can't marry American girls when that happens."

Mr. Kennedy sat looking helpless, his large pale mouth gaping a little, but he was not helpless. He was listening and thinking. He knew perfectly well what his Josephine, his little Empress, could make out of all this. He understood what his son was talking about. Hadn't Southern men always known? And their wives let them go so far but no further. The tides of the sea were not more regulated than the inner dominion of white women in the South.

"Your mother is never going to like it," he said in a pallid voice. "She wouldn't have minded the other thing. I reckon our women are used to that. But having a young woman—who isn't white, mind you—coming in here as her daughter-in-law is quite something, and I don't know that she can take it. I'd better go upstairs."

He hoisted himself up on his large flat hands and trod heavily across the floor to the stairs, and mounted them slowly, planting his feet solidly on each step. When he reached his wife's bedroom door he rattled the handle gently.

"Open the door, Sugar!" he called.

He waited and after some moments he heard her move across the floor. Then the door opened and he went in and took her in his arms with a patient familiarity. Her head went to his shoulder and he patted her hair.

"Did he tell you?" she said against his coat.

"Yes, Sugar."

"What shall we do?"

"I always say, Sugar, that the best thing is to do nothing at all. Just let things take their course."

"But he'll bring her here!"

"We'll have to let her come."

"I won't!"

"Well, if you won't, that's something, too. I reckon then he'll leave the house and they'll set up somewhere else."

She pushed him away and he sighed and stood waiting while she walked about the room, rubbing her temples with a cologne-drenched handkerchief.

"I have a splitting headache."

"I was afraid you would have."

He sat down carefully in a low rose taffeta chair. He was too large for it and he felt uncomfortable but he knew it to be the only chair he could sit upon in this room.

He waited while she dabbed her temples, loving her, knowing that in spite of her pettishness, her possessiveness, her domineering ways, she was a good woman, a good wife, and that the strength of the nation was in her. If everybody were like him there would be no order and maybe no decency. The house would be a shambles and everybody in town would be taking advantage. He wished that she could have been a little more passionately in love with him, but a man couldn't have a good wife and a mistress at the same time. If he had been more energetic he might have fallen into the temptations of other men, but it was too much trouble. He loved peace, and in his home he found it after his fashion.

"Sugar," he began gently. "You're too big a woman to take it like this. I know how you feel. I feel something like that, too. I kind of wanted Cynthia to be the mother of our grandchildren. But our boy wants something different and he's done it. We can't take it back. We have to accept it. Let's see what we can do to make it a success."

She was twisting the handkerchief, knotting it and then untying it, her flushed face, still so pretty under the slightly graying curls, bent upon the nervous task. "How can it be a success?" she demanded. "Marriage is something more than just two people, Tom. It's building a family. And they mustn't have children. They just mustn't!"

He did not reply. He knew what she meant. The picture of little half-Japanese children running around this house was unnerving indeed. "Maybe they won't have children," he said, somewhat feebly.

"You know they will," she retorted. "Haven't you read about the birth rate over there? All those Oriental women breed like rabbits. No, it's got to be prevented."

He was too delicate minded with women to ask just what she meant and so he said nothing. He sat looking large and tired, his face the color of his sandy gray goatee and eyebrows and hair.

"Allen has to be brought to his senses," she said. "He must see for himself that it simply won't do."

"But if he's married?" he suggested.

"He can be divorced."

He saw a lightening look in her face, a brightening hope, an idea. She dropped the handkerchief.

"Tom, maybe they aren't really married!"

"He says they are, Sugar."

"But maybe they're not. What is Buddhism, anyway? That's no real religion. And certainly a temple isn't a church —it's full of idols. Those Japanese probably took advantage of him."

He felt sorry for her now. "That won't mean anything to Allen. He wants to believe he's married to her."

"Not yet—but wait. When he sees that it simply won't do—oh, Tom, you can't think of a slant-eyed woman walking around here in our house or even in the town! Who'll invite her to parties? It will be the end of our whole life."

She was capable of anything, whether evil or good. "Sugar, I still think with a woman as big as you are here in this town, you could carry it off. You make the best of it and people will think the better of you."

She shook her head, bit her trembling lips, and put her hands to her hair to hide her face. "I can't, Tom. I shall just pretend it isn't so—and then try to get Allen to see it as I do."

He got up. "Well, I've given my advice for what it's worth. I'll give a little more. Take care you know your own son, Sugar."

He ambled away then, feeling that the most desperate need of his life was a stiff drink of Scotch.

After he had mixed the drink he sat sipping it slowly on the front porch, reflecting upon the problems which encir-

cled any person who allowed desires, standards, public opinion, station in life, and all the common cries of humanity
to become of any personal significance whatsoever. If the
little Japanese creature came into the house here, he would
simply go on as he was. There was nothing she could do
that would upset him. If he could not have both his wife
and his son happy, he would at least be happy himself, and
his happiness was well founded in the spiritual meaning of
pleasant food, a regulated liver, the most comfortable bed
in the nation, and the ability to sleep all night. He was aware
that he had missed some stimulating human emotions, but
he did not wish now to be stimulated.

Meanwhile he was grateful that the bad news was broken
and that his wife had faced it, although with what consequences yet he was not sure. If he knew her she would not
talk about it any more. Her plans would be laid and she
would proceed to carry them out and sooner or later he
would know about them, though probably not until it was
too late for him to do anything. She was too well bred to
allow an atmosphere of hostility in the house, and when she
came down to dinner tonight she would be her usual self.
Allen had a good deal of his mother in him, and he too
would probably behave as usual. The mere passage of time
was healing as well as revealing and maybe by living with
a fact for a while they would end up by living with it for
the rest of their lives. They might get used even to slant eyes.

When Allen came out of the house he found his father
half-asleep, his empty glass on the floor. At the sound of
footsteps Mr. Kennedy woke up and saw his son with a suit-

case in his hand, his topcoat on his arm, and a hat on his head.

"I'm off for a few days," Allen told his father.

Mr. Kennedy barely opened his slumberous eyes. "Where to?"

"Washington."

"What you want to go to that hellhole for?"

"I might ask for a job. And I want to see what is entailed in getting Josui over right away."

"Did you tell your mother?"

"No. Say good-by for me, will you? I'll only be gone a few days, likely. If I get the job, I'll have to come back and get my things."

"All right, son."

His eyelids drooped, but Allen paused. "How is Mother now?"

"She'll be better," his father answered drowsily. Whisky always made him sleepy.

He watched his son climb into the car they had kept for him carefully during the years he was away and then he went soundly to sleep.

Mrs. Kennedy had never believed in inevitables. Not believing she never accepted them. She had no confidante among her many friends, although each one thought herself close enough to know everything that Josephine thought and did. Certainly she never told her husband anything except what she wanted him to know and he was glad that she did not. To know the whole mind and heart of this willful woman would have horrified him. She suspected that he was pleased to know as little as possible, and that his sympathy, in so far as he would allow himself to be disturbed by it, might be for the innocent Japanese girl, who was expecting to come to his house. He would conceal this sympathy as a piece of contrariness on his part, since he could not do anything about it, but he would side secretly with Allen. Men were shaped more by rebellion than by love. Mrs. Kennedy sometimes thought maybe rebellion was the stronger. Well, she could rebel, too.

The life in the house went on much as usual while Allen was away and Mr. Kennedy grew used to hearing his wife's pleasant voice answering the telephone. "Oh, my dear, we don't take it seriously! You know how we mothers have to expect incidents from our boys—it can't be helped, do you think, and it is the unfortunate part of a war. No, he isn't really married! I think they went through some sort of engagement ceremony in a Buddhist temple, though whether even that would really hold over here, I very much doubt. At any rate, we just aren't talking about it now."

The beautiful days stretched one into another. Roses in the garden began to bloom again, the late roses never quite so large or so gay as those of spring, and yet more fragrant. Allen sent postcards now and then, each declaring that he would soon be home for his trunks and then he did not come. There were delays he did not understand. Washington was a maze in which he felt lost. So far he had only a promise which might not mean anything.

Mrs. Kennedy read the cards aloud to her husband at mealtimes with a look of detachment on her face. She had sent air-mail letters to the Colonel's wife in Tokyo, grateful for warnings and asking for more help.

"Is it possible," she urged, "for Allen to be sent to Europe? That would be the most wonderful solution. If he could be sent away at once, before he has time to bring the girl here, it would spare us all."

Therefore in Washington, going from office to office, Allen found a curious and baffling delay. It was quite easy not to return to Japan. That was arranged almost at once. The next unexpected proposal was that he go to Europe and there do exactly what he had been doing in Japan. It was recognized that he had unusual ability in making analyses of political situations in foreign nations and there were aspects of some of the nations surrounding Germany which needed such analysis.

The stout and astute but somewhat illiterate officer who urged him put it to him thus: "You can write plainly and that is more than most college graduates can do. When I read your stuff I know what you are saying."

"Thank you," Allen said, resolving that somehow he would never go to Europe, at least not until Josui had come and could go with him. Europe was another world. He had already lived in too many.

He went home in a state of compromise. It was understood that he was to be given time to think things over, and therefore that he would have unofficial leave for as much time as he needed. If he did not want to go to Europe—well, there had seemed to be nothing for him right now in Washington. He digested this news with incredulity and suspicion. It looked as though someone were working against him, but he did not believe it was his old Colonel who was certainly eager to have him return to Japan. He could not imagine anyone else who could reach as far as Washington. Anyway, he told himself as he drove through the rich red fields of Virginia, he would send for Josui at once. That much he could do, for he had arranged that while he was in Washington. There was no barrier possible, because she had been born in this country. Fragments of forgotten Scripture heard unwillingly as a restless boy in church compelled to listen to the rector's voice, drifted across his mind. St. Paul, the outcast, standing before an official of Rome, so declared himself. "With great price," the haughty Roman official said, "did I buy my freedom."

"But I," said St. Paul, lifting his proud head, "I was born free."

Josui, too, was born free, even as he, Allen Kennedy, was free. She was an American, before the law. He would hold fast to that unchangeable fact.

When he got home one night it was still early and his parents were playing chess in the living room. They were good chess players but his mother was slightly the better of the two because she wanted to win and his father did not care enough.

"Hello, champions," he said as he came in.

They looked up startled, pleased, his mother reserved, he thought. But she did not allow what she felt to mar the warmth of her welcome. She rose impulsively, kissed his cheek, and clung with both hands to his arm. "Oh, I am glad you're back. I hope you couldn't get a job, darling— not just yet! The house feels so empty without you."

"Well, I couldn't. Rather, I didn't want what they offered me. Europe, if you please! Why should I go to Europe and waste all I have learned in Asia? Who's winning? You, I'll bet!"

"Sit down," his father said. "Tell me what to do. The queen has me cornered, as usual."

"Oh, hush," his mother cried. "Allen's hungry. Have you your dinner, son?"

"Not a bite." He felt suddenly gay. They weren't going to be hard on him, these two. His mother in her own oblique way was trying to let him know that they weren't. She would never say she was sorry, she could not, but this was her way. He relaxed and felt suddenly very tired. Everything in the world was complex, involved, pulling a hundred ways at once, but here at least life went on as it always had. Little Josui could slip into the open door and life would not be disturbed. His parents had the power as long as they lived of keeping the peace, and when they were gone he would take their place. By the strength of his will and his determination he would keep this one house as it was and always had been, world without end, amen.

Josui read the letter as she always did, first quickly, dwelling upon every word of love. This was most important. Then she read it over very carefully, that she might understand every direction and description and bit of news. Thereafter she read it several times a day so that she might feel close to him, their minds in communication, their hearts in touch. Through the letters she had come to know him. Strange how the nearness of flesh could be a barrier to understanding!

When she was in his arms, even when she simply saw him coming toward her, the mind stopped and thought fled. But with the sea between them, it was through the mind that they could live in the presence of each other, and so thought flowed freely, and understanding throve.

She had in these weeks of separation begun to see him as he was. He was not as strong as she had first thought. He too was somewhat dependent upon his parents. This surprised her for she had imagined that young men and women in America were totally free of their families and that they did as they pleased. Obedience was not required or given. Now she saw that while this was so, nevertheless there were demands, and in his house it was the mother who demanded, instead of the father as here. She pondered this a good deal. It was not Allen's father but his mother whom she must please. Well, this could be understood, for even in Japan the mother-in-law could make a young wife happy or sad. Allen had sent her small photographs of the house and of his parents. She studied the faces of the two elders often and long. She used her magnifying glass, brought home from her biology class, and examined their features and the expressions upon their faces. She belonged to an old race and she had inherited a certain human wisdom, and by this long secret meditation she came to know surprisingly well Allen's parents. Once she had been uneasy about a girl named Cynthia. Cynthia knew of their marriage first, but Cynthia, he hoped, would be her friend. He sent no picture of her and now did not mention her.

His letters were all about her coming and this letter today at last gave her the definite command to come and above all it contained her airplane ticket. This was treasure. She examined every part of it, reading every word. It was so simple and yet so valuable, her permission to enter heaven. His directions were clear. Nothing would be hard. She had her passport, she must get her visa, she would get the plane in Tokyo, and he would meet her in San Francisco with his car and they would have their honeymoon while driving across the country alone together.

When she had read the letter several times she went to find her mother, and together they would tell her father when he came home tonight. She found her mother feeding the fan-tailed goldfish in the small pool and stirring the water slowly and gently with a bamboo stick to rouse the fish. They were sluggish with cold but it was too early for them to hide under mud.

The sight of her mother's slight crouching figure in the silvery blue kimono, in the misty sunshine of the morning in the garden, smote upon Josui's sight like a suddenly presented picture. She would miss this little mother! Somehow she had not thought of it in her longing anxiety to be with Allen. Her mother was so silent, so retiring, so often unnoticed, and yet when she thought of being far from her, she was aware of a reluctance that was almost pain. She knelt beside her mother on the dying grass and for a moment did not take the letter from her bosom.

The fish were slipping out now from under the rocks, waving their wide cobwebby tails and fins, not caring whether they ate.

"They want to sleep," Josui said.

"They know winter will come," her mother replied.

Her mother did not look at her for a moment, absorbed in her task. Then as though she knew Josui had come with a purpose she looked up half startled. "Is there something?"

"Yes," Josui said. She drew out the letter. "He wants me to come. He sends the ticket." She drew out the ticket, and her mother took it and turned it over and over, unable to read it.

She gave the letter, the envelope, and the ticket back to Josui.

"What will my father say?" Josui asked. "He has never wholly believed that Allen would send for me."

"He will believe it now." Her mother rose to her feet and fastened the lid tightly on the small jar of fish food.

They stood looking down into the water. The fish became suddenly sprightly as they tasted food. They had forgotten but they remembered again that they liked food. There was still time to eat before they slept.

"It will be a long time before I see you again," her mother said. "Perhaps I shall never see you again. Your father will never go to America. He has told me so."

"I will come to see you," Josui promised. She curled her hand into her mother's hand as she used to do when she was small.

"If there is a child—" her mother began, and stopped.

This child! What would he be? It was inevitable that he be born. But did they wish him to be born? Each woman asked herself the question. When there is love, must there not be a child? Mrs. Sakai knew that there was a sort of love which she herself had never experienced but whose magic she had seen in Josui. Through Josui she had felt its power, a changing energy which had made her daughter into a woman ready to leave her parents. She herself had not felt it and yet when her parents sent her to America to marry a man she had never seen, she had gone without question. It was her destiny. Josui was more fortunate than she had been, for she would be going to a man she knew. Yet could a Japanese woman really know an American man? This remained to be discovered. After all, Sakai had been a Japanese man and not different from other Japanese, though superior. Thus she knew that her children would be Japanese, black-haired, black-eyed, golden-skinned, but how could Josui know what her child would be? He might even have light-colored eyes like the father's. What then could be done? She looked startled at this possibility and Josui saw the look.

"What is the matter, Mother?"

"I have had a thought," Mrs. Sakai replied, bewildered, "Josui, I have thought of something!"

"What, Mother?"

"American women—they can never know what color eyes and hair their children will have! Is this not an embarrassment?"

"Mother, will this matter to me?" Josui asked.

"I think it matters," Mrs. Sakai said with much concern. "It would matter to me, Josui, if when I saw you, your eyes had not been black. How can I feel the child is my grandchild if his eyes are not black?"

"Oh, Mother—"

Josui tried to laugh, but she too felt unhappy for a moment. If the child had blue eyes, would she herself feel strange? Yet if the child was altogether like her, Allen might feel strange. This was indeed, as her mother said, an embarrassment.

"I may not have a child," she said.

Her mother shook her head. "You cannot say so," she declared in a practical voice. "If it is a time for a child to be conceived, he will be conceived and nothing can stop his life. The spirit waits at the threshold for its appointed time. When it is time to live, we live, even as when it is time to die, we die. The cycle cannot be hastened nor can it be stayed. The lives of some are short, the lives of some are long, but all is destiny."

So was explained her mother's patience, her nonresistance, her acceptance, the source of her immense and simple strength. Josui could not answer it, and feeling her mother's dignity, she bowed and went away.

For the first time, after this moment of insight into her mother's heart, she felt the inevitability of the child.

When her father made no protest whatever to her going she was surprised, or felt that she should have been surprised, and yet the conviction of inevitability included this also. He arranged for her visa, accompanying her to the proper office in Tokyo. He told her that he had some money in a savings bank in San Francisco which he had left for Kensan, and when he died, there it had remained. He would put it now in her name.

All went so easily that it seemed gods ran before her to make the path. Her birth certificate, proving that she was born in Los Angeles, her passport included with that of her parents and now needing only separation and a new photograph were all within regulation. The only difficulty was of her own making. She wished to use her new name on the passport, Mrs. Allen Kennedy.

This her father forbade. "No, I will not allow it. You must use my name and yours, Josui Sakai. It may be that you will need this name again."

She was angry with him. "Father, how can you say that? You will not believe in me. You distrust me."

"I distrust life," he said.

She yielded. Life itself must prove her right. He would see for himself when all happened as she knew it would. The elders were unbelieving. When all was arranged, they went home again, and she was touched by her father's effort to be amiable. He would not speak of her leaving, but from the train window he pointed out to her certain sights—a man with a tumor growing on his neck, or a child whose eyes were diseased. He opened the window to call to the man, who was only a porter. "You there, with the lump on your neck! That could be taken off. Why do you not go to the hospital in Tokyo? Or come to me in Kyoto?"

The man was ignorant and he shouted back, "My life is contained in this lump. Shall I cut off my life?"

Dr. Sakai sighed as he shut the window. The task of the physician is hard. First he must tell a man that he can be healed and then he must force him to believe. The act of healing is the last and easiest part of it all.

He discussed for some time with Josui the stubbornness of the human mind, especially the ignorant mind, in which he included most of mankind, and especially, Josui felt, the young and the female.

Yet nothing could dim her happiness. Now that the day was set, the very hour known, time went skimming past. Morning came soon and the hours of the day flew upon the wings of joy. She was so happy that she was cruel and did not know it. She did not see the red berries in the garden, which each year gave her father such serious pleasure. She forgot twice to tend the tokonoma, but her parents did not reprove her. To them she was already lost.

She was aware of this sadness yet she knew she was not able to share it, for she was brimming with love and excitement and her heart had already crossed the sea and was waiting impatiently upon the further shore.

Therefore when the moment of departure arrived, when she bade farewell to the house and garden, to Yumi, to her mother last of all, when she set out with her father for the airfield, when she knew she was only a few hours away from Allen, she still felt numb with joy. It was impossible to think only of her parents or of what she was leaving.

She received through the mail a few days before her going, a short letter from Kobori Matsui. It was friendly and kind, he wished her happiness and he wrote that he would send to America a small wedding gift. He might even be coming to America some time in the next year, if business opened as he and his father hoped it would, and if she were willing he would like to call upon her and make the acquaintance of her new relatives. He would value always her friendship and she would possess his, whether she needed it or not. She read the letter, knowing it was like his goodness to send it, and yet unable to feel even such goodness. She burned the letter in the incense urn, not wishing to keep it and yet not wishing to leave it behind.

For a moment, when the plane was taking off, she had a brief perception of what she was doing. She looked from the small window and saw her father standing on the ground outside, straight and tall, his loose coat fluttering in the wind. His hands were clasped together upon his cane, his feet planted firmly apart, his head lifted and facing her. She was not sure he could see her, but in that instant she saw him clearly indeed. The day was fine, the sunshine piercingly bright after three days of rain and storm, and this light fell upon his lined and handsome face. She saw a noble sadness there, a dignified sorrow, an unrelenting regret beneath his determined composure. A pang of understanding pierced her heart.

It could not last. The great bright wings lifted her up into the sky, and the earth grew small. Within a short time she was high above the sea and her thoughts, her dreams were already flying far ahead.

# Part III

Part III.

A T the airport in San Francisco Allen saw her descend and hesitate a moment, as looking from side to side she searched for him. He pressed forward through the small crowd, ashamed that he had been a moment late, ashamed that this morning of all others he had overslept.

"Josui!" he called.

She saw him and her face changed with her smile. For the first moment, seeing that sober anxiety upon the face he thought he remembered so well, he had felt a light but sharp disappointment. She was not quite as pretty as he had remembered her, or was it the gray suit she wore? But the smile, so charming in its reserve, brought her back again. She was distinguished by the smile and by the half-shy grace with which she moved toward him. He seized her in his arms, safe in the midst of strangers. Yet he was instantly aware of curious glances, aware that people were looking at a tall young American man embracing a Japanese girl. No one said a word, and all went about their business, too hurried to spare more than a second or two of curiosity. He led her along in the curve of his arm, ignoring the eyes of strangers. But she too was aware of the darting looks of surprise and she withdrew herself delicately, although she let him hold her hand.

"We'll go straight to the hotel," Allen said. "I've taken a suite there. We'll stay a few days, darling. There's no hurry. I want time—time—time with you. And we'll take a long time to get home."

By then they would know what to do. He would tell her exactly how everything was at home. That is, he would tell her in so far as he knew, but he knew almost nothing, although he felt a great deal. His mother had simply made up her mind, so far as he could see, to ignore everything. But how could she ignore Josui standing at the door? And he would be there beside her.

He brushed aside such thoughts. For these weeks they would be alone. He wished that Cynthia had not chosen to spend the season in New York. Cynthia could have been a great help. Well, he did not need help!

"You are very silent, darling."

"There is so much I see."

He had his car here and they climbed into it.

"It is yours, Allenn?"

"It's ours, darling. All that is mine is yours."

She smiled, and he reached for her hand.

"Better you drive carefully," she said after an anxious moment.

He laughed. "This is America, Josui. Have you forgotten it?"

But he went slowly, for so he could fondle her little hand with his gold signet ring upon it, the ring he had put on her finger at the ceremony in the temple. That night, when they were alone in that shadowy beautiful room in the house now far away from them both, he had taken the ring from her finger and put it on again. Then he had repeated the sacred words, "With this ring, I thee wed."

She had not quite understood. Well, now he would make her understand.

They reached the hotel, she still very silent and he supposed bewildered, and he gave her bags to a bellboy and they went into the elevator up to the seventeenth floor where their windows looked out over the sea. He tipped the boy and locked the door. When he took off her little hat, which was not, he decided, very becoming, he slipped her coat from her shoulders, and held her in his arms. Oh, the fragrance of her skin, the sweetness of the curve of her neck, the pressure of her little breasts against him! He could not wait. And why should he wait? He saw her eyes so dark, so luminous, and the softness of her young mouth. She knew, she understood his need. She was the essence of all that was woman, a woman of the Orient, instinctive in the ways of the heart.

"Do you still love me?" He stayed to demand so much, to hear at least those words.

"I do love you," she said, not in a whisper, but in a voice lovely and clear. "I come so far for love of you, Allenn."

When was the mortal life of the child begun? They did not know at which moment in the day's brightness or in what shadow of the night his spirit stepped from the eternity before birth into the world of life. Whether it was in that first screened room now across the sea, or in the high room looking toward the west, whether it was in the mountain cabin where they spent a handful of days, reluctant to leave the snow-crowned peaks, whether it was in the upper room in a little hotel in a small town on the endless plain, or in the rolling hills of the Midwest, they did not know. Somewhere in the glorious months, at some place of love in the chain of days and nights of love, the world child was living, but still they did not know. They were not thinking of him but of themselves.

"We must tell your parents exactly when we come," Josui said. Of this they both had been thinking, each secretly from the other, each reluctant to acknowledge that one day soon this transcendent journey must end, the glorious days, the shimmering nights be past. The heavens were kind and the autumn warmth made the mystic atmosphere in which they moved or lingered. It had to end, they knew it; this was not life, it was only love, and somewhere there had to be fusion of the two. Josui, the more practical, thus suggested the last day. Sensitive to his every look, she knew already that he dreaded it. Something loomed ahead, she did not know what, but she prepared herself as best she could. If she were very careful, very dutiful, very helpful, if she considered the elders always first, perhaps they could be happy together. She was the key figure, that she understood. At night while he slept she considered her increasing knowledge of this man and though she loved him more and more, though she yielded herself to him wholly, yet she was beginning dimly to understand that the woman could yield no more than the man wanted. The capacity to receive must equal the capacity to give. Did he want her whole? Of this she was not sure.

"Unless we stop somewhere a couple of days," he said, "we can't help getting home day after tomorrow."

"You don't want to go home?" she inquired.

"Oh, I do, of course. We have to settle down. I have to think what to do about a job. Maybe I'll give up the army entirely. I can—my time was up several years ago, for that matter. Maybe I'll just be what my father is—a country gentleman."

She followed everything he said with an exact attention, but she did not always understand the over and above, the extra meaning, the allusions of idiom. Each English word contained its dictionary definition for her and no more.

"We must tell them the hour we come," she said, returning to her concept of duty.

"Day after tomorrow, about six o'clock in the evening," he said.

"So tomorrow, Allenn, please, you telephone to your parents," she said, coaxing.

He found her attempts to control him as charming as the dictates of a child. She was so sweetly anxious to guide him while she adored and obeyed. It was so necessary in her eyes that he behave always at his best, at least toward others. She laughed when he was what she called "naughty" toward her, when he would not get up in the morning, when he left his pajamas on the floor, when he rumpled her smooth hair or her fresh dress, when he teased her to make her argue with him, which she did seriously and with such earnestness that his eyes betrayed him. When she saw the glints of his laughter she cried out at him, "Naughty Allenn!" and put her small right hand over her mouth to hide her own laughter. She spoiled him outrageously, he acknowledged. She expected no help from him in the little housekeeping duties of the places where they stopped, she waited on him as a matter of course, holding the towel ready when he bathed, washing his shaving things when he had finished.

At first he had cried out against such service. "Here, you little thing, you're my wife, not my slave!"

But she persisted and he found himself yielding to her, for this was her way of expressing her love. It was very pleasant, he had to say so, it was pleasant not to wait upon himself. It gave him a feeling of leisure and freedom from detail. She showed herself Japanese at heart. An American girl would never have so served him. He began to understand why men said it was impossible to love an American woman if one had known a woman of the Orient.

"So this morning you telephone your parents?" Josui suggested sweetly the next morning.

"Oh, sometime," he said carelessly. Another matchless day had begun in the haze of purple upon the Alleghenies. He did not want to think of its end.

Yet soon he saw that she was troubled. She sat beside him in anxious restraint, and he felt her anxiety.

"Relax," he told her. "I'll do it, Josui."

"Yes," she agreed, "so nice to do it now, isn't it?"

He laughed suddenly. "All right, at the very next public telephone we stop. Watch for the little blue bell."

She saw it first and within ten minutes in a cluster of houses that was scarcely a village. "There—there!" she cried, pointing with her middle right finger.

He was compelled to it then. He stopped the car. "You

can wait here," he commanded. Now that the moment had arrived he was troubled and reluctant. He was not so childish as to be frightened, whatever happened. He could take Josui away and they could live where they pleased in the world. But he did not want to leave his home. The years abroad had deepened his love of his own country, his own state, his town, and the big house which his great-grandfather had built to shelter the generations to come. It was a way of life which might be doomed but it would last his time, at least in America. He wanted to live it, to be able to be the sort of man his father was, wise, leisured, content.

He stood in the booth, thinking such thoughts while he waited. And could Josui take his mother's place?

"Here's your party," the operator's voice sang over the wires.

"Hello, Dad? This is Allen." He had called his father, person-to-person, dreading the impact upon his mother without the presence.

"Yes, son?" His father's voice came to his ears surprisingly strong and vibrant. "Where are you?"

"In the Alleghenies. I wanted you to know that we'll probably reach home tomorrow night, or maybe the day after, if we dawdle along, as we may."

"Yes, well—" his father hesitated. "Allen, I reckon you better stay in a hotel the first night, son. You and I better have a talk."

"What's the matter?" he demanded.

"I can't tell you right now. We better have a talk. Suppose you stay over in Richmond. I'll go up there in the afternoon and wait for you. You call me at the club when you get in."

"All right, we'll be there." He wanted to get there. Whatever it was his father said they must talk about, he wanted to know it and face it.

"Good-by, Dad. See you tomorrow."

"All right, son."

He hung up and loitered a moment in the little general store. He bought some chocolate bars and waited for change. This was to allow him time to remove anxiety from his face. Josui's eyes were so keen, she could read his very thoughts, she caught the atmosphere of his spirit. He did not want to hide himself from her except to save her hurt. He had begun to know her, too, and he discerned in her a rock bottom of quick despair, a readiness to give up hope and to believe in the worst, which he recognized as a characteristic of the Japanese nature. She must not give up hope now at the very beginning.

When he went back to the car he was smiling and he offered the chocolate.

"Oh, thank you," she exclaimed. He liked to give her little gifts that he might hear the heartfelt sweetness of her polite gratitude, her thanks spoken in that warm accepting voice. "And did you talk with parents?"

"Yes, with my father. We'll stop the first night in Richmond, though, in a good hotel. My father said he'd meet us there."

"Oh, how nice and kind he is," she exclaimed. Her eyes suddenly misted with tears. "I hope he is not too old. Such trouble! And your mother?"

He improvised. "She'll want to stay home and have the house nice."

Josui was very happy after that. She fed him bits of chocolate while he drove, ate a very little herself, and she
wrapped what was left neatly in the silver paper and then in
some newspaper and put it in the glove compartment for
another time. Her economical ways touched him. She was
careful about scraps of food, about his garments and hers,
about half sheets of writing paper and penny stamps and all
small items which might be wasted. She had lived among a
people taught to save and make the most of everything material. How, he wondered, would she take the vast wastefulness of the big house, the four servants, the baskets of food
taken home, the food thrown away, the carelessness about
money and clothing and all material goods which here could
so easily be replaced? He was troubled as he thought. There
was something adamant about her. Underneath all the seemingly soft yielding she had principles which could not be
moved. Right was an absolute in her clear, even hard young
mind. Though she was swept by her love for him, right remained. She had a zeal for whatever she considered proper,
in attitude, in speech, in behavior. She did not expect the
same zeal in him, but with herself she was relentless. He
could foresee a future wherein she was zealous in his defense, earnest to guard his money, his sources of food, his
happiness. He would not be able to persuade her that wastefulness could be right, or that the mild pilfering of old servants was not theft. All would be done for his sake, but he
foresaw that this love, too, though passionately tender, might
be inexorable.

He chose to stop at a small hotel that was on a quiet street in Richmond, and he was honest enough to acknowledge that he did so in order to be less conspicuous when he came in with Josui. He must accustom himself to the curious looks, the unspoken question. There must have been the same curiosity and question about him in Japan, but he had not noticed it. Had she, perhaps, and had she not told him? He would not ask her now lest here she had not noticed, and lest he might put into her mind a wound that she might be spared.

The hotel was pleasant. Josui liked the rather old-fashioned quiet, and when they were settled in a small suite whose windows gave upon a little square park where a few trees were still bright with autumn color, Allen telephoned to his father's club.

Mr. Kennedy was awaiting the call. He had arrived the day before and had spent the time visiting a few old friends, not in their homes, where he never went if he could help it, but in their offices. Leisure seemed abundant, and each man was glad to see him because he carried with him a store of knowledge. Tom Kennedy was better than a newspaper.

"I'll be right over, son," he replied to Allen's voice on the telephone.

He hung up the receiver, ambled across the large pleasant room which he rented regularly in the club, put on his loose topcoat of grayish-brown tweed and his somewhat shapeless brown felt hat, and walked down the wide curving stairs. There was no elevator and he would not have used it if there had been.

Outside the air was muggy with a belated damp heat and he stopped a taxicab. "Take me to the Mansfield," he ordered, and then sat oblivious while the cab wound its way through the city. He had no intention of concealing from his son the long talk he had had with Josephine. The sooner Allen knew what he had to face the better it would be. Time must pass before anyone could know the end. He got out at the hotel and paid the fare and shook his head at the small black bellboy loitering at the door.

"I'm not stopping here. I've just come to see somebody."

He was astonished at himself. Why did he not say, "I have come to see my son?" Was there some damned unwillingness in him, too? If there was he would root it out. He despised prejudice. He believed, within the privacy of his own skull, that the day would inevitably come, and the sooner the better, when all people would be the same color. Let everybody be a dirty brown! What did it matter? So the more quickly would be removed from the tangle of human affairs one source of trouble. Once he had been in New York and there had encountered at a public dinner an earnest female savior of the nation.

"But what, Mr. Kennedy, shall we do with the color problem?" the insistent woman had asked.

Safe among strangers and far from his native South and those who knew him, he had attacked the toughest fried chicken he had ever met upon his plate. "Fade 'em out, fade 'em out," he had said cheerfully. The woman had not spoken to him again.

He ambled now to the desk. "Tell Mr. Allen Kennedy that his father is coming upstairs," he ordered the pallid clerk.

"Yes, sir," the clerk said, staring at him.

So people stared, did they? He would not notice.

"Elevator is that way, sir," the clerk called.

"I'll walk," Mr. Kennedy replied. It was only one floor up. He hated exercise and salved his conscience by stairs. They were wide and easy and the upstairs corridor was deeply carpeted. His footfall made no sound and he knocked heavily on the door—twenty-two, Allen had said. He heard a little cry through the open transom, a girl's voice, and then Allen's reply. "It's my father."

The door opened immediately. The room was empty except for Allen, smiling at him. "Josui has gone into the bedroom to touch up her hair. She's fearfully anxious to look her best. Come on in, Dad."

"I reckon all women are fussy about their hair," Mr. Kennedy said.

He came in and allowed Allen to help with his coat and take his hat and cane. Then he sat down in the most comfortable chair and looked around the little sitting room. He must delay no longer, but he did delay enough to light a cigar.

"Before she comes in, son, I ought to tell you that your mother is in no good frame of mind. I don't like to talk about it before your wife, but you and I will have to think things over."

Allen stood where he was, transfixed by the dejected solemnity of his father's face.

"You mean she doesn't want us to come home?" he demanded.

Mr. Kennedy looked miserable. He turned his head away and drew on the cigar. "I'm afraid not, son. At least, she

210

isn't ready yet to have your wife come home. Of course she'll always be glad to see you. In fact, she told me especially to tell you that you are always welcome. She said to tell you that your room would be kept just as it is, always, ready for you whenever you want it."

"Wait a minute—"

Allen darted out of the room into the bedroom and closed the door between. There was a long silence, a long wait. Mr. Kennedy kept drawing on the cigar. It was long and thin and when he held it a long thin curl of smoke came from its end. He hoped that Allen was not telling the girl. It was much easier to manage solutions if the women did not know. But like most bridegrooms Allen probably thought he had to tell his wife everything. It took men a while to learn, and a father could not teach his son anything either.

His mind went back to his own wife and the wretched evening they had spent. He had told her the truth, that he was going up to Richmond to meet Allen and his bride. Instead of being grateful, she had blamed him bitterly, apparently for that which certainly he could not help.

"We've got to make the best of things," he had argued. "Who does it hurt if we don't? You and me and that's all. The young people can go off and make a life of their own somewhere. It's you and I that will be left alone in this house. We can't disown our only son, Sugar."

"I'm not asking for that," she had retorted. "I simply say what I have said all along, that he cannot bring that girl here."

"They're married, Sugar," he had reminded her.

Upon her pretty face there had come something which long ago he had acknowledged was a sneer. The first time he had seen it was on their honeymoon, and he had forgotten why. He remembered only the shock that it had been to him to see that lovely mouth, made for his kisses, twisted into a shape to repel even his love. But in those days he had not known that love cannot change even the beloved. In the years since then he had not ceased to love her but he no longer loved her whole. There were hours and days and certainly many moments when he preferred not to think about her and when his love waited.

"They are not married," she had declared crisply. She spoke with a soft sweet drawl, the gentlest of women when she wished to be, but there was also this harsh crisp voice that he feared.

"Sugar, why do you say that again? You know I told you that a temple is just the same thing as a church—"

"I don't care about the temple," she said.

He had not at all liked the look of triumph on her face. He had seen it there before, two or three times, once when she had entered Allen in a military school against his wish and the boy's. He had let her have her way because to have insisted upon the boy's withdrawal would have created a public commotion.

"It's not what you care about—" he began.

She cut across his meandering with a whiplike cry, "You're right! It doesn't matter what I think or what you think. It's the law. The law of this state forbids marriage between the white and colored races."

She faced him and compelled his answering stare.

"Josephine!" he said loudly, "you know that law was made against the niggra!"

"It's the law," she repeated.

He had got up and left her, but before he could sleep he had called his own lawyer, Bancroft Haynes. It was true. The law of the state did forbid Allen's marriage, because the girl had in her the blood of Asia. Now he had to tell the boy somehow.

The door opened and Allen came in with Josui. Mr. Kennedy had dreaded this moment and here it was. He rose slowly to his feet, staring at the girl his son held by the hand, a shy lovely girl, whose cream-white skin was flooding pink and whose great dark eyes were humid with fear. Why, he thought, what a sweet face, what a timid child, a suffering child, anxious to please, pleading to be understood! All his pity, ready and trembling, rushed toward her.

"This is Josui," Allen said.

Mr. Kennedy crossed the room heavily and put out his large soft right hand. "I am glad to see you, ma'am," he said with his finest courtesy. "You have come a long way and I make you welcome." He felt her small firm hand in his and he pressed it gently. "You must be tired and maybe a little homesick."

"Oh, no, thank you," Josui replied in a voice just above a whisper. She was overpowered by Mr. Kennedy's size. So big a man, but instantly she saw how kind. She smiled, her lips quivering and her eyes larger than ever as she looked up at him.

Mr. Kennedy gazed down on her almost tenderly, relieved to see her so obviously not colored. Why, there were

213

plenty of girls in the best Southern families who were darker by a good deal. He would certainly tell Josephine.

"You're a little bit of a thing, aren't you?" he said. He turned to his son. "Are they all as little as she is?"

"Josui isn't so little, Dad," Allen replied. He was heartened. His father had responded at once to Josui's delicate, almost touching charm, and he was proud of her. His father would understand how a man could fall in love with her. His father would be on their side.

Between the two tall men Josui suddenly smiled. She was no longer afraid. This big fat good man who was her father-in-law would help them and everything would be nice. She liked him, she could never be afraid of him, she would be very happy living in his house. It was no wonder that Allen was wonderful, he being the son of such a father. And she also would be a perfect daughter-in-law.

She pulled away from Allen. "Please, Father, sit down," she exclaimed. "Allen, we don't have some tea. Call, please, and tell downstairs to bring up tea and some little eating things."

"I don't want anything to eat," Mr. Kennedy said in the same tender voice. She was such a cute little thing! "I've only just finished my breakfast and Allen will tell you that I'm a hearty eater at breakfast. But then I eat very little in the middle of the day. Night is when I have dinner."

He sat down and she hovered about him. "Some whisky-soda?" she coaxed, "or a coke, maybe?" She had learned to drink and say coke, while they traveled, because she did not like alcohol.

"Well, a whisky-soda, maybe," Mr. Kennedy said to please her.

So Allen must order it and she was not at ease until the boy brought it up on a tray and then she would not let Allen touch the glass or the ice, but she must do everything herself. Only when Mr. Kennedy was served, when she had carried a little table to his side and had set everything exactly upon it and had actually seen him with the glass in his hand, was she at ease. She stood waiting and anxious until he had taken a first sip.

"It is nice?"

"Perfect," he replied heartily, willing to say anything to please her. "Now you sit down, honey, and rest yourself. I want to hear you talk. I want to know how my son is treating you. He better be nice to you!"

"Sit down, Josui," Allen commanded.

She sat down at once, not answering, her graceful little body still unrelaxed, looking from one to the other of the two men.

"Does she spoil you like this all the time?" Mr. Kennedy asked of his son.

"It's the Japanese idea of what a woman ought to do," Allen said, smiling.

"They're wonderful people," his father said.

Then he remembered. Long habit made it easy for him to forget what was sad or hard or troublesome and for the moment he had forgotten. But of course he couldn't talk before this little creature. Her heart would be broken and it must not be. He and Allen must think what to do. He must help

215

his son to do the right thing. But what was the right thing exactly?

He became grave and Josui, reflecting at once the mood of those nearest her, looked at Allen and was afraid again. She wished that he could speak Japanese, for then she could ask him what she had done that was wrong. He did not look at her, and then suddenly she could not bear the silence and the father's almost sorrowful gaze not at her or at Allen but at his glass, the carpet at his feet, the window. She stole across the floor to put her hand on Allen's shoulder. "Do I something wrong?" she inquired in a whisper.

"No, of course not," Allen said in his natural voice. "But I think my father wants to talk to me alone, Josui. Suppose you go in the other room."

She knew instantly that something was very wrong but she obeyed like a child. She walked away to the bedroom door, opened it, went in and then closed it noiselessly behind her.

Mr. Kennedy knew then that he had to face it. There was no escape. He put down his glass. "Son, I have bad, bad news."

Allen waited, not answering.

"Had I better give it to you straight?" Mr. Kennedy asked.

"Of course, Dad."

"That's what I thought you'd say."

He leaned forward in his chair and put his elbows on his knees and his big soft hands hung between his knees. He clasped them, his fingers twisted. "Son, your mother is right, I guess. It's not a legal marriage."

"What do you mean?" Allen demanded.

"Not in our state," his father said heavily. "There's an old law, forbidding marriage between the races. Your mother found it somehow. I reckon some of the ladies she goes with heard about it somewhere. Maybe she knew all the time but I don't believe she did."

"That old law was meant for the colored people," Allen said coldly.

"That's right," his father said. He was sweating terribly and big drops burst out of his high forehead and ran down his cheeks by his ears. "But it seems—forgive me, son—that it includes everybody not white."

"Who said so?"

"I asked Bancroft Haynes and he said it did."

He got up and went to the window and stood looking out so that Allen could get over it by himself for a few minutes.

"We don't have to live in this state," Allen said.

"Of course not," Mr. Kennedy turned around, relieved that thus his son spoke. "The thing to do is to go to another state and go through a civil marriage. Then you're safe. If you're sure what you want to do."

"Why do you say if I am sure?" Allen demanded. He was suddenly angry with his father, outraged at the implication of doubt.

Mr. Kennedy answered peaceably. "You know your own mind, son. I'm just saying."

"We will certainly go to another state," Allen continued in the same angry voice. "We'll go to New York. I'll find a job there. You can tell Mother that I'll never come home again."

"I'm not going to tell her any such thing," Mr. Kennedy

said reprovingly. He sat down again and took up the glass and drank it half empty and set it down again. "I don't think it would be right of you even to think it. I hope you'll come home often. You're her only son."

"She doesn't treat me like one," he retorted.

"Now you're acting childish," his father said. "She loves you too much, I reckon. She can't cut herself off from you and that's the trouble. The placenta still bleeds. It's not just you but it's all the life that she looks for from you. When she found she couldn't have another child, I thought she would kill herself with crying. I thought she'd never get over it. I held her in my arms all night long, sitting up in that old chair in my room. We couldn't either of us sleep. I don't think she's ever forgiven God for that. She doesn't say her prayers at night—hasn't for years, though she goes to church every Sunday. But she holds it. She even holds it up against me in some way I don't understand, though God knows it's not my fault."

"She wants everything her own damned way," Allen growled.

Mr. Kennedy evaded this. "She's a pitiful, wonderful, childish creature," he said with musing tenderness. For the first time he spoke to his son as to a man. "She's so strong and capable and managing and bossy that sometimes I can't hardly stand her. And then I remember the other side of her, the stricken child she is. I reckon you can't be expected to understand that, son. But I do. She's everything in her own way, and I've found her interesting. I couldn't have loved a woman that wasn't interesting."

He glanced at his son with a shy almost placating look,

an unspoken plea, implicit in the revelation. Allen was touched and embarrassed. He could not see his mother in the role of wife. It was a nakedness that must be covered at once. He got to his feet almost briskly, eager to evade it.

"I can see that you have done your best for us," he declared. "Now it is up to me, Dad. You'll stay for luncheon with us, won't you? We'll get on our way this afternoon, I think. I'll be sending for my clothes and my books."

"I won't stay today," Mr. Kennedy said. He felt very tired and he was not sure he wanted to see that pretty child again. "I'll come and see you again when you're settled."

"I'll let you know," Allen said. They clasped hands strongly, and he resisted an impulse to put his head down on his father's heavy bowed old shoulder. Instead he held his head high, and spoke in a resolute and strong voice. "I am glad you gave it to me straight. It makes everything clear. I know where I am."

Mr. Kennedy cleared his throat and tried to think of something worth saying. He felt his knees tremble and he wished that he could lie down for a while.

"Well, son, good-by. Call on me if you need me. I'm always the same."

"I know," Allen said. The familiar phrase was freighted with pathetic memory. His father had spoken these words at every parting. And yet there was never anything really that he could do.

He smiled steadily until he closed the door upon his father's retreating form and then he sat down alone and leaned his head in his hands.

In the other room Josui waited. Honor forbade her to look

or to listen when father and son talked together. Nevertheless she knew that something had been said, something told and heard, which was dangerous to her. She stood immobile in the middle of the hotel bedroom. She was tired, not only from the journey but because it had been many years since she had sat on chairs and slept on beds lifted from the floor. The muscles of her legs ached from strain, and her back was sore from the soft mattresses. She was weary, too, from determination not to feel bewildered and certainly not to appear so. How little she and Allen really knew each other! A heavy burden is put upon love when upon love must lean also understanding. Her love was strong enough but was his? She had thought so, and she did still think so.

She heard the door of the other room close and when he did not call her she opened the door between them softly and looked in. He sat there with his head in his hands. What terrible grief had befallen him?

"Allenn!"

He jumped at the sound of her voice, and as though he had forgotten that she was there. His hands fell from his face.

"Allenn, what is it?" she cried. She came in swiftly and knelt at his side. "Tell me, Allenn! How is it?"

He was ashamed to tell her. How could he explain to her the need, which he supposed was real, for this law forbidding such union and how explain that which could not be explained, that a net laid for others had caught her, for whom it was not first designed? As well explain how a barrier, laid for wasps, prevented also a butterfly!

"My mother isn't well," he said awkwardly. "My father

says we must wait until she feels better. For the time being we must find a place to live by ourselves."

He saw her look change and he hurried on. "You know, Pittysing"—this was his playful name for her, devised from the play of love—"in America we don't live at home with parents. I assure you it is not done. Most young people here would hate it, and I don't think the older ones would like it for long. Maybe by Christmas we can go home for a bit. Meanwhile—"

He got up, thrust his hands into his pockets and walked about the room, talking while she knelt there watching, her white face composed and her great black eyes expressionless as they followed him.

"New York is the place for us, a great city where all sorts of people live and live together. You see, Pittysing, my home town is such a small place, and everybody has lived there for generations—a dozen families or so and their servants and satellites—put it that way. I don't believe they have ever seen a Japanese."

"Then it is me," Josui said.

He had allowed too much to escape him. He stopped in front of her and stood, trying to smile, as he looked down into her upturned face.

"Remember how your father felt about me? Well!"

"But in America?"

"Oh, yes, in America, my love! Especially in America! Had you forgotten? You were in Los Angeles until you were a big girl. Don't you remember?" His tone was bitter.

She did remember. She let her head droop and tears hung

on her long straight eyelashes. "I thought it was changed," she whispered.

"Changing, perhaps," he admitted. "I am part of the change, so are you."

She lifted her head at this, and met his eyes fearfully. "This makes me feel lonely," she said in a small voice.

"Two wandering stars," he agreed, "seeking to make a universe of their own. It can be done, Pittysing."

He took her hands and pulled her to her feet. "No more kneeling, please, Mrs. Kennedy," he said. "And I think I shall not call you Pittysing any more. It's a honeymoon name. The honeymoon is over, my girl. Life begins. I shall call you Jo Kennedy. That's good. Sounds American, eh?"

He was brave with anger, courageous with rebellion. To hell, he thought, with the old and the past. He would get out of the army, go to New York, and find a job. He would become a good husband and provider. A father? He recoiled at the thought. Well, if so, an inconspicuous place, no neighbors, a cell in a beehive, a little apartment where nobody asked anybody anything.

"Come along, Jo," he said. He gave her a resolute hug, an embrace fired with no passion except wrath. "Get your things together. We're going north."

Outwardly the change was easy. He was able to get a job without difficulty with a weekly magazine. His references were excellent, and he had the look and the experience. He showed his honorable discharge from the armed services, and his pay check was enough for the small apartment he found on Riverside Drive. Josui even found friends, a

Chinese girl married to a Columbia student, and a Japanese couple studying education and child psychology.

But the change had come between them. She and Allen began each to have a secret lonely life, while they clung together in determined love and for a time with passion more intense than they had ever known. And they were not children of the slums to whom this neat little apartment might represent a sort of heaven. They were not even children of apartment houses, elevators, little terraces, and high sooty roof tops. They were children of space and plenty. She tidied her tiny kitchen and thought of the vistas of her home in Kyoto, the latticed screens drawn away and one room opening into another as far as eye could see. He hung his clothes in a yard-square closet and thought of his rooms in the big-pillared house, his house by inheritance, a possession which could not be taken away from him who was the lawful heir. They thought in secret of gardens and pools, and Josui sleeping dreamed of the splash of the waterfall thousands of miles away. To her, too, belonged the waterfall, the pools and the latticed house, the treasures of the tokonoma. Neither would for one instant have given up their love, but each dreamed of what they did not have and perhaps would never have.

And each, too, kept secret a deepening hatred of the city. It was a transient life. Who can live in a honeycomb of cells and call it life? An embryo, perhaps, but not a living moving feeling human being, Josui thought in that secret life she guarded so well from Allen that he never dreamed it there, possessed as he was by his own furtive dreams. He could not yield his hopes, indeed, his determination, to find a way to gain his home again.

He became increasingly angry with thwarted love of home and childhood and parents. He thought incessantly about his parents, living in the house he loved, and he was angry with his father even more than with his mother. The man should insist and demand, should force his will upon the woman. Not to do so was weakness in the male. He did not know that he himself was a man very different from his father. Though he had been too fastidious to enjoy a prostitute who belongs to any man, yet the subjection of a conquered country had changed him as it changes all men. There are men who feel compelled to force conquered women to submit to them, it is the final phase of war, the completion of personal victory. He would have declared himself not one of these, and yet he was. He was arrogant as his father was not, insistent for himself as his father was not. He was one of a generation who are physically dominant, who have conquered by body strength, and by so much did he differ from his father, who had no wish to dominate or to control anyone.

So thinking, day after day, Allen became unconsciously more insistent, more demanding, more forceful even with Josui. She was astonished, not understanding why what she did was so often wrong. She was a perfectionist, a creature so anxious to do right and only right that she could spend hours arranging a bowl of flowers on the table in the corner of the small living room which was also a dining room. Yet attention to one detail did not prevent her determination to complete everything before Allen came home. She had no maid and wanted none, remembering that few women in America have servants. Also how would she occupy her time? She planned that when winter came, when she could not go out into the parks, she would attend some school. The city was full of schools. She sent for catalogues and studied them while she waited for Allen to come home on the nights when he had to work late. Every week there were such nights, and always one final night of madness when the magazine was, as he told her, "put to bed." Sometimes it was dawn before he came in and always she waited.

If she were going to school, she could be studying during these hours. As it was, she read books which she rented from the neighborhood library. Sometimes they were good books and sometimes not. She had no guide except her own polite request to the elderly librarian for books which told about American life. These she read with increasing surprise and puzzlement. Where did she belong among these women and their many problems? Her life was contained in this small apartment, with the one whom she loved.

And yet, could this last forever? There were hours when the house was a box too small, when her good mind was restless and reaching. Was this indeed all there was?

"Allenn," she said on one of these days, "do you have no friends, my dear?"

She had made him a pleasant little dinner, a sukiyaki dish which he liked, and a mound of feather-light rice.

"Friends?" he repeated.

"For us to talk with," she went on. "I could make such a nice dinner like this, maybe for two friends, and we could talk, lady and gentleman."

"I haven't had time for anybody outside the office, Jo," he replied. "Later, maybe."

She invited the couple whom she had met in the park one day, the two young Japanese-Americans, born and bred in Seattle, now students at Columbia. They were pleasant but reserved. Josui's husband, they felt, was still the young American officer. It was hard to forget that they themselves had lived in an arid Arizona camp behind barbed wire. Still, the evening was pleasant. The young Japanese, while prisoned, had made a hobby of carving roots, the twisted roots of desert sagebrush, and at Josui's urging they brought some of their best pieces, none for sale.

"We keep them, to remember," the stocky little wife said.

There was hearty forced conversation and much praise of Josui's cooking but they went home early. She did not invite them again. "You are thinking they are not your kind of people, Allenn?" she inquired when they had gone.

"That doesn't matter," he said really kindly. "They are very nice. I want you to have friends."

Then suddenly all restlessness disappeared. One day when she returned from the market where she did her daily shopping she felt very weary and she lay down upon the bed. There had been signs which made her afraid, delays, small changes in herself which she thought imaginary. She had never been regular in her physical female life. The shock, a doctor had told her once in Japan, of the departure from America and the end of all that she had known at a time when she was ceasing to be a child, was becoming a woman, the breaking off of deep emotional ties, not only with her friends but with familiar landscapes, the necessity to conform to the Japanese background, at once her own and yet alien, had set up restraints upon her spirit, certainly in her mind, which affected her body. She had wondered a few weeks ago if she were pregnant, had feared and doubted, had tried to prevent, by her own disinclination, the conception of a child. For what sort of home was this to give a child? It was not only the boxlike compartment in which they lived, with no garden in which a child could play, it was also the park, where she had seen white women guarding their children from the children of darker color. She would not take her child to that park. A child!

"No, no," she muttered.

Suddenly today, as she lay at rest, she felt a stir within herself, movements feather light, but not her own. The signs which she had refused to recognize fell instantly into their place in the pattern of certainty. She felt in her body the thrust of another life. It was there, it had begun, it was too late. The child lived.

She lay immobile in horror, and then she turned over upon her face and wept into the pillow.

Lucky it is that the child unborn does not know when the mother weeps. He begins gaily to live, wanted or not, and his mother's agony does not embrace him. Wisely he lives alone and apart, preparing for a world of his own creation, greedily growing, sleeping the deep sleep of the unborn, which only death, the last sleep, can equal in peace and in forgetfulness. But each day he wakes a little more, he sleeps a little less, thrusting his legs out, stretching his arms, preparing himself for the crisis of birth, the first great separation of himself from eternity. For him time begins.

So with the world child Lennie. That his mother often wept he did not know. He was absorbed in his own process, unthinking, and yet growing. To whom he was to be born he neither knew nor cared, he was not aware of the mighty fusion in his infinitesimal frame. He slept, he absorbed his food through his navel, he moved now and again with increasing restlessness and he did not know that his existence was a profound secret between himself and his mother.

For Josui would not tell Allen of what she had discovered. She discerned that this American whom she had married so passionately, and whom she still loved most passionately, was not happy. He worked desperately hard, he was kind to her, he loved her, she believed, for there were hours of the utmost tenderness between them, hours when she lay in his arms and was given up to him, when they were melted together in love, all thought quieted, all feeling lost in the cosmic fusion of their bodies. And yet she was always aware now of the secret third. Did that one partake of this fusion? Did he wonder, did he feel his private sea disturbed by outer storms?

"What is the matter with you?" Allen asked. "What are you thinking about? You are off somewhere. Come back to me."

"I am here," she said putting out her hands. "See, I am here, with you."

No, no, she would not tell him. For she was not his whole life. She had known for a long time that he had secrets from her. He lived apart, he had thoughts which he could not share with her. These were not merely the thoughts of his home, his family from which she had separated him, his childhood which she now could not share. There was very much which she did not understand about the world which was his. He was interested in politics, and she did not understand this interest. He read books which she could not read, he grew very angry sometimes when he heard the news over their small radio, and he frowned over the daily papers. To her none of these things mattered, but if they did so much matter to him, should they not also be her interest? When she tried to understand them, asking him many questions, for whom had she to teach her except him, he answered her with impatience which he tried not to show. Nothing broke her heart more finally than his hardly controlled impatience, which grew more and more sharp.

"It is too much for you to teach me," she decided aloud one day.

"No, it isn't that," he argued. "I am tired when I come home."

But it was that. Had she been able to go to school as she planned she could have learned about America. But there could be no question of going to school. It would be no use, now that the child was coming. She could not prevent the child, though once she tried. She talked with her Japanese friend, they went to a doctor together and he told her that the child must be born. It was too late. Also he did not do that sort of thing. She was almost glad, after all. It was not fair to the child to destroy him before he was born. It was not his fault that he was a world child. This was his destiny.

The autumn passed and early winter came. She grew thin with worry over the secret, and many times she nearly confessed it to Allen, but never did she quite do it. When the words lay heavy upon her tongue she could not speak them out, not that she was afraid of him, for indeed she was not, but she felt the instability of her life. Even the lease of this little apartment was by the month. How could one live month by month?

"One of these days," he said, "we'll go home. The time will come. Even if my mother refuses while she lives, she will die one day. But she won't refuse."

"Allenn!" she cried out, horrified, "do not speak so of your parent. You will be punished."

He was strangely callous. "Death is natural. It is a good thing that the old die. There is no progress until they are dead."

"Allenn, she is your mother!" Josui put her soft palm against his lips.

"She is a limited woman," he retorted, taking away her hand. "She has been born and reared in that little town. She cannot or will not understand that everything changes."

"You love the little town," Josui said.

"I know I do," he replied, "and I find it hard to forgive that she will not allow me to live there."

"I will not wish her dead," Josui said firmly. "I cannot wish death upon anyone. I would fear to do so."

He said, still strangely, "That is because you have never killed anyone. Why, look here, Josui—I've been taught to kill people. It isn't hard. Sometimes when I sit listening to our managing editor, I can't keep from thinking how I would kill him, supposing he were the enemy. I can see the vulnerable spots in his big hulk. I would know just how to defend myself against him, the soft spot here, in the neck, or under the ribs. The bayonet would slip into his fat."

She stood looking at him, transfixed with increasing horror. She was wiping a dish, a little pink apron tied about her waist, and she held in her hands the glass dish, which suddenly she clutched.

He laughed. "Don't worry, Jo, I shall never do it. It was simply part of my training. I tell you to explain why death is not monstrous to me any more."

She did not reply. She turned to the sink and began washing the dishes again in the hot soapy water.

He did love his mother, of course. He would not be so angry with her if he did not love her.

"I ought to go away," Josui thought humbly. "I keep him from all that he loves best."

How could she go away? She had that little money in the bank in San Francisco, but she had nowhere to go. If she wrote to her father he would send her more money perhaps, but then he had told her not to come back. Yet what sort of life would it be in her father's house, and oh, the child, who would want the child except herself? It would not be possible for the child and her father to live in the same house. She would be always a buffer between them. She saw the little creature, looking like Allen, doubtless, for she had heard that white blood always predominated over any other, that white blood can never be hidden, and could such a little child grow up happily in a country where all people had black eyes and black hair and golden skin? Would he not be very unhappy there? He must stay here among other people like him. So how could she go away?

It became hard even to be with her Japanese friends and gradually she withdrew herself from them. She could not tell the woman what she thought day and night, so she made excuses that she did not feel well, that she must rest a great deal. The husband and wife were busy in school together, and so gradually she saw no one at all.

Then one day Allen telephoned that he was bringing a friend with him, Cynthia, the girl he had told her was his childhood playmate. She had come to his office to see him, and she had asked to meet Josui. So he was bringing her that night, and Josui must please cook a fine sukiyaki. His voice sounded gay over the telephone, and Josui was glad to hear it as she had not heard it for months.

She cleaned the small apartment, she bought a handful of small chrysanthemums and then, tempted, she bought three huge yellow ones, such as her father grew by the hundreds in the garden in autumn, and she spent two hours in arrangements, striving for the effect of space in these rooms where there was no space, and using the window finally, and borrowing the space of a patch of sky and some roof tops for background.

Oh, and the food to be prepared so carefully, the rice to be washed again and again until there was not a particle of the white starch to make it sticky when she had steamed it dry to perfection, and the radishes sliced into flowers, the bits of cress and endive designed to decorate the clear chicken broth, the fish, which she must have head and all, for she could not bear the decapitated body which the Americans presented. A fish was beautiful whole but hideous without its head, and could anyone fail to see this? She polished her bowls and dishes, she cleaned the kitchen until the child protested and she must lie down to quiet him.

She had named him. One had to call a child something even before he was born. She had pondered much on this matter of a name. What name ought a world child to have? A name of his own, certainly, not his father's nor one like his mother's. There was an American name, Joseph. But she did not like it. She had thought of taking her dead brother's name, Kensan. But had this child the right to her brother's name? She did not like to use it without permission, and there was no one to give it. She imagined the child's little face, not looking like anyone she knew, and yet looking like everyone, a world child indeed. She would not name him Allen, when the mother of Allen would not allow his existence. Allenn—Allenn! So why not simply a part of his father, and let him be called Lennie? The moment she spoke the name to herself it became the child's name. She saw a small lively face, large eyes whose color she could not distinguish, but a vivid little face that she could see, and just such a child as the name Lennie would fit. So it became his name, and she talked to him, calling him Lennie. When he was impatient with her running about the apartment and cleaning and dusting and wiping, when she stood long chopping the vegetables ready for sukiyaki, she scolded him sweetly.

"I could sit down, Lennie. It is true I could sit down. But I never saw any woman sit down when she cuts the vegetables small. We always stand. So you must if you please be quiet."

But he would not, and so she lay down resting.

This woman, this Cynthia, would she discern what Allen did not? Would she be friend or enemy?

The moment she saw Cynthia, she knew it was friend. A tall beautiful girl, so blonde, so graceful, came into the room with Allen, and Josui looked up to her with humble and instant admiration. This of course was the girl whom Allen should have married. It was to be seen at once, and at once she understood Allen's mother completely. Oh, of course, Cynthia was the one, and had she known there was such a woman, she would have refused Allen because she loved him so much.

She put out her hand, unable to speak, and Cynthia took it in both of hers.

"I have wanted so much to meet you," Cynthia said in a big warm voice, "I have known Allen all my life. We are like brother and sister. I hope he has told you so."

"He has told me," Josui said.

She hesitated, she was not able to take her eyes from the wonderful fair girl, the eyes the bluest, the skin so white and smooth, the sweet full mouth.

"Take off your hat, Cynthia," Allen said. He was careless with her but he was glad to see her. "Make yourself at home, Cynthia, a poor place but our own. Josui, where are your manners?"

"I am so surprised," Josui murmured helplessly.

"Surprised at what?" Allen demanded.

"So beautiful," Josui said, still helplessly. "I didn't expect. You didn't tell me so."

They laughed at her, looking at each with understanding enjoyment. "Oh, you cute little thing," Cynthia said ardently.

234

"Allen, you didn't tell me how cute she is. I don't wonder that you are crazy about her. Why, I could pin her on my jacket, like a flower."

Josui laughed too then and fell in love with Cynthia. Oh, she was very glad to find her like this, a big kind girl, though so beautiful.

"Please sit down," she said, recovering herself. "I will get some tea. Allenn says tonight everything Japanese, please excuse me."

She bowed herself out of the room and into the tiny kitchen where she shut the door. She sat down on the stool for a minute to breathe. "Lennie," she scolded the unborn silently. "Do not jump, please. The apron covers something but not everything. You are not invited. Help your mother, please!"

He quieted at once as her heart quieted and then she got up and made the tea and poured it.

The room beyond the closed door was very quiet, too. She could hear their voices but not their words. They were talking, perhaps about his home, about his mother, things they would not say before her. This was natural, though she felt a little lonely, nevertheless, and she lingered over the tea-making to give them time.

". . . Allen, she is adorable," Cynthia said. "If your mother could see her just once, I believe it would make a difference."

"I thought that perhaps at Christmas—" Allen stopped.

"I thought of that, too," Cynthia said with sympathy. She was rich with sympathy. It glowed from her eyes and in her half-smile, in the ardor with which she leaned forward in her chair, toward him. She was without consciousness of

235

herself, and he saw this and he wondered, detached and yet half sadly, if he had never seen Josui, whether Cynthia would have or could have loved him, or he her. If his mother would believe that they could never have loved each other, it might now make her less invincible.

"I feel I can say anything to you," he told Cynthia.

"So you can, Allen," she told him.

"You know what my mother always hoped, about you and me."

"Oh, yes," Cynthia said instantly. She did not flush and her bright eyes were as tranquil as ever.

"Even if I had never met Josui?" he asked.

"Oh, I never thought of you so," she said robustly. "I am terribly fond of you, Allen, you know that. Dear me, I couldn't imagine life without you, then or now, but I don't believe that sort of fondness leads into marrying love, do you, honestly?"

"I suppose not," he said almost unwillingly.

"Why do you talk about that?" she inquired.

"If you could persuade my mother," he suggested. "Mightn't it help?"

She grew thoughtful, her fine white hands interlaced on her knee. "I see what you mean." She entered into the play. "Why not? I will do my best. I'll entice your mother in spite of herself, I'll tell her what a darling this little creature is—Josui—do I say her name right? And we'll see—we'll see."

"Cynthia, if you would—"

"I will," she said heartily. "Those eyes, Allen! So big and black, and the straight lashes. Are all of them like that—everybody?"

"Josui is much prettier than any girl I ever saw in Japan," he said with the restraint proper to a husband.

"Prettier than any girl I ever saw in America," Cynthia said generously. "I don't blame you for loving her. I'm all on your side. I declare war against the opposition!"

"You're a host, Cynthia." He felt excited. She justified what he had done and perhaps indeed she could do what he and his father had not been able to do.

"If your mother won't yield," Cynthia said, "I shall invite Josui to see me, and I'll invite everybody to a party and then we'll see."

"Oh, I don't know—" he began in alarm.

"Allen, no cowardice! We'll force her hand. You'll be there for Christmas."

She overwhelmed him with determination and optimism and warm energy. Perhaps, perhaps!

Josui came in at this moment with the tea, and Cynthia began to ask her about the tea ceremony which she had heard about and read about but which she did not understand, and Josui lost her timidity in explaining. No one else had asked her anything about Japan, and she enjoyed talking about her home, her father, her mother, the flowers, the tokonoma. Cynthia was charming in her curiosity, a genuine eager interest, Allen saw with some astonishment. He knew what Josui meant when she said no one had asked. Americans did not ask, it was true. They told, but they did not ask. It did not occur to them. He listened to Josui's sweet, rather hesitating voice. She had quite forgotten him. She was talking only to Cynthia, enjoying it. Had she been lonely? He sat watching her, tender toward her, remorseful that he had been so often grim. Did she understand the torture of his doubts of what he had done? Perhaps Cynthia would help them both. It might, it must, end well.

The fragrance which Cynthia's presence infused had its permanent effect, when she was gone. Her large sincerity created a glow of tenderness in Allen, and for the first time in many weeks he turned to Josui with something as nearly humility as he had ever felt.

"You were sweet," he told her, "the sukiyaki was the best I ever tasted. Cynthia thought the flowers were beautiful and I told her that no one could arrange them as you do. You're so pretty, little Jo—Cynthia said so."

He was seeing her true again, doubt had dimmed his eyes but now he was seeing her through Cynthia's eyes. Josui was pretty, she had a kitten charm, her little frame, her tiny hands, so neat in their precise movements, her careful absorption in all she did, all was charming once more. He could depend upon Cynthia. It was only a matter of time. His mother would believe what Cynthia said.

They were almost happy enough again. Allen was so kind that Josui nearly told him about Lennie. She would have told him except that she perceived his happiness was still bound up with his home, his family, his town, the world he had been sheltered in during his childhood. She could not be sure of happiness until he could make a world for themselves apart. When he could do this, when she was sure that he had transplanted himself from the past into the present, when they could leave this little box in which they lived and find a small house somewhere with a garden which he could consider his home, then she would tell him. But would all this happen in time?

"I am eating too much," she said, trying to laugh. "I am getting so fat. The air here in America is too good for me."

She made her pretenses and hid herself behind them, waiting. But until when? Cynthia wrote a letter to Allen. It lay on the table by the door and Josui did not dare to open it. There was something between these two, the long memories of childhood, and she had no right to come between. She trusted Cynthia with her whole heart, but there were the long memories. When Allen came home she held up the letter.

"Today, for you, Allenn."

He tore the letter open quickly just as he stood and she watched his eyes slip over the big pages of thick creamy paper. This was an important letter—she could see that upon his face. He crumpled it suddenly, threw it in the waste basket, and strode toward the bedroom.

"Not for me to see?" she called to his retreating back.

"Read it if you like," he replied without turning his head. She had to know sometime, he thought bitterly.

So she picked it out of the basket and straightened it carefully before reading it, smoothing the paper. Such beautiful paper it was, so soft, almost like handmade paper, except that nothing in America was handmade, she believed.

Dear Allen—[so Cynthia wrote in big loose letters, flowing across the page, the ink a dark violet]

I went to see your mother as I told you I would. I told her about our darling little Josui, described her, said all I felt.

I wouldn't let her get in a word—you know how she is, her voice just runs on like a silver stream, and she outtalks anybody when she wants to. I did the talking and she had to listen. I thought I was making great headway and I was mentally planning our Christmas party. She let me finish without answering a word. But I should have suspected that she held the trump card all the while. You know that look she gets, that adamant, diamond-bright certainty, when, damn it all, she really is right.

Allen, why didn't you tell me about the law? There's a law. That was her trump card, "My dear," she said, "even if I did what you want me to do, there's the law."

I wouldn't believe it until I talked with your father. Isn't it queer how you can grow up in a place and never care about the laws? There is a law, Allen. You can't be married to Josui in our state. Your father said it would be impossible to change it—he said people have to be ready for such a change. Feelings make laws and the feeling has to change. But nothing has changed in our town since it was begun, two hundred years ago.

I keep thinking about Josui. You're a man and you're on your own ground. I reckon you had better build yourself up somewhere else, Allen. What a mess the world is!

Yours as always,
Cynthia

Josui read every word carefully and understanding welled up in her mind and seeped through her being like poison. The gates of America had closed on her again. She was not married to Allen at all. The law forbade it. She could never be married to him. Lennie, Lennie!

She put the letter into the drawer of the small desk. She

went into the kitchen and basted a pleasant little roast she had bought in the morning and she lifted the lids of the two pots where vegetables waited, steaming hot. Why had Allen not told her? But she knew that he could not bear to tell her. So he, too, had his secret, a fearful secret. She understood everything now, why he had been so sad, why so often impatient, why so restless. He was very restless, and she had wondered if this was true of all American men. He could not sit quietly in the evening, even with her. His impatience was a rising energy, exploding at last into a tempest of passion that was almost ferocious. Then he slept, exhausted. But the cycle would begin again. She had wondered so many times why there was no peace in his love. Now she knew. Tears burned her eyes and dropped upon the floor. Her love was transmuted into anguish. What would they do?

When he came out of the bedroom, changed into his slacks and an old shirt and his leather bedroom slippers, she ran to him with outstretched arms.

"Oh, poor Allenn," she sobbed. "I am so sorry. It is my fault to marry you. I make you unhappy when I like happy. How can I do?"

He held her hard in his arms and spoke bravely. "We'll live somewhere else, Pittysing." Oh, it had been weeks upon weeks since he had called her the precious silly name. "We'll build us another home. We'll forget the old house in Virginia."

"But your ancestors made that house for you," she mourned. Ancestors were like gods. Can gods be forgotten?

He patted her back, he soothed her shoulder with nervous quick movements. "I reckon they made it for themselves. I

241

reckon we can make another for ourselves. I'll get rich. I'll make a bigger house. I'll shame them all."

She felt his heart thumping under cheek. He was angry, he was hurt. He wanted his own way. She stood, feeling the angry heart beating not for her but for himself, and she grew still and her tears dried. She must keep her secret, after all. A world of peace and safety cannot be built upon anger. No, she must think, she must wait, she must consider what to do. The child would be born against the law. Love had made him a tiny criminal, innocent as he was. They were all innocent, but upon him the punishment must fall. They could part, they might even forget, but Lennie would have nowhere to lay his head. Oh, what thinking she must do about this!

"Come," she said. She drew away from the thumping angry heart. She wiped her eyes on the full short apron that somehow she never took off, pretty little lace-fringed aprons that seemed merely to decorate her frocks. "I have a nice roasting beef, Allenn. We will eat and we will feel better then. Come—come."

She twined her fingers into his and they sat down and she put the hot food upon the table. She enjoyed cooking and each dish was served with the touch of taste that was natural to her, a fringe of fruit or vegetable, a dash of color, an arrangement to entice the eye first. He noticed it now though often he did not, and he caught her in his arms, "Josui, I swear it will make no difference!"

She made her usual gentle protest. She put her warm square little palm on his mouth. "No swearing, please, we just live, that's all."

To his surprise, she seemed exactly as usual. He could not believe that she understood the full weight of Cynthia's letter. He was never sure of how much she understood, he had never fathomed the gaps in her knowledge of American ways. She seemed to know all, to accept everything, and then suddenly he would find that some crucial point she had not grasped, or comprehending had rejected it as insignificant. With her robust sense of life and living, perhaps even the law made no difference to her. Suddenly his spirit relaxed. He was glad she knew. Now he would wait, live, as she said, do his work, and solution would be found perhaps simply in living. He ate heartily and after his meal he felt weighed down with sleep.

"Wonderful dinner, Pittysing," he muttered. He flung himself on the couch and fell into sleep.

Josui never asked him what he would do. She did not mention the evil day, the letter from Cynthia. She continued unmoved, he thought, careful to please him, and now no longer puzzled, she appeared settled in calm. He was immensely relieved. She understood in her Japanese fashion. She was grateful to him, and she would make no demands. When Christmas approached his father wrote him that it would make them happy if he could come home alone, even for a day.

"I suppose that being a Buddhist, your wife will not have association with this day, as we have," his father wrote apologetically. "I would come to you, if I were alone. But your mother would be cheered by your coming. She has not suggested it. This is my idea."

243

He took the letter to Josui and she read it without change of countenance. "Of course," she said instantly. "It is your duty. You must go. I shall be quite happy here. Maybe I will ask Mr. and Mrs. Sato to invite me to dinner also. Please make me happy—obey your father, Allenn."

But she did not go to Mr. and Mrs. Sato, although he was gone day after day. No one came to see her, and so she was alone with Lennie. Being thus alone with him, she communed with him, explaining that she did not know what to do for him. She asked his forgiveness, kneeling as though he were born and grown and standing before her, a man.

"You understand, my Lennie, this is not as I wish it." Thus she spoke to him in the silence of her being, in direct communication with his, and her feeling words crept into his unawakened mind. "There are two good houses," she told him, "in each of which you have a right to be born, my father's house, and your father's father's house. Why there is no room for you in either I cannot explain to you now. In Japan my father, your grandfather Sakai, is angry with me. When he learns that the Buddhist religion is of no value here, where there is a law, he will certainly be very angry. I shall have no reply to make to him because he is right and I am wrong. I thought because I was born a citizen here, I was right. But there is a law against you and me, Lennie. I cannot change it and your father cannot change it. Therefore I cannot tell him about you. Do not ask me why. Please forgive me."

Words like this she spoke in silence to him almost every day. The law, that was the great rock in the road, the impediment, the immovable obstacle that even love could not destroy. For she understood now that Allen loved not only her. He loved also his ancestors, his parents, his home, the place where he was born. These were all good loves and she could not blame him for them. But they divided him from her and she was a stranger to these old loves. It was necessary for him that he love within the framework of his own people and she was alien to that. He was not strong enough, she knew now, to leave the old and cleave only to her, to make with her a world that neither knew before. This she could do but he could not. He must not be blamed and she explained this to Lennie.

And all the time she was not lonely. She even ate very well, remembering that Lennie was now growing into a strong child within her. But what should she do when Allen came back? It was impossible to hide herself always from him. She could think of no answer to this question and so she simply went on living.

On New Year's Eve, though Allen had not come back, she heard a knock on the door. She went carefully tiptoe to open it, somewhat alarmed, although perhaps it was only Mr. and Mrs. Sato, come to bring her a small holiday gift. She opened the door cautiously. There stood Kobori! She saw him, solid and tall, garbed in correct western garments, hat and cane and gloves, his large smooth face smiling, and in his hand a box of flowers.

"Kobori!" she cried, unbelieving and suddenly happy.

"I told you I was coming to New York on business," he said.

"Oh, come in—come in," she cried. She was glad she was wearing a Japanese kimono. She had put on this dress when

Allen left her, obeying some impulse she did not try to understand. She had just now brushed her hair, for she had slept most of the afternoon. But there was nothing to eat in the apartment, not even a few sweetmeats.

He was in the room, taking off his coat and putting down the hat, the gloves, the cane.

"Are you alone?" he inquired, his voice amiable.

"Allenn is gone to his home for a few days," she said easily.

"And you?"

"Oh, I am well," she replied, robustly. "So well!"

"But you do not go to his home with him?" He stood large and quiet before her.

She shook her head. "Not yet."

"Ah," he said. He sat down, and she sank upon the small couch. "So!" he murmured, continuing to gaze at her kindly. "Tell me the truth, please, Josui. We are old friends."

"I will put the flowers into water first," she replied. She took the box which was still under his arm, and found that he had brought her Chinese lilies, exquisitely fragrant. At this season of the year in Kyoto, one could buy great knots of the bulbous roots, already sprouting thick creamy white blades tipped with jade green.

"I was afraid it was red roses," she confessed.

He shook his head. "Would I be so stupid?"

Then of course he saw what Allen had not seen. He perceived the existence of the child.

"So," he murmured again. "You are not alone here. There is a little third one."

She bowed her head over the flowers while she arranged them. "Allenn does not know."

Kobori looked astonished. He opened his eyes wide, and pursed his somewhat full lips. "How can a husband not know? Does he not wish a child?"

She sat down then beside the table where the flowers stood in the bowl, and breathing their fragrance, she told him about the law. She told him everything in very few words. It was all simple, plain, unchangeable. She found that she could say everything easily and without tears. He understood, and he listened without interrupting her, his big calm face moving slightly now and then.

When she finished he sighed deeply and leaned back in his chair. "Yet is it fair not to tell your husband? It may be that the child will change him entirely."

"Oh, no," she said quickly. "You do not understand. Here a child is not so important. It does not change everything as it does with us. Here the generations do not depend on one another."

"Nevertheless—"

"No," she said, impetuous and adamant. She found that she had really made up her whole mind. She would never tell Allen about Lennie.

"Josui, what will you do?" Kobori inquired gently. He was overwhelmed, aghast at what he had discovered here.

He had loved Josui well in his placid fashion, and when he knew he had lost her, he suffered, but not angrily or long. The pain now had subsided into an aversion to marriage with anyone. He expected this, too, to pass, and had indeed planned that when he had seen Josui once more in her happiness he could release his heart to a prudent and suitable marriage with some young woman his parents might choose for him, and provide them with grandchildren and himself with a family of his own generation. A man must have children.

His plans were demolished at once by Josui as he now saw her and he was as near agitation as he had ever been.

"I don't know what I should do," she said, head drooping again over the lilies. "I only know what I will not do."

Kobori said, sighing, "It is better for you to return to your father's house. At least let the child be born in Japan. There are such children there in the orphanages, you understand. The American men have made many children like this one. He can simply be one more."

"No," she said again.

"Not that either?" Kobori murmured.

They sat in silence, feeling mutually the fearful weight of inevitable birth. She saw him stretching his soul, his heart struggling.

"And you, my dear," he said after a while but in the same low voice, "do you still love the American?"

She lifted her head sharply at the question. It came from Kobori, but she had asked it many times of herself. Yes, she did love Allen, but it was with a dead love. She would always love him, but without hope. They should not have met. They were born apart, they should have lived and died on opposite sides of the world. Allen was not her mate, and she was not his. The gods had put them asunder, but they had disobeyed the eternal laws of the gods. She felt no rebellion and scarcely despair. She felt only a sorrow as deep as her life.

"It is no use to me to love him," she said simply.

They sat in long silence again, each musing. He spoke at last, hesitating, and with great delicacy. "I wish to say something. I do not know how to say it. Forgive me if I should keep silent, and do not."

"Please speak," she replied, not turning her head.

He moistened his lips. "If ever you wish to return alone to Japan, please return to me."

The sweetness of the lilies was suddenly too much and she pushed the bowl away. She understood at once. If she did not have the child, that is, he wanted her for his wife.

"I have the child," she said.

He did not meet her eyes. He looked down at his large pale hands clasped upon his knees. "I wish I could take this child," he said. "I wish indeed that it might be so. For myself, were I alone, having no parents to consider, no ancestors, I would do so. At least, I believe I could do so."

He was honest, troubled, yearning to be generous and certainly to be kind. She understood all this, but her sorrow was not lightened. "I thank you," she said. "Sometime I may remember this that you have said. I do not know."

She got up resolutely. One word more would be too much. Sorrow brimmed her being. She would break if another word were spoken.

"I must make you some tea," she said in a bright voice and she moved toward the kitchen. "At least I have tea. I am so lazy that I have not gone out to buy sweetmeats."

He let her make the tea, watching her through the open

door. It did not occur to him to help her, for he was used to being served, and she did not expect him to be otherwise. She brought in the lacquered teapot and two bowls of fresh green tea, a small luxury which she kept in the house for herself. Green tea, the Japanese tea, was rich with vitamins and she drank much of it. She drank now when she had served him, holding the black and gold bowl in the curve of her hand.

"Tell me about my parents," she said. "They have not written to me, though I have twice sent letters to them."

"I know," he replied. "I called upon your father before I sailed and he told me he is still bitter. He does not believe that you should have disobeyed him."

She set down the bowl. "Please," she said bravely, "please tell him he is right."

He was amazed. "Josui, you who are so proud!"

"I am proud no more," she said humbly. "I cannot fight against the law of America. It is in the hearts of the people here. It is a feeling. They make their laws from their hearts, and they have such feelings. What can I do? Where shall I go that the child may be born? He has nowhere to lay his head."

Oh, when she said this, she suddenly lost all her pride and all her control. The dead calm in which she had spent these days broke away from her heart and she began to weep aloud, and terribly, holding her hands to her face and rocking back and forth.

Kobori was distressed to agitation. He put down his bowl and he stood alone here, wringing his hands. It did not occur to him to touch her. "Now," he said, "now this is very dangerous for you. Please, Josui, for your sake, this is so bad."

He waited, sighing and murmuring, until suddenly she stopped, ashamed. She wiped her eyes on her sleeves and spoke rationally, to his great relief. "You are staying here in America?"

"For several months," he replied, relieved. "I shall stay now, of course, until you know what you should do. Please tell me what you do. I beg this, at least. Here is my address. If I go away it is only to some neighboring city for a few days for business, and I shall leave the name of the city, so that you can reach me."

She took his card and set it under a small empty box on the end table. "If you do not hear from me," she said, "it means that I have no need to write."

"But indeed you must let me know," he insisted.

So she promised, seeing that he would not leave until she did. "Very well, Kobori. I will write to you what I decide. It may not be soon."

"I have your promise," he replied.

He went away then, careful of his hat, his gloves, his cane. They bowed deeply to each other at the door, and she waited at the door until the elevator came for him and they bowed deeply again and again while the elevator man stared. Then she went back into the room and locked the door. It was now perfectly clear to her what she must do, entirely for Lennie's sake. There was really no place for him in the world.

Josui had said, her face flushing with shyness, "Allenn, I do not write to you while you are at home."

251

He had been about to put his clean dress shirt into the suitcase. "Now why not?"

"I think it is disobedient to your mother," she had said. "It is to enter secretly the house she forbids."

He protested. "You are being absurd. You aren't angry because I am going?"

"Oh, no, Allenn. Just I don't write, for being polite to your mother. I wish to obey her."

So he did not expect a letter. At first he had not thought of it. When he entered the great welcoming hall he felt the old childish excitement, the relief, the conviction that here all was well. In the old days when he came home at Christmas from the military school in Lexington, he remembered this easing of the spirit, this blessed relaxation of the mind. Here was peace, here approval, here he was the beloved.

It was so exactly like the old days that when his mother came with her swift grace through the opened doors of the long living room, he turned toward her with the old compulsive love. She came with arms outstretched, the thin draperies of her silver-gray chiffon gown floating from her arms and foaming about her feet.

"My dear, dear boy!"

Her arms were about him, and the familiar fragrance enchanted his nostrils again.

"Well, Mother—" his hearty man's voice showed no trace of the quivering boy soul within.

"Welcome home, darling—"

"How did you know I was coming? I thought it was to be a surprise."

252

She held him off, laughing, her pretty face, so young under the silvery curls, all alive with triumphant laughter.

"Your father can't pretend, not for a moment, not with me. Oh, I knew! What—at Christmas? Darling!"

The gray chiffon enveloped him again like soft cobwebs. He felt her strong thin fingers twining and holding his right hand. "Come in to the fire. We have not finished the tree. You must reach to the top for the star just as you used to do. I didn't have a star there all the years you were away. Cynthia's here for tea."

She tossed out Cynthia's name lightly, leaving him no time to suppose a reason. Cynthia's here for tea. "Cynthia, here he is. I told you he was coming. I knew!"

Cynthia was wearing a holly-red jersey with her black suit and she had holly berries in her blonde hair. As usual they met exactly as though they had been together until ten minutes ago.

"Sit down," Cynthia said. "I've been pouring the tea. Your mother has one of her lazy fits today."

"That's because I'm so happy," his mother cried.

They heard the creak of the heavy library door, the shuffle of leather slippers and his father came in. "Who said tea? Watery stuff! Tell Harry to mix me a martini. Allen, you'll have one with me? Leave tea to the ladies."

"Very well, Dad." They clasped hands strongly and parted quickly.

Harry came in so soon that he must have had the martinis ready and he greeted his young master softly, "Howdy, Marse Allen, it's good to see you home again. Merry Christmas, suh—"

253

Well, such perfection still existed in this little town just beyond Richmond in the state of Virginia, and with all his strength, Allen thought, he would preserve the perfection in a wholly imperfect world. Perfection was rare, it was precious, it must not be lost, island in a stormy sea, safety in the whirl of disaster. He was suddenly acutely perceptive of every beauty in the room, the yellow roses, greenhouse roses that his mother grew in a world where the atomic bomb was also made, the dull-blue draperies drawn away from the western window to show the last of the winter sunset, the fire leaping up from wood laid across bright brass andirons, the satin-covered chairs and sofas, the polished floors and deep carpets, room opening into room, and all shining and clean, apparently without work or effort or cost to any one, though he knew well the cost. But he had the right to his inheritance, unless he chose to throw it away. Folly!

And Cynthia sat there by the small inlaid rosewood table whereupon was set the silver tea tray that was an heirloom, his to inherit with all else, and she would look like that, whatever her age, for she was blessed, too, with beauty, and here she belonged. The law was here, the protecting forbidding law, and he could take shelter behind it if he must.

The days passed in the traditional stately march of the days. He set the star aloft and he played a child again. They hung their stockings under the white marble mantelpiece that his great-great-grandfather had brought from a house in France long ago, and they laughed on Christmas morning at the freakish gifts, the toy monkey, the tiny bear from Berne, but in the toe of his stocking he found the black pearl tiepin which had been his grandfather's and this was treasure.

His mother met his reproachful eyes with a smile.

"Sometime, so why not now? I don't believe in heaping everything at once. I've told your father that I want to settle on you now what I have to give you, darling. We'll talk about that one of these days."

One of these days was always the next day and the next, and finally delayed because the family lawyer had gone to Miami for Christmas and could not be back until after the New Year. And New Year's Eve, surely, his mother said, was really as important as Christmas, because of the dance. Cynthia was holding many dances free.

So it was while he was dancing with Cynthia that this conversation took place.

"We've managed not to talk at all," Cynthia said.

"I've managed not even to think," he retorted.

"Still no plans?"

"None."

"While your mother weaves her webs?"

"Is she weaving?"

"Of course! When a woman loves a man, even if he is a son—only of course your mother loves you because you are her son, and she loves you much more than she ever loved anybody—a woman weaves her webs."

"Are you a weaver, too?"

"I try never to be," she replied almost brusquely.

He imagined a strange hostility in her blue eyes, she looked at him fearlessly and without evasion, but her eyes were not soft.

255

He ought, he told himself as they danced with all the old familiar ease, he ought, of course, to have gone back to New York, certainly not to have waited for an inheritance except that he had some greedy private notion that if he had more money now it would be easier to insist upon his marriage with Josui, easier, perhaps, to build his own house somewhere, change his roots, grow into his own created world. This justified delay, but he wrote to Josui after the dance that night, honestly troubled because he had felt stirred by the nearness of Cynthia, tempted perhaps by her unusual reserve, her steadfast attitude carefully maintained that of course he was married and therefore safe.

Josui did not reply, but he did not expect a reply. He would join her in a few days, at most. The New Year passed in exchanged visits, house upon house, friends in and out, and he dashing hither and yon between visits to make calls of his own, and never, not once, in any house was there any question asked concerning Josui, or his living away from home, no questions, and only the old sweet welcoming acceptance; the accustomed rapturous cries—"Why, Allen, you precious old thing, it's been ages!" all the high feminine cries, tinkling silver bells, meaning nothing because they pealed for every comer and meaning so much because they spoke a warmth of heart that was true.

It was a way of life, his way of life, and he could not be exiled from it, even by love. Yet what could he do to be saved?

In the night, when after another day still no letter had come from Josui, and still he had not telephoned her which he might have done, except she had said that this, too, was disobedience, in the night lying alone upon his boyhood bed, he considered desperately what he might do. It was of no avail now to beseech his mother or goad his father. The law was there, inexorable, beyond them all, sheltering his mother. Upon the law she could and would throw all her guilt and unwillingness. He could see her lovely eyes widen. "Why, Allen darling," he could even hear her voice. "It's not my fault, darling! I didn't make the law." But others like her had made it.

He took the only refuge he knew, and this was to stop thinking. He sank back into the comfort and the beauty of the solid and ancient house.

When Mr. Haynes, the lawyer, came back from Miami he was summoned to the library, and there he heard what his mother had done. She sat tense at the end of the long mahogany table, the winter sunshine falling across the room through the gold velvet curtains that hung from ceiling to floor.

Mr. Haynes nibbled the air when he talked, a small tight-faced old man, red nosed, and just now peeling from Florida sunshine.

"Allen, your mother has done a generous thing. She has put the house into your name. It belongs now to you."

He was dazed, he stammered out something, "But I thought the house was yours, Dad—"

His father sat in a chair near one of the tall windows. He said dryly, a dry gray figure in the glowing room, "I gave this house to your mother when we were married. We both understood, of course, that it would go to our eldest son, as it had come to me from my father. I felt that a woman ought to have a house. It is her safeguard against life."

"You'll leave me my corner, darling," his mother said. "I trust you for that."

"I don't approve of this," his father said.

"I don't want it," Allen said.

"Please, darling," his mother pleaded with him. "I want it to be so."

"I don't like it," he said again. But he did like it. He looked about the great room that now belonged to him. He might have suspected her of weaving her web, except that the law stood as it had stood before, whatever she did, sheltering her from good and from evil.

"I can't live here," he said abruptly.

"Perhaps someday you can," his mother said gaily.

So, he still unwilling and his father not approving, it was done as so much had been done all his life because his mother wished it. And when it was done he had a strange revolting sense of possession. It would have been his anyway, he told himself, trying not to exult. It was now his only a little sooner. Even if he had built himself a house somewhere, this would have been his, and then he would have had to decide finally and forever where he would live.

He left that afternoon for New York. It was night when he reached the city, night when his taxi drew up in front of the apartment house. A strange elevator man took him up, a man he had never seen before, someone newly engaged, he supposed, and he did not speak to him. He rang the bell of his apartment, expecting Josui to open the door instantly, and his remorseful heart quickened. Oh, he had a great deal to make up to her somehow.

But the door did not open. He rang again, for she might be asleep. She had a kittenlike way of sleeping at any time, curling up on the couch, or even among cushions on the floor. But the door did not open. He had at last to fumble among the keys in his pocket and find his own key and open the door himself. The apartment was dark. The air was close and dry with steam heat. The silence was absolute.

"Josui!" he called loudly.

There was no answer. He had turned on the light as he stepped in and now he ran into the bedroom. She was not there. The bed was neatly made, the floor was clean. He flung open the closet door and saw only his own garments hanging there. She was gone.

The conviction fell upon him with terrifying weight. She was gone! How could he find her? He knew so well the possibilities of despair in her Japanese heart. She had reached some ultimate unknown, hidden from him under her careful pleasantness, her dutiful sweetness. What she had seen, how much she had comprehended, he would never know. He sank down upon the edge of the bed, suddenly faint, overcome with grief and self-reproach. Then he hid his face in his hands and cursed himself in his heart, not because she was gone but because, in the midst of remorse and consternation and shame, he knew that he was glad she was gone.

# Part IV

Part III

J osui walked down the street quietly. Every day now
while she waited for Lennie to be born she took long
quiet walks, speaking to no one, and none speaking to
her. She remembered this street. It was surprising how much
she remembered of Los Angeles, how all came back to her.
It was familiar and yet it was not home, for more vivid than
anything else, she discovered, was the violent departure,
the anger and fury of her father when he knew that they
must leave the city. She had walked once to see the house
she remembered so well, it was occupied now by a cleanly
placid Negro family. She did not go in, but she saw the children playing in the small yard where she had used to play
with Kensan. Even their old swing was there; her father
had used metal ropes, and they were as good as ever. The
little dark children were screaming with joy, crowding the
swing.

Today, however, she was taking the next step in duty. She
had got up early, had bathed herself carefully, and had put
on a dark-blue suit, newly bought, the jacket pleated full
over her figure. The money which her father had left in the
bank in San Francisco was quite enough for this and for the
room in a cheap boardinghouse kept by a Mexican woman
who spoke little English, and enough, too, for her food. For

all else she must depend upon charity. Let charity do what love could not, let charity, too, allow what the law forbade. She had inquired carefully of a stranger the way to a child welfare agency and now she approached the house on a side street where the rents were cheap. She went in, the door being open, and sat down in a waiting room. Two other women were there, not women, girls. One was perhaps fourteen, a colorless child, with tired eyes. She was pregnant, her body swollen, her lips pale. She had no charm, no prettiness, nothing at all, except the simple femaleness which she had traded to some boy for a little pleasure in exchange, perhaps a date to go to a movie, perhaps even only an ice cream soda. Who knew? Her miserable garments were rags. A bit of torn and dirty lace hung from under her rayon skirt.

The other girl was weeping, a blonde girl, her hair dyed silver, her lipstick smeared by tears. She was thin and she coughed as she wept. Her legs in cheap nylon stockings were as thin as sticks, her hands were loaded with costume jewelry, and she wore no wedding ring.

Josui sat down and folded her hands neatly and waited. The young girl was called into the office and after a while came out again, looking cheerful. The blonde girl went in and Josui heard her break into loud crying. After a long time she came out, pulled down her veil over her swollen face and she too went away. The office girl looked uncertainly at Josui.

"Your name, please?"

"Miss Sakai," Josui said.

"Come in," the girl said.

264

So she went into a little inner office and saw a mild-faced elderly woman sitting behind a shabby desk.

"Miss Sakai."

"Yes, please."

"What can I do for you?"

"I hear you take care of children," Josui said uncertainly. For how did one begin to tell what she had to tell?

"You are expecting a child?" The elderly woman was professional and kind.

"Yes—not at once. But I must prepare."

"Have you no family?"

"None," Josui said.

The woman was writing down what she said in a neat clear script.

"You wish to keep the child?"

"No," Josui said. "I am alone. I cannot keep him."

She had practiced saying this and so the words came almost easily.

Oh, Lennie, Lennie, whom she cradled in her innermost being, how still he lay, as though he knew what she had spoken!

"My name is Miss Bray," the woman said kindly. "Can you tell me something about yourself?"

"I am alone," Josui repeated. "There is nothing to tell."

"Will you tell me who the father is?" Miss Bray asked. "I only want to help you."

"He is American, white," Josui said. "I am American-Japanese."

"I see," Miss Bray said reluctantly. She took time to look at her visitor. A beautiful young woman, reserved almost to

265

coldness, and how unfortunate it all was, for who wanted a child half-white, half-Japanese? But it was getting to be a common story with these wars breaking out in so many ungodly places. Only two days before she had been compelled to accept a Korean baby, two months old. Who wanted a Korean baby? Even the boarding homes did not want them. Mrs. Kisch was one of their best boarding mothers, but she said the Korean baby had given her the creeps with those eyes. Miss Bray had put him into a Negro orphanage, and had been uncomfortable ever since, because a Korean was really not a Negro.

"Will this man not assume some responsibility?" Miss Bray asked.

"I do not wish him to know," Josui said.

Miss Bray remonstrated. "Oh, my dear, you know that's not right, really! Men ought to know. They get off so easily and they ought not. Please! I could talk to him for you."

"No, thank you," Josui said, with finality.

Miss Bray lost patience. She had never in her life had a lover and she could not understand girls who did not want men to know what they had done. She put down her sharp pencil and straightened the eyeglasses on her thin nose. "Now, Miss—"

"Sakai," Josui said.

"Oh, yes—foreign names are so hard to remember! Miss Sakai, I was about to say it will be very difficult to place your child in any home. Adoption, you know, is almost impossible. No one wants to adopt a child of mixed blood. I have tried it before, and it just cannot be done. Neither side wants the child."

"I know," Josui said in a still voice.

"You must have some family," Miss Bray urged.

"None," Josui said faintly.

"You mean they will not have him?"

She could not answer, for she was determined not to cry and all her immense will knotted in her throat.

Miss Bray sighed. "Well, we will see what to do. Perhaps he won't look too queer, since he is partly white. I might find some boarding mother."

"Boarding mother?" Josui repeated.

"Someone who will take him for pay," Miss Bray explained. "Could you contribute toward his keep?"

"Yes, I think," Josui said.

She felt dazed. She had not really considered what might happen to Lennie, except that she supposed somewhere there might be an orphanage where children played on the grass under big trees. She remembered seeing such a place once long ago, somewhere near Los Angeles. The children looked happy, but then she had not seen them close.

"It would help if you could pay," Miss Bray said.

She took up the pencil and began writing again. "Where do you expect to have your confinement?" she asked.

"I don't know that," Josui said. She had triumphed against tears and her throat eased. "Wherever you say, please."

"You had better go to a hospital—I'll give you this address. Ask for Dr. Steiner—she's a woman doctor, a refugee, but kind and good. We'll take the baby from the hospital. I suppose you won't want to see him—"

"I do wish to see him," Josui said.

Miss Bray looked up from her writing. "If you are sure you don't want to keep him, I advise you not to see him."

"I must see him," Josui said.

Miss Bray shrugged her shoulders. She finished her writing. "What is the probable date?"

"I think in June," Josui said.

"Your address?"

She gave the address.

"Go to see Dr. Steiner now and then," Miss Bray advised. "You had better be checked regularly. If you change your mind about anything let me know."

The interview she had dreaded was over. Lennie could be born and he would be taken care of somehow. Josui rose and bowed gracefully. "Thank you, Miss Bray," she said.

"Don't mention it," Miss Bray said politely, thinking about something else.

Out in the waiting room three more women now waited, young, unhappy, not looking at each other. Josui stepped quickly past them and out into the mild morning. There remained now Dr. Steiner, whom she must see, but not today. She felt tired, and she was alarmed because Lennie lay so still. Did he know already that they must part?

She went to a small park and sat down to rest. Two or three mothers were there with their children and she watched them. They were all white mothers, and their children were white and this was pleasant, for such mothers and children could stay together. She did not allow herself to think of Allen. Whenever the image of him came into her mind she shut it away, blotted it out. He knew by now that they would never meet again. She had left no note, nothing, she had simply gone away, taking her clothes, her trinkets, everything she had brought, the little that it was. By now he would have let the apartment, and he would be at home with his parents. Only Kobori knew she was here, and she had forbidden him to come to see her until it was all over, until she knew what she should do.

"I wish to live alone until I have seen my son's face," so she wrote him, but she gave him her address, asking that he not come.

She reviewed again the desperate possibility that she might keep Lennie somehow. But how? Could she too live without home and family, only with a child? She understood very well how Allen had felt. She did not blame him. What he longed for was natural, and in itself it was good. Simply it could not include Lennie, even as her father's house, too, could not include him. No one was to blame, except the law was there, it was the law that forbade and yet could not prevent Lennie's birth because it had not been able to prevent the love that had compelled his conception. Law never considered love. She still loved Allen. She would always love him, as one loves the dead, whom the living cannot replace.

Dr. Steiner regarded with curiosity the beautiful Japanese girl. The pale and youthful face was expressionless, a *Noh* mask, one could imagine the eyes were dark holes in the mask. It was a strong face in spite of delicate features and that delicate skin which Oriental peoples seem always to possess. The strength perhaps was in the determined calm of this young girl who had obviously prepared herself for tragedy. Miss Bray had told her to expect Josui Sakai, and she had anticipated the experience. She had never known a Japanese, even though her native Germany had during the war considered Japan her hope in the East.

"And so you do not wish to tell me?" She now repeated for the fifth time.

"Please no," Josui said, without passion and without yielding.

Dr. Steiner was short, fat, and quite aware of her own square and ugly face. She bore no resentment toward anyone for her appearance. Early in life she had accepted the course of her life. It was hardly to be expected that any man would want to marry a girl who looked like a primitive hewn from gray rock. She was therefore extremely grateful for her excellent brain and giving up all thought of romance she became a scientist, but warmhearted. The last fragment of wistfulness in her heart was betrayed only by the humility and admiration with which she looked at any beautiful human being, man, woman, or child. This look she now bestowed upon Josui.

Josui, however, after many weeks, was far beyond reach either of admiration or of pity. She felt continually cold, spiritually and mentally, and this coldness penetrated so deeply into her being that she was chilled in her very blood. Actually her hands and feet were cold to touch and Dr. Steiner noticed this as she lumbered about the table upon which Josui lay under a sheet.

"Why are you cold, my dear?" she exclaimed. "The day is quite hot, for me, at least."

"I am usually cold," Josui replied.

"Relax yourself, please," Dr. Steiner commanded. "I cannot examine such stiff muscles."

But Josui could not relax. She continued to lie as stiff as a marble statue, which indeed she resembled. She was in a tensity of waiting. She did not think, she did not feel, she would not remember. Every week she received a letter from Kobori, a kindly long writing, full of pleasant detail and steadfast goodness. He did not press her for decision, but she knew his expectation and put it aside. First she had this great task of birth. Until she was separated from Lennie she could not decide where she would go or what she would do with her life. As far as possible she waited without thought or feeling. Yet sometimes in the night when she could not sleep, when she lay upon her narrow bed, the mattress so thin and hard beneath her, and she dared not take a sleeping medicine because at least Lennie must have his full chance to live, then sometimes, very suddenly, she began to feel, not to think, only to feel, as though blood broke from a bandaged wound. Then all her feeling was agony not for what was past, but because she would never see Lennie, never live with him, never watch him grow, never hear him speak or see him smile, never bathe his active body, never know him as he was to be.

For, after long searching feeling, she had come to believe that Miss Bray was right. She must not see Lennie or she would not be able to leave him. She knew, or she feared, that once having seen his face, it would be so. Then she mourned with a grief passing all other grief that women know, a broken heart indeed, but broken because it was her own doing, and mingled in the sorrow was the sense of wrong to

Lennie. So small, so helpless, so innocent, so unprepared, she must leave him to make his way alone. For here it was—even if she kept him it would do him wrong. Here it was, that he had done no wrong. He had marched into life by all the laws of nature, love had performed its duty, the call had summoned him from the previous shade, and he had come joyously. For he was a joyous child, of that she was aware. The movements of his body within hers assured her of his vivid happiness. He swam like a little fish at dawn, when the mountains first tremble with the light of day. He waked her from a night of weeping to assure her of his laughter, waiting to be loosed. This was the crisis of her pain, that she would never hear him laugh.

"You are getting on nicely," Dr. Steiner now told her. "Everything is normal. You are healthy. Your body is functioning in spite of all."

"Thank you," Josui said. She got off the table and began to put on her clothes. Being modest she turned her back and Dr. Steiner gazed at the shapely form, the ivory-pure skin, the soft and dense black hair.

"Please come to see me each month," she said abruptly, her accent very strong and German. "At the time of delivery I shall be with you. There will be no trouble, I think."

"Thank you," Josui said again in her gentle voice. She put on her last garments quickly, twisted her hair again, and went away.

When she was gone Dr. Steiner telephoned Miss Bray. "I have examined the young Japanese girl," she said in the loud voice she always felt it necessary to use on the telephone. "She is an extraordinary creature—very beautiful and very healthy. Surely someone will adopt this child. It is clear the girl is an aristocrat. Such a female does not choose a stupid male, therefore the child will be intelligent as well as handsome and healthy. Is there not some one among your waiting parents who will understand this treasure?"

"You would be surprised," Miss Bray's voice came over the wires nasal, dry, and pessimistic as ever. "We have a waiting list of three hundred and seventeen pairs of would-be parents, all clamoring for children who do not exist, all blaming me because I can't produce children for them, but I can bet you a dollar that not one of them will want this baby."

Dr. Steiner shouted. "Hah! Such democracy makes me think about damned Hitler! I myself am one-eighth Jewish, but for Hitler I was a whole Jew."

Miss Bray did not answer this. She was prudent and long ago she had learned to believe the worst about every human being. She rather liked the oblong squat woman doctor, who said exactly what she thought, and she knew that Dr. Steiner liked her also in an abstract fashion. The two had often occasion to work together, Dr. Steiner always quarreling when Mexican and Negro babies were relegated ruthlessly to overcrowded orphanages.

"Nobody wants them," Miss Bray said patiently again and again. "White people wouldn't think of taking them and the Mexicans and Negroes already have too many, don't you see?"

"I do not," Dr. Steiner snorted. "A child is a child is a child, isn't?" She made a grimace instead of a smile. But Miss Bray had never heard of Gertrude Stein and she imagined that Dr. Steiner was merely being German in some obscure way of her own.

Seeing this Dr. Steiner had once demanded abruptly, "You never had a child did you, Bray?"

Miss Bray had blushed and then turned white. "After all I've seen I wouldn't think of bringing a child into the world, even if I could. I'd like to stop the whole business for a hundred years."

"Then start over?" Dr. Steiner said with interest.

"Only with legal permission and documents to show that the child can be provided for," Miss Bray said with more spirit than she had ever shown.

Dr. Steiner had chuckled. "Maybe there wouldn't be any parents at the end of a hundred years."

"There'd be somebody who sneaked and had a baby," Miss Bray had declared with habitual hostility to reproduction.

"Well," Dr. Steiner demanded sharply now over the telephone. "You don't speak?"

"I am thinking," Miss Bray said rather feebly. "I can't think of a thing. I guess he'll just have to go into the west-end orphanage."

"They haven't three feet to put another child in," Dr. Steiner shouted.

"Well, what shall I do?"

"This is your business, Bray," Dr. Steiner shouted in the same loud voice. "I bring the child out alive and good. That is my business only."

She slammed the receiver down and wiped her sleeve across her forehead. She always sweated when she was angry and she was often angry. She shouldn't allow herself, because she was so fat. America was full of good things to eat and she did eat, after the starvation in the camps in Germany. Her shape was of no interest to anyone. Never mind —she had no wish to live long, even in America.

She bellowed to her timid nurse. "Next case—quick!"

The strange months slipped by. The days were empty and the nights were hollow shells of darkness. Josui wept less and less often as the moment of parting drew near. Her mind receded and her heart slept while her body made ready for its ordeal. Birth is a battle between woman and child. The child fights against the mother for its own freedom, and the woman hoards her own life. She shelters herself that she may live to bear again, or even merely to live. Her task is finished, the duty of the body to her generation is done, she withdraws, she lies back fainting.

"Ah, ha!" Dr. Steiner gloated.

She drew out the child for whom she had been waiting, a small plump little boy, perfectly formed, a few days late, all details complete. She had been waiting with astonishing interest and even impatience for this child. All during the spring she had noticed at first with amusement at herself and then with excitement, her absorption in this unwanted child. He would be extraordinary, this child, a world child she had begun to call him, an adventurer, born in spite of all laws and hatreds, a bold child, creator of a new world.

"Ah," she said softly, looking down at the child. She knew that his eyes could not focus but he seemed to see her. He had enormous black eyes and a gay tiny face.

275

"A little boy!" she called to Josui.

Josui, sleeping under anesthetic, did not reply.

"Do not take the baby away," Dr. Steiner ordered the nurse. "I wish to tend him myself."

The nurse wrapped him in an old clean sheet and placed him on an empty bed. Dr. Steiner went to the bed and gazed down at Lennie. Little indeed did the young mother say, but this morning just before she went under the ether she had held the cone delicately away for a few seconds and then she said very distinctly to the waiting doctor.

"Please, two things to be remembered. I do not wish to see the child. He is to be named Lennie."

"No surname?" Dr. Steiner asked.

"None," Josui replied. Then, gripped with pain, she had put the cone resolutely over her face.

"Lennie," Dr. Steiner repeated experimentally. The name suited him. He had a smooth little face, quite pale, with no redness, and his tiny body was perfect. He was a small baby, only a little over five pounds, and he had been born easily. Indeed, when he emerged from his prison it was almost sportively, carelessly, certainly lightheartedly.

He looked up at her now, impatient, or so she imagined, for laughter. She was amazed, for did not newborn babies simply continue their long sleep? Not so Lennie. He was ripe for life, and the ugly tenderhearted woman felt a turning within her breast, a stir, a yearning. She was not maternal, she had not longed for children, perhaps because she had never allowed herself to hope for a child. Her approach to the newborn was one of respect for an unknown human being, an arrival, who must as carefully and thoroughly as possible be prepared for a long and healthy life. The body was her concern, indeed her duty, and beyond that she had never allowed her thoughts and curiosities to explore. But Lennie was someone the like of whom she had never seen before. Wrapped in his white sheet, his tiny hands clenched under his chin, his black eyes, huge and already clear, regarded her with appraisal. "So you," the child might be thinking, "you are a human being!"

Pity that this gaze did not fall upon the young mother! She turned to the patient and watched the tasks which the nurse now performed about the bed. They were quite routine. Josui slept as though she did not wish to wake. She lay relaxed and unconscious, and so pale that the doctor again felt her pulse. No, it was young and strong. She was quite normal. She simply did not wish to wake and the wish made the anesthetic more potent.

"Take her away," the doctor said. "She does not wish to see the child."

Two orderlies waited outside the door and at the summons of the nurse they came in and wheeled the bed away. Another nurse appeared for the child. Dr. Steiner commanded her to wait.

"I wish to examine this child very thoroughly," she said. "I will wash him myself."

The nurse did not reply. Every one in the hospital knew the stubbornness of this woman doctor, the German that she was, incomprehensible, demanding an exactitude of performance that created rebellion everywhere, and yet so competent that reluctant admiration compelled obedience. In this mixed mood the young American nurse, half contemptuous, half understanding, brought a basin of warm water, soap and clean gauze, a sterile towel. Without the slightest hurry, forgetful of other patients who waited, Dr. Steiner washed the tiny boy carefully, noting every detail of a frame sturdy and yet minute, the square set of the shoulders, the good shape of the intelligent head, the composure of the small mouth, and then again and again, the extraordinary eyes.

"A very remarkable child," she remarked to the nurse. "There is something here. It is more than the individual, you understand, nurse? There is a racial bounty here, which one often sees when races mingle. This is what Hitler never understood. When old stocks cross, something new is born. Ah, yes!"

The nurse scarcely listened. She was a red-haired young woman with a pretty pink face and her mind was on her own affairs. She had yet an hour to go before her eight-hour shift was over for the day. Then she had a private program for the hours until midnight, each item delightful and to be spent in the company of her present young man whom she might or might not marry. He was certainly not Japanese or Jewish or German, or any of the strange breeds. He was a good American.

Nevertheless, she was not cruel, and when Dr. Steiner placed the child in her arms she received him with the semi-tenderness which her training had told her was the proper attitude for small babies. It was now accepted that a baby did better if there was at least an imitation of tenderness in his early life. Every day each baby in the nursery was held for fifteen minutes by appointed nurses, and thus the infants received the impression of maternal warmth.

"Place this child in the corner crib," Dr. Steiner ordered. "I shall come every day myself to see him."

"Very well, Dr. Steiner," the obedient nurse replied. She carried him away, removed from the corner crib a small girl who was the seventh child of an Irish policeman, and put Lennie in the crib. She should have changed the sheet, but the newborn child was half-Japanese, he could not easily die, and the Irish girl baby was also healthy. The hour was speeding by and she had many small details yet to finish before she could hope to pass the head nurse without fear of delay. Quickly she put the few necessary garments upon Lennie, laid over him the pink flannel blanket which had been over the little girl, and left him to sleep. When the new nurse came on she would report the change in babies, that Dr. Steiner would come herself to see this baby, that details must therefore be attended to with care if the doctor's always short temper was to be avoided. The German was not afraid of anyone and when she was angry she bellowed long harsh German words which no one understood but which were unspeakable in sound and meaning.

Before Dr. Steiner went home that night she tramped into the nursery and went at once to the corner bed. There he lay, the incomparable child, and now he was peacefully asleep. He lay stretched out, not curled as are most new arrivals from the womb, but testing his tiny length, his hands relaxed. She took one of the hands, so infinitely small, so perfect. Yes, it was quite relaxed. She had read that the children of Asia did not clench their fists as the western children did. These fingers, delicate, pointed, were as softly loose as flower petals. Such children came into life, perhaps, accepting their fate, unresisting, wise with the wisdom of ancient peoples in their blood. Interesting speculations upon which she brooded, there was so much beyond the body which could be only imagined now but which someday might be known, someday when the human brain concerned itself with life instead of with death. And then, still gazing at Lennie, it occurred to her to remember his loneliness, how nowhere in the world was there a single human being who cared whether he lived or died, none who waited for him, now that he was born. Where would he go when his brief days in the hospital were over?

She left the crib abruptly, and went home by her usual circuitous route of two trolley cars. Her house was a small ugly modern bungalow outside the city. She had tried to live in an apartment and had found it unbearable. A house she must have although she was a bad housekeeper. She locked the door when she went away and now she unlocked it, as usual jamming the key because she pushed it too hard into the keyhole. She always got up early in order to leave the house reasonably clean. Now here it was as she had left it, and as she liked it to be, graceless indeed to any eye but her own, the table piled with books and pamphlets, except where a straw place mat held a knife, fork, and spoon, a plate and a cup. She went about the small house, the two rooms and a corner cupboard of a kitchen, a bathroom into which she had to insert herself sidewise, and she talked heavily and aloud in German as she trundled about the rooms bathing and putting on a faded cotton wrapper, and then heating the soup and spreading the thick slices of brown bread which made her supper. Muttering and guttural, she inquired of herself whether she was mad, what she would do with a child, how could she afford to hire someone who would understand that this child was a miracle, a human being not expendable, a creature too valuable to be thrown away. She sat down at the table and carefully removed her false teeth, both upper and lower plates, and then in comfort she chewed upon her bare gums, the bread softened in the soup. She had lost all her teeth in the concentration camp. Some of them had been knocked out, some had fallen out. She wore the plates for the sake of those who had to look at her, but when she wished to be comfortable, to be herself, she took them out. Sometimes when she had a difficult and dangerous operation to perform she startled the nurses by wrenching them out of her mouth and handing them to the nearest one. "Take care," she commanded most sternly. "They cost me very much—a fortune!"

When she had eaten she brushed the teeth carefully and dropped them into a glass of antiseptic by the kitchen sink. She washed her dishes, set the straw mat again for the morning, and then sat herself in a large stuffed chair covered with faded red velvet. Beside it was a square table, and upon it were a telephone, magazines, books, pamphlets, manuscripts, a cigar box, a saucer of kitchen matches, and a cracked plate for an ash tray. She opened the box and took out a cigar, lit it and smoked in outer calm but in furious inward thought.

Then after ten minutes or so she reached for the telephone, dialed, and holding the cigar in the corner of her mouth, securely wrapped about by her wide lips, she conducted a conversation.

"Bray, is that you?"

Far off she heard the fatigued voice of Miss Bray. "Yes, Dr. Steiner."

"The baby was born today."

"What baby?"

"Bray, please, do not be stupid! The baby you sent me to be born from the beautiful Japanese mother. How can you forget?"

"Oh, yes."

"Bray, can you hear me?"

"I could hear you better if you didn't talk so loud."

Dr. Steiner could guess that Miss Bray was tired and inclined to be pettish.

"How can it be you don't hear me because I talk loud?" she demanded. "This is nonsense." She raised her voice. "Bray, I have made up my mind. I take this child."

She waited for the effect of this enormous announcement. Miss Bray remained silent.

"You hear me, Bray?"

"Yes," Miss Bray said afar off, "I hear all right. But we aren't supposed to give babies to women who don't have husbands."

Dr. Steiner snorted. "How many husbands in the orphanage? You told me you put this child into that orphanage. He will get diarrhea and die. Ten babies this year it has been so. I will not have him the eleventh. I keep him. If you get into some trouble, let them come to me."

The day had been long and hot, and there had been an

unusual number of sullen young pregnant women. Miss Bray was weary of sex and all its consequences and she did not for the moment care very much whether she lost her job. She had been thinking for some time that she would apply for work in the county home where the men and women were old and where even though they sometimes fell in love there could be no possibility of pregnancy.

"Oh, all right," she said quite crossly. "I suppose they won't notice one baby more or less. I know I can't get him adopted."

"I adopt him!" Dr. Steiner shouted.

"Well," Miss Bray said in a dry voice. "I hope you won't regret it. I'll get the surrender from the mother and turn it over to you."

"Good," Dr. Steiner bellowed. She banged the receiver into place and sinking back into the chair she smoked ruminatively upon the shrinking cigar.

When Josui was confronted with the paper of surrender, she hesitated. This was what she had decided upon and she must sign it. Yet she felt unable to do so because of a strange feeling of unfulfillment. Upon this paper there was no name on the surrender except the name of the agency, and she did not know where the baby was going. Yet it seemed quite beyond her strength to put her name upon a piece of paper which gave Lennie to nobody except an agency.

"Is no one to take the child?" she asked Miss Bray.

"It is better for you not to know about that," Miss Bray said dryly.

Josui heard this without answer. Then in a sudden little

spasm she bent her head and hastily she wrote her name on the line marked *Mother*. Her eyes fell upon the word. Yes, she was the mother, she alone could give the child away and now she had done so. Tears rose to her eyes and hung upon the long straight lashes. Miss Bray did not look up enough to see them. She took the paper and blotted it.

"I guess that's all," she said. "If you ever want to know how the baby is, you can write to us, or if anything happens to him we will let you know, but no news is good news, and I advise you just to forget about him."

"Thank you," Josui said faintly. She got up, wiped her eyes, and took her handbag. "Good-by," she said, still more faintly.

"Good-by," Miss Bray replied.

So Josui went out into the sunshine, feeling bereaved, though it was her own doing. She had promised to return once more to the doctor for a final check, yet she would not have kept her promise had it not been that the doctor was unusual, someone strong and kind in spite of bad temper, and above all, a woman. She had once or twice thought that she would talk to the doctor about herself but she had not done so. It was better simply to remain as she was, unknown. As soon as this examination was over, she would write to Kobori, he would meet her, and when they met she would decide what she would do. She knew at least that she would never write to Allen, never see him again, for though her love remained, it was for someone dead, or who perhaps had never lived. Life as it must be lived was familiar. It did not occur to her that a life of renunciation could be

284

lived here in California. California was remote for her now, though she walked upon its streets and under its sky.

She entered the doctor's office, looking composed and pale. Dr. Steiner was waiting for her impatiently. Miss Bray had told her that the young woman knew nothing about the baby and that she was to be told nothing. Dr. Steiner, snorting, had been prudent for once and had neither agreed nor disagreed. She had made up her mind about what she would do, and she began at once as soon as the young woman sat before her, holding her handbag tightly in both ringless hands.

"Now I tell you," Dr. Steiner said briskly, gazing at Josui with renewed pleasure in her pale beauty. "I want you to know, but say nothing, please, to Bray. I want not a quarrel with that good soul, who is always stupid." She leaned forward and lowered her voice importantly. "Now I tell you, I shall keep your baby! I want you to know he is with me, and also that he is extraordinary. He cannot be wasted, you understand, on some people who think he is not valuable. I keep him, I teach him how he is valuable, how he brings together in his one small being the whole world!" Dr. Steiner reached her short fat arms in a circle around the world. "I will make him a great man. How? Because he is something great already!"

Josui heard this with amazement and emotion. She, too, leaned forward, her bandaged bosom aching with its burden of useless milk, an unusual fountain of milk, enough, the nurse had complained in the hospital, to feed triplets. "So I may know," she breathed, "I know where he is!"

"You may know," Dr. Steiner said firmly. "You should

know, my dear. And I tell you he is wonderful. And I wish that you take the child for a while if you like to do so. You come to my little house and stay with him as you like."

"Oh, thank you," Josui said. All her resolve crumbled in wild desire. "I cannot stay long, please, but perhaps for one night?"

"You come," Dr. Steiner repeated. "Here is the key. You go there by yourself now and I bring him. You will sleep in the bedroom where is already a crib I have bought for him, and I sleep on the couch in the living room. Two days, anyway, you keep him by yourself. I am busy here. Stay more if you wish."

"But how will you—" Josui looked about the crowded office.

"I have arranged," Dr. Steiner said, "I have a good neighbor woman, kind, a grandmother but not too old, her children gone. She takes him when I am in office. It will do. Old women are best lovers of children—we know that children are the true meaning of life, the link between yesterday and tomorrow for us. Go now, and be ready for him. I am bringing him myself during the lunch hour."

Josui took the key from the blunt fat hand. She bent her head for a moment and laid her cheek against that hand and then she went out, unable to speak. She walked slowly, trying to think what she was about to do. Then she was to hold her baby, after all, her child and Allen's. She could hold him and wash him and feed him, and while he slept, what would she do? She could sew for him something to wear, little gifts, which perhaps the kind harsh woman would put away for him until he was grown, so that he might know his mother loved him. So she turned aside into a shop and there she bought pink and blue bits of flannel, needles and silk thread of pretty colors, and with this parcel under her arm she got on a trolley car and so came at last to the house which it seemed to her she recognized because somehow it looked like the doctor. She opened the door with the key and went in. This was Lennie's home. She stood looking about her, never to forget the impression of the one large room, the solitary place at the table, the book-lined walls, the big shabby chair by a brick fireplace full of ashes. Beyond the door was opened into the bedroom. She saw an old iron bed, very clean, and a new crib, painted pale blue. New small sheets and blankets were piled there, the bed still unmade. Her heart swelled and choked her, but she would not weep. She took off her hat and her jacket, and she began with her usual neat and compact movements to spread the sheets and blankets, and so to make Lennie's first resting place.

Thus began the holy week.

For it was a week before these two women could part. Lennie came home in Dr. Steiner's arms, and she laid him upon the bed which Josui had made. It was noon and the day was hot, but inside the house the air was cool. Josui had turned on the electric fan and had set a pan of ice below it. She set a second place at the table, she opened the refrigerator and found food and made a luncheon of what she found, a dish nearly sukiyaki, a cold salad, some thin toasted bread. She found also a box of bottles and a sterilizer and tins of milk and dextrose. These were for Lennie, but she did not know how to make his food. And then she felt her breasts ache again. Could she not let him drink at her breast?

When he came in she besought the doctor with her eyes, with the gesture of her hand at her bosom, unbuttoning the fastenings of her blouse.

"Poor creature, do so," Dr. Steiner said heartily. "I will dry up the fountain when the time comes. Take him."

So Josui, in a daze of happiness, received Lennie, and she went into the bedroom and closed the door, and there alone with him she fed him her milk. He seemed almost strange with her, he mouthed the nipple, so much softer than the one he had known, the rubber, the hard glass. Then suddenly he understood and he began to drink deep draughts of the blessed milk, his great eyes fixed upon her face. And she looking down into those eyes felt her sorrow round itself, she was complete in grief, so that she wept and her tears fell on his face. She wiped them away with her palm, and continued to gaze at him, trembling with love.

He slept soon, filled with milk, and she laid him in his bed. She hung over the crib, studying his face, his hands, his shape, his bare feet. She recognized Allen's mouth, the sweet curve of the lips, yet the firm chin denied the sweetness, this chin was like her father's. But the hands were hers, and the square shoulders came from someone unknown, hers being gently sloping, and Allen's not like these, either. Then she saw the eyelashes. They were American, for no Japanese had such lashes, long and curling upward from the Asian eyes. His eyes were of Asia, encircled with these western lashes. But whose lashes? Not Allen's, but from some ancestor of his, whose name she would never know, the extravagant lashes of a beautiful American woman, living or dead, whom she would never know.

The door opened and Dr. Steiner came in and silently the two women stood adoring the child.

Thus the holy week began. For one night and two days were only the beginning of the communion between the three of them. Josui told at last the brief history of Lennie's life. When she talked, she remembered things she had forgotten, or perhaps not even noticed when they happened.

"When we first stood together under the wisteria," she told, "that is, you know when we first—kissed—"

"I do not know," Dr. Steiner said. "I have never kissed a man. What happened to you?"

"We felt a stir of air, a whirl of some small breeze, although the day was still and there was no wind," Josui said remembering. "We felt another presence with us. Do you believe it could have been his unborn soul?"

"I do not disbelieve," Dr. Steiner said.

It was not only Josui who told Dr. Steiner. The doctor had remained silent in America in the presence of those who could never understand sorrow because they had known so little, those who had never known death because they had not seen the death of a million innocents, young and old, and now she told to Josui what she remembered and must remember until her brain was dust.

"At first, you must know, we could not imagine that they really killed little children of mixed blood. It was not your blood, but it was my blood, mixed with the Germans. They said we must have only pure blood—as though human blood is not pure wherever it is found! Your blood, my dear, is not different from mine. We bleed the same red stuff, though I am ugly old Jewess, and you are such delicate young Oriental girl."

And holding Lennie on her broad lap, her full skirt spread between her thick knees, she tried to tell Josui how he was the triumph of her faith. "He is so beautiful, this child. He proves what I know, that human beings in any crossing and in any mixture can be superb. You understand superb, my dear? It is a height."

Lennie had no time to sleep in the bed except at night when they were compelled at last to give over talking and sleep, the doctor lest her hand shake with fatigue when it held the knife tomorrow, and Josui because she was young and stretched upon a cross of love and loss. He slept in the arms that held him, the soft slender arms, the strong short arms. He slept when he was carried about the rooms, when he lay upon a wide and comfortable lap, or against a swelling bosom where he fed. He was wrapped in love. He was adored by the two, all his hidden first memory, enough to last his lifetime out, was of love and love and love. He was the most welcome child in the world.

And so there came the last day of the week, and Josui made ready to go. In the earlier days she had dreaded this last day, but now that it was here she found herself able for its arrival. She would not have taken Lennie away from this house. He was safe here. Outside there was no welcome, no waiting. But here he had no rival. The huge heart of this woman, who had lived through life and death, loved no one except all humanity and him. He was safe.

"Stay, my dear," Dr. Steiner urged. "We will live together, three of us. I earn enough."

But Josui would not stay. "He does not belong to me," she insisted. "If I stay, one day he will ask for his father. I cannot hear him ask the question I cannot answer. Let me go."

She was determined to go, determined to leave Allen even in this child, in whom she was startled sometimes to see a look that made her remember another look too like it in Allen's face, a laughing happiness that broke her heart because it had ended soon.

So she took the medicine to dry her breasts, she bound them tight again, she made ready to leave the house. She would go to San Francisco where Kobori waited and when she saw him she would know what she could do. Peace she bore in her soul, the peace of finished love. When the moment came to leave, she held Lennie in her arms. Upon his feet he wore small pink and blue shoes that she had made and embroidered in butterflies. Then she put him in Dr. Steiner's arms and stepping back, she bowed her deep Japanese bow. "Thank you," she said. "Thank you now and for all my life and his."

"Come back," Dr. Steiner said, holding Lennie against her shoulder.

Josui bowed once more. "Thank you," she said again. But she did not speak what she knew, that she would never come back. Her gift was final. Between the past and future no link held.

At the railway station in San Francisco Kobori waited. He had dressed with care, amused with himself as he did so.

Nevertheless, it was pleasant to look one's best, and whatever life destined for him, he could accept it the better for grace in detail. So much was beyond his control that it gave him some satisfaction at least to perfect small matters which he could control. He had chosen to wear a custom-tailored suit of a heavy cream-colored Shantung silk, correct for the somewhat unusually hot day. A mist hung over the distant mountains, and might by evening creep down to the shore, but as yet the sun prevailed.

The train was on time and he saw Josui before she saw him. She was beautiful and slender again, and though his heart rushed to meet her he knew better than to show impatience. She had, he hoped, recovered from the experience of love, but the newly recovered must not be overwhelmed, and he must in decency give her every chance to refuse him. He was depressed by his own honesty, for he could not enjoy good fortune unless he let her know the news that the papers had published since last they met. He had decided, after hesitation, not to write her the news but to tell her, so that face to face with her he might watch those glorious eyes and catch their least light of hope, which would on the other hand convey wisdom.

He took off his hat and approaching her quietly, he put out his hand in the western manner. This was less conspicuous on the railway platform than the Japanese bow.

"Josui," he said.

She had not seen him, but at the sound of her name she turned toward him.

"Kobori, how kind to meet me!"

She took his hand lightly and withdrew hers soon.

"I thought it was understood that I was to meet you," he replied.

They walked together closely along the platform and through the station, the porter following with her bag. He could not keep from looking at her face. She was not pale as he had feared she would be. She seemed calm, she looked well, there was a delicate color in her cheeks and her dark eyes were content, though remote. She was older, more quiet, more contained, but for him these qualities deepened her beauty.

He summoned a cab and helped her enter and then took his seat beside her. "I have arranged for us to have luncheon together," he said hesitating, wondering if he had decided too much.

"That will be pleasant," she replied.

He gave the name of the restaurant to the driver and then leaned back. She sat at a distance from him, her gloved hands folded over her brown leather handbag. She wore a light-tan suit, very plain, a white blouse ruffled at the bosom, a small brown straw hat. She looked somehow more American than he remembered and he felt mildly distressed by this, until he remembered that he had not seen her in western dress until now. Then he was surprised to see that it did not dim her beauty as it did for most Japanese women. Her features stood the test of severity, her profile was clear under the strange little hat.

But he found nothing to say. What should he say? He did not wish to ask any questions about the child. He did not wish even to know whether the child lived or what she had done with it. The child had nothing to do with him or now with her, unless of course the news he had to tell might change her mind, whatever her mind was, and that he did not know.

Josui turned to him after some minutes with a slight smile. "You are well?" she inquired politely.

"Quite well," he replied.

"And your parents?"

"They are well," he replied.

"That is good news," she said.

"Now," he said, "you are also looking very well."

She laughed. "Then we are all well!"

Fortunately the restaurant was near, the cab stopped soon, he paid the driver and tipped him too much and they got out. He would have liked to take her arm as he saw American men take the arms of women they escorted, but he was too shy to do so, and he led the way into the restaurant, a small expensive place, where he had already engaged a table and ordered the dishes. It was a Creole restaurant, the food was of New Orleans, and while he would have preferred a Japanese place with good Japanese food, he felt it better not to be recognized until Josui disclosed to him her mind.

The table was by a window which provided a good view of the bay and the cloth was white, the silver polished and the dishes clean. All was correct, and upon the table were some flowers he had bought, pale-purple asters and lemon-colored lantana.

He sat back in his chair which was too small for him and for the first time he felt happy and at ease. "Now," he said, "you must eat what I have ordered. It is considered the best

Creole food. It is not too different from the food of Asian countries, though spiced more than our own."

"I am hungry," she declared. "My appetite has returned now that I am no longer sad."

It was good news that she was no longer sad and he smiled broadly. Then he remembered his own news which in honesty he must give her. But he would wait until the soup came. The waiter was bringing it now, a silver tureen, not too big, and two bowls, and the ladle. When the bowls were filled, they looked at each other, he invited her to begin and they drank the soup without conversation. Both had been taught that one does not divert the mind of host or guest from good food.

There was, however, a long wait until the next course. "These shrimps," he explained, "which are to be the main dish, cannot be prepared until we arrive."

"We are not in a hurry, are we?" she replied.

"No," he said again. He wiped his mouth with his white linen napkin. "Not at all." He cleared his throat. "In fact, I welcome this time. I have some news for you. I do not know whether you will consider it good."

"News?" she repeated. Her mind flew to Allen first. But what news of him? Or perhaps it was news of her parents.

"Within the last fortnight," he said with painful care that she comprehend, "I have learned that in this state of California the judges of the court have decided that it is now possible for white persons to marry Japanese."

He looked at her with a deep penetrating gaze. She understood its passionate inquiry and she returned the look fully.

"What is this to me?" she asked.

"I thought you ought to know," he said. "I thought it might make a difference. That is, if you wish, you could write this news to the American whose name I will not speak. It is now possible for you to live here together."

"It is not possible for us to live together anywhere," she said. "It is no longer possible."

His heart was a big lump in his bosom, it slowed its beat, and he could feel the heavy muscle contract. "You mean you do not wish it?"

"It is not a matter of wish," she replied in a steady voice. "It is a matter of cannot." Then she broke, only a little. "Do you not see, Kobori, that I cannot? The law no longer matters. I know him now as he is. It is not enough for a life."

His lumpish heart actually shook his bosom.

"Do you mean you no longer have any—"

She spoke the word for him. "Love? Perhaps not—perhaps, yet, I have. That, too, does not matter. Love is not enough, either. It is not enough for me. Perhaps it is enough for Americans, but not for me. I know that now."

He drew in his breath with a long hissing sigh. "Does this mean that you will come back to Japan?"

"Yes, Kobori, as my father did."

The waiter came inopportunely at this moment carrying a tray and upon the tray was a fine pottery dish of shrimps. He set it down before Kobori with pride and placed the spoon and fork at his hand.

"You, Monsieur, will wish to serve Madame yourself," he suggested.

Kobori was surprised, and with awkward hands he took

296

up the utensils. Then he looked helplessly at Josui. "I have never done this before."

"Let me." Josui put out her slender hands and with quick grace she took the silver fork and the flat spoon. She was adept, she was skillful. "Hold out your plate, Kobori. I will serve you."

Gratefully he held out the plate. "Thank you," he murmured. He thought, watching her, how fortunate was it that he had kept the pink pearls from India, the true pearls, and he said tenderly, "Though I am the host, yet you do everything better than I."

She smiled and did not answer. It was quite natural to serve this large helpless man. She would be doing it, she felt, for the rest of her life.

The day was hot, too, in the little town in Virginia, a silent day in midsummer, lifeless, though the trees hung green and flowers glowed hotly along the guarding wall.

Mrs. Kennedy was fresh from her afternoon nap, and coming down the polished staircase, a slender figure in cool and cloudy blue, she paused to look out to the swimming pool. She had been wakened by the sound of voices and splashing, and for a moment she had felt a fury of indignation that she had been waked. Then she recognized the voices, Allen and Cynthia, and fury fled. The two were coming together. She had been so careful not to talk about Cynthia, not to take her for granted, ever since Allen came home last winter, sick with a terrible cold, an unexplained fatigue, a weariness almost sullen. They had gone at once to White Sulphur Springs to stay a month, and she had asked no questions until he had talked to his father. Even then she asked no questions. Tom had merely told her that the Japanese girl had packed up and left, not even leaving a note. Allen had resigned his job and given up the apartment and come home.

"Tom, it's a mercy." That was all she had said.

He had not replied to this but she was used to his unanswering silences. It was now understood that there was really nothing more to be said. It was nobody's fault, and perhaps the girl, foreign though she was, perceived that a woman could not give up her only son. She had been patient with Allen as she had never been, for her love had always been impatient, critical, demanding his homage. Oh, she knew when she offended because when she was crossed she could willfully offend. But now she let him contradict her and treat her with a new ruthlessness.

"Please let me decide for myself." He said that over and over again about the smallest matter, as, for example, when she urged him to try the blanc mange. He disliked the dish but she had tried a new recipe and it was delicious, the milk and eggs so good for him in his rundown condition. He was very disobedient and troublesome, almost as he had been when he was a little boy, but now she yielded to him everywhere because he had come home again.

She stood by the window looking fondly at the two who stretched themselves under the sycamore tree on the terrace. They were dripping wet but the day was so hot and never mind. They were beautiful, both so tall, but she must warn Cynthia not to allow herself to get heavy as she grew older. Married women, especially after the children came, were inclined to fatten, though she herself had never put on a pound.

She let the silken curtain fall and walked across the long cool room and touched a bell. Harry, the old butler, came at once, fresh and clean in his white duck suit.

"Harry, you mix some drinks and take them out to Master Allen and Miss Cynthia," she ordered.

"Yas'm."

"Make sure you have plenty of ice and take them on the silver tray, you hear? I don't like that old painted tin tray you keep using. Take out four glasses. Mr. Kennedy and I may join them."

"Yas'm."

He went away and she sat down, wondering if, were she and Tom to go out, they would be interfering with what might even be a proposal. For the last month she had thought that any day, any night, Allen would come and tell her, "Mother, today Cynthia has promised—"

She leaned back, careful not to damage her curls, and closed her eyes, smiling, waiting.

Cynthia was rubbing her hair dry with a green bath towel. Allen, lying on the grass at her feet put an idle question. "Do you choose a green towel because you like green, because you know you are most beautiful in green, because your bathing outfit is green—"

"I just picked up the towel as I came through the bathroom," Cynthia said. "But then maybe I did take it because it was green. Anyway, I wouldn't have chosen blue, let's say. Maybe it was conscious."

"Fully conscious as usual," Allen suggested, still teasing. "Maybe."

He lifted himself to his elbows. "How foolishly we talk!"

"We always have," Cynthia agreed. "I remember when you were about ten I used to think you were the silliest boy I knew."

"But you liked me?"

She hesitated, always wary. "Sometimes maybe I did."

The wariness irritated him and he seized it suddenly, determined to grasp it, to crush it as one does a thistle if one must.

"Look here, Cynthia, it's about time we came to grips."

She rubbed her blonde short hair furiously without answer.

"Cynthia, put down that damned towel," he commanded, and leaning toward her he seized one end of it and jerked it from her hands. She caught it and held it and they tugged.

"Silly again!" she cried.

He let go his end abruptly. "All right, but I am tired of the way you behave toward me. You know perfectly well what I want to say and you won't let me say it. You can't fool me—I know you too well."

She threw down the towel. "All right—say it. Let's get it over."

"Cynthia!"

Her blue eyes were burning, her lips were pressed together, and he felt vaguely frightened. Had he been too sure?

"Say it," she commanded.

"Damn you, I will," he said, suddenly angry. "I want you to marry me. You know that. You've known it a long time."

"All right, I don't want to marry you. It's time you knew."

She flung the words at him and he could not receive them, he heard and he could not believe. He had counted on her, he had thought for weeks now that she would marry him. Because of him, he thought, she refused all other lovers.

"I cannot think you mean what you say." He was suddenly dignified, he sat up and brushed the bits of grass from his bare legs.

Cynthia stayed the drying of her hair, she let the green towel fall, and looking down at him sorrowfully, she wondered indeed why the very possibility of love was gone. She was not articulate even when she was alone, she did not examine her motives, she was a creature of attractions and repulsions, and she had not for months found him attractive. The old habit of companionship held but the pleasure was gone. There was no more excitement in his presence.

"I am afraid I mean it," she said wistfully. "I wish I didn't."

He knew then that she did not love him, impossible though this was, made for each other as they were, so his mother had always said and his mother was right.

"I cannot accept it," he said gravely. "I realize now that our marriage is what I have lived for all these years. If you are thinking of Josui—"

"I *am* thinking of her," Cynthia said.

"You need not," he told her. "It is over. It is as though it never was. I wonder that I ever let myself be caught. I was away from home so long and though this may not mean anything to you, Cynthia, yet I hope it will—I never went

301

about with other Japanese women as some or most of the men did."

He could not be sure she was listening. Her hair drying in little curls about her face gave her an air of fresh almost childish grace. She stood as still as a statue, the green towel trailing from her hand.

She said, gazing across the lawns, "I think I know why Josui left you. I think she found she was going to have a baby."

"No!" he cried. "No, that at least is not true. She would have told me."

"I don't think she would tell you," Cynthia said, almost dreamily. "I think she just wanted to get away and be alone somewhere because she must have known that if your mother didn't want her, she wouldn't want the baby."

"Stop blaming my mother!" he cried passionately. "It wasn't her fault and you know it. You know there is a law—"

"Oh, pish!" She threw down the towel and leaning against the sycamore tree she folded her arms. "As if Virginia were the only state in the Union!"

"My home is here," he said.

"Oh, pish," she cried again but the tears came to her eyes.

He got up when he saw the tears and went over to her with his arms outstretched. "Cynthia, darling—"

She drew back, she cried out against him. "Don't touch me—I can't bear it!" And stooping she caught up the green towel and ran across the lawn to the gate in the low stone wall which opened to the grounds of her father's house.

He stood watching her flying across the grass, such a desolation in him as he had never dreamed of. Now actually his world had come to an end. When he left the apartment that day months ago he had been wretched enough, his head aching so that he was barely conscious enough to drag himself homeward for healing. Cynthia, that was what he had thought, Cynthia was at home, waiting for him. Given a decent interval, a time for wooing, weeks in which to forget and to persuade himself that he had not really loved Josui at all, he would take up his life again and be whole. Now he could never be whole. How could they go on living, she on the other side of the stone wall, and he on this?

It was not to be endured. He walked slowly across the grass to the house and nearly ran into Harry, bringing a silver tray of cold tall glasses. He suspected the hand of his mother and he ordered the old man sharply. "Take those back into the house, Harry. Miss Cynthia has gone home."

He strode ahead, and found his mother at the door, hovering, anxious, he could see. Better to have it all over with at once!

"Mother, I want you to know once and for all and then please don't speak of it, I have asked Cynthia to marry me and she has refused."

"Allen!" she cried in a whisper. "Why?"

"She gave no reason." He made a thin smile. "Perhaps I am not attractive to her."

He stood looking down upon her, tall, handsome enough to break his mother's heart, she thought, and behind his pride she saw his agony. "I think I'll go back to the army, Mother," he said uncertainly.

"Oh, darling," she sobbed and put out her hands.

"Please," he said, and refusing her he turned away and mounted the stairs to his own room.

Dr. Steiner sat with a huge white bath towel across her knees. "Now," she commanded. "Lift him up, Mrs. Markey. Sit him here upon my knees. I dry him, I put the powder on him—so."

. Mrs. Markey, a thin elderly woman in a neat gray calico dress sprigged with small white flowers, lifted Lennie carefully from his bath and set him upon the expanse of the waiting lap. He sat as erect as he could and smiled at Dr. Steiner bravely, though uncertainly. Unless he was in pain, which was never unless one of these two awkward and loving women stabbed him with a pin or delayed his bottle, he smiled at either or both of the faces. His Asian eyes, large and softly black, the slightest slant enhancing their size, were fringed with those extravagantly long and curled-up lashes, never seen on Asian eyes before. His sturdy upright body, small but fat, his square shoulders, his exquisite petaled hands, his little face amiable and gay, his mobile mouth and turned-up nose, sent ecstasy through Dr. Steiner's blocky frame. She paused in her meticulous and scientific drying of the beloved child.

"Mrs. Markey," she said in her lecturing voice, "observe, please, Lennie's hands. See how the fingers assume such positions. The first and the fourth fingers outspread with the thumb, the second and third folded, it is the movement of the dance in Burma, also in Siam, from there translated to other countries, doubtless also Japan. That is to say, the creators of the Asian dance forms took the first movements

304

of the living child as the primary expression of the human hand."

Mrs. Markey was an unlearned woman, but she looked respectfully at Lennie's hands. They were flying free as birds, he was all but dancing upon the secure bottom of his seat, trying, it seemed, to rise into the air if he could. He was bright with dimples and smiles, as vivid as flowing water and sunlight, different, as she well knew, from her own somewhat stodgy babies, one of whom, grown to manhood, lay moldering and undiscovered in an island jungle. Neighbors, when she boasted of Lennie, said to her, "How can you be so crazy about a Japanese baby?"

"Lennie ain't Japanese," she retorted. "He's different from any baby I ever did see."

"Especially," they said cruelly, "when your son was killed by a Jap."

She still bled at heart when her Sam was mentioned but she said, "It wasn't Lennie that did it, for sure."

But how could stupid neighbors understand how she felt?

An alarming change now came over Lennie. One minute he was as bright as the morning and then suddenly a look of consternation spread over his small intelligent face. He looked reproachfully at Dr. Steiner whom already he recognized as the central figure in his world. His rose-red mouth quivered, large tears hung on his lashes—a new gift, this accomplishment of tears.

"Quick," Dr. Steiner shouted in agitation. "He grows hungry. We waste too much time. Yes, yes, my wonderling! The bottle, Mrs. Markey!"

Mrs. Markey ran for the bottle. Dr. Steiner felt it carefully when it was in her hand. It was not cold, not hot. She set it down and slipped a small short-sleeved shirt over Lennie's head and pinned a diaper about his fat and compact thighs. He barely endured the delay, exerting the greatest effort of will, his feet and hands in a fury of flight.

"Now, now," Dr. Steiner said in apology. "I am too slow, I know it. Here is the bottle."

He stretched out his hands, far too early for his age, as she noted, he grasped the nourishing shape and inserted it into his mouth, where now was concentrated all the pain and ache of his hunger. He lay back upon the pillow of Dr. Steiner's large forearm, his body stilled in fulfillment, and he gazed contemplatively at her kind big face, bent above him. Small noises which he ignored were simply Mrs. Markey emptying the bath and removing the remnants of the daily ritual of cleaning, while Dr. Steiner, as usual when all was at peace, discoursed on Lennie.

"I have yesterday completed the tests, you understand, Mrs. Markey?"

"Did you, now," Mrs. Markey murmured rebelliously. She considered it cruel and even wicked to test so tiny and perfect a creature, as if Lennie needed testing, as if anybody couldn't believe that he was the finest child anybody ever saw.

"I finished all tests, including neurological," Dr. Steiner said in her loud decisive voice. "His intelligence quotient, I like to tell you, is the highest I have ever found in a human being this age, wonderful high, indeed."

"I wish you wouldn't just call Lennie a human being," Mrs. Markey said sharply.

Dr. Steiner stared at her. "Why not?" she demanded.

"It sounds like he was just ordinary," Mrs. Markey said. "He ain't only a human being. He's the cutest little baby, the darlingest little boy."

Lennie, hearing her voice, slanted his eyes toward her, and she became maudlin with love.

Dr. Steiner rumbled out laughter from her abdomen. "Markey, you don't like him."

Mrs. Markey put her hand in front of her mouth to hide her broken teeth when she felt compelled to smile. "I dunno why it is—I dunno, with all the children I've had, too, and one of them gone forever, and still when this here little Lennie looks at me, I feel like meltin' ice inside."

Lennie pushed away the bottle, milk ran down his chin, he smiled the smile of an angel in heaven and turned with interest to the big woman. What would she say to this?

Dr. Steiner looked down into his laughing face. She thought suddenly of little dead babies, starved, killed, bayoneted, tossed into heaps, babies who died because of what their parents were: Jews, Catholics, rebels, the hated, the feared, the despised. She could not bear to know that Lennie saw these memories even in her eyes. He was so sensitive, so wise, in his brain were garnered the gifts of all the world. She lifted him against her shoulder and felt his soft red-brown hair against her cheek. Already this baby was strong, calm, humorous, intelligent. She recognized him for what he was and she humbled herself before what he was to be, she the chosen one, weird old virgin that she was. Ignorance could not discern him, the ignorance of the narrow in mind, the small in heart, but she, she could know. Among all who were lost, this child she had saved.

"What flowering," she muttered, "what flowering is here!"

And she sat, triumphant, rocking to and fro, gently patting Lennie's back.